THE MYSTERY

BOOK TWO

By

Melody Huttinger

THE MYSTERY

J BAR X PUBLISHING

Printed in the United States of America

ISBN-978-1-7328715-1-9

Cover Art by Maura Dorn

Edited by Heidi Thomas

Map art by Marilyn Wiley

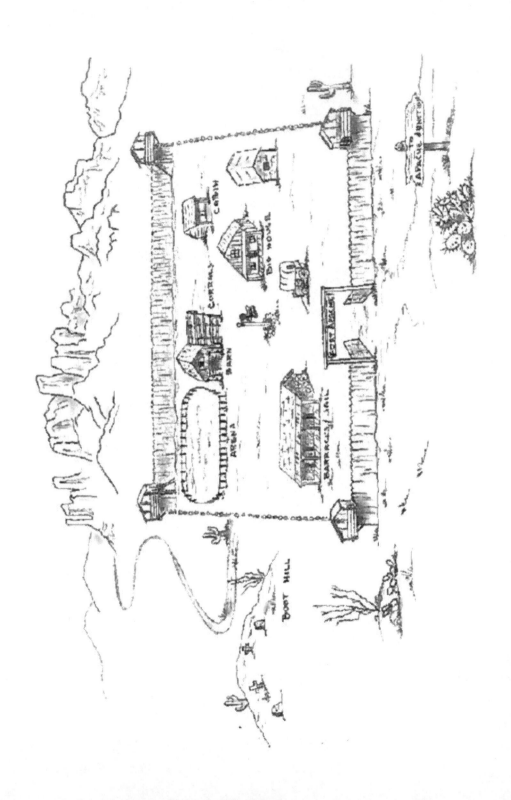

Contents

Chapter 1

Scottsdale 1960

Meadow Shepherd crouched low over the neck of her Arabian mare, racing across the desert floor as though they were being chased by bandits. Not far behind, with long legs pumping, her black Kelpie dog tried her best to keep up. They maintained the fast pace up a narrow ravine to the top of a knoll. Plump Barrel cacti and spidery Ocotillo dotted the sandy landscape where she reined Foxfire to a stop. Her mare stamped impatiently, eager to keep running.

"Easy, girl. Let's just catch our breath." She patted Foxfire's burnished copper coat, then glanced around to find Kelsey. Her dog lay collapsed in the shadow of a greasewood bush, panting. Meadow smiled. Faithful Kelsey, never complaining, always ready for a new adventure.

The knoll proved to be a perfect spot to take in the late afternoon sky, painted with pink streaks overtaking the blue. Spectacular sunsets were some consolation for the loneliness she felt now that they were back in Scottsdale for the winter.

Foxfire shifted and Meadow quieted her, at the same time absently tucking back a brunette strand that had escaped her ponytail. She breathed in the clean desert air. It was beautiful here, with the massive Saguaros and lonely vistas, but Meadow yearned for the mountains and Brighten Hot Springs where they'd spent the summer.

It had been two weeks since her family moved back to Scottsdale. Dad had arranged to rent the same property as last winter, with its old adobe house, green lawn and citrus trees. The place was perfect for them, mostly because it had a large barn for the horses. But it wasn't Brighten.

There were some compensations, though. At least now she had her own bedroom and there was an indoor bathroom. All summer she'd been relegated to a cot in the kitchen of the small cabin at Brighten stable, so a real bed and some privacy was nice for a change.

Dad had procrastinated about moving down from the high country, saying that the weather was still too infernally hot in the desert. As a result, Meadow and her older brothers, Monty and Mike, started school a week late. Not that she minded missing school, but dreaded coming in late with everyone staring at her like she was a red-headed step-child.

Her father, an original free spirit, didn't pay a lot of attention to rules he felt were unnecessary. He said his children were above average and would be up to speed in short order.

Meadow's mother fretted about them missing the first week, worried they would have a hard time making friends. Last school year had been pretty rough on all three of them, since they'd just moved to Arizona from Oregon.

As she watched the sun fading, Meadow ached for the unbroken freedom of last summer. She missed riding to Hidden Valley to see the wild Andalusian stallion she called Arrow. Solitary rides on Foxfire, with Kelsey trailing, helped to ease her unrest, so every day after school she mounted and raced away.

She felt for the pendant under her shirt, Meda's sacred amulet. It warmed to her touch. Arrow was free now—at least for the time being. In the spring, Meadow would have to bring him in to the Bowman Ranch to prove he would come when she asked. She puckered her brow. It was a long time before spring. Anything could happen.

Meadow was still watching the colors play out over the horizon when a vision of Meda appeared, smiling down. Behind the Medicine Woman stood an Indian brave, as if protecting her. He looked remarkably like Colt the day she'd first laid eyes on him. The scene was so beautiful and real to her that she caught her breath and a small tear escaped and rolled down her cheek.

Sighing, she turned Foxfire toward home. Before long, her mother would have supper on the table.

Her father's old truck was parked in the driveway by the time she arrived at the house, with Nueme's pickup parked next to it. She smiled. Oh, good, Dad was back after a two-day trip up to the Navajo reservation to replenish his trading stock. And she was always glad to see her dad's best friend, Nueme. He was of the Shonto tribe, and Dad had known him since boyhood.

A little shiver of anticipation ran through Meadow as she suddenly remembered it was her fourteenth birthday. Before putting her mare away, she rested her cheek on Foxfire's sleek neck.

"There'll never be a present as good as you, Foxy." She chuckled. "Remember when Dad interrupted my bubble bath when I turned seven? You were just a baby and it was so cute when he led you right into the bathroom. I thought Mom would have a conniption fit."

A knot formed in her gut thinking about Dad. She'd always been his favorite. She knew it, and suspected the boys knew it, too, even though he was strictly fair in dealing with them. But their close relationship had suffered when she'd found the Indian cliff dwelling last summer. Colt told her she had a Native American heritage, but her father wouldn't acknowledge it. There was some secret in his past that he kept from the whole family. It was painful to think he might be ashamed of his heritage.

Lost in her thoughts, she was still idly petting her mare, when Kelsey looked up and gave a low woof, as though to say, hey, what about me? Meadow dropped down to dog level, ruffling her fur.

"And what would I ever do without you, Kelsey?"

Meadow led Foxfire into her stall, and noticed the large corral behind the barn had five new horses milling around. Her father was doing a lot of trading again, now that they weren't working the riding stable at Brighten.

Curious to see what he'd brought home, she made her way to the corral and peered over the rail. The horses were various sizes and colors, but all bore the distinctive Bar N brand on their shoulder, indicating they were from the Navajo Nation. They were mostly underweight from running loose out on the dry range and were busily chewing on the piles of hay strewn about the enclosure. Her father often brought home starved-looking horses, and then fed them up until they were fat and glossy before re-selling them.

"Don't worry guys, you'll get plenty to eat around here." A black and white paint eyed her for a moment before burying his face back into his dinner.

She watched them for a bit longer, and then with the last of the light fading behind the mountains to the west, turned from the horses and sprinted to the house, with Kelsey close on her heels.

"Sorry, girl, you can't come in. You know Mom doesn't like dogs in the house."

Kelsey sat, knowing the routine, but seemed ever hopeful that someday she would be allowed in. She sympathized with her dog's earnest look, but knew it was highly unlikely that Mom would ever relax the rule about animals coming inside. Meadow's asthma was the reason they made the move from Oregon, and her doctors had been very specific that household animal dander could trigger an attack.

Her mother turned with a smile as Meadow came into the kitchen. The oven door was open and she smelled the delicious aroma of roast pork coming from it. On the counter was her usual favorite birthday cake, Angel Food, iced with her mother's famous fluffy white frosting.

"Did you have a nice ride, honey?" Her mother wiped away a trickle of sweat from her brow.

"Uh huh. Where is everyone?"

"Out on the front lawn where it's a little cooler." Her mother turned back to the stove and pulled the roast from the oven.

"That smells yummy, Mom. I'm surprised you're baking on such a hot day, though."

"Well, it *is* sort of a special occasion . . . ."

Her mother's dark hair was held in place by a scarf, the same material as her dress. Meadow touched the soft Robin's egg blue fabric. "You look pretty in that color. Is that the outfit you were working on yesterday?" Her mother was a whiz on her Singer sewing machine and had tried in vain to interest Meadow in learning to sew.

"This and some other things. . . ."

"Whew, when's it ever going to cool off around here?" Meadow could hear the old swamp cooler rattling and hissing, but it hadn't kept up with the heat of the day combined with the oven.

"Soon, I think. It's almost October. Go wash up, then you can set the table. Nueme is joining us for dinner." Her mother turned back to her preparations.

"Oh, good." Meadow hoped Nueme might have some news of Arrow and the wild herd.

After taking a quick shower and pulling on some clean cut-off shorts, Meadow set the table, then stepped outside. Her father sat on a lawn chair, his long legs splayed out in front of him, with Nueme seated nearby. Her brothers lounged on the grass, trying their best to soak up some of its coolness.

"Well, here's the birthday girl," her father said.

Meadow smiled. "Daddy, I'm so glad you're back."

"And fourteen, at that," Nueme added. "Shonto girls are married by that age." His dark eyes danced.

"Heck, I don't even have a boyfriend." She frowned, thinking of Brett, who seemed to have forgotten her already. With the exception of one terse letter, saying he hated everything about military school, she hadn't heard a word from him.

"Maybe boys would like you better if you acted more mature." Her middle brother, Mike, was a royal pain.

She made a face at him, then sank onto the grass. "Did you have a good trip, Daddy?"

"Yep, did you see the new ponies? Some of 'em will be dandies after they put away a few groceries."

Mom stuck her head out of the door. "Hey you guys, time for dinner."

They all got up and headed for the new walnut dining table her father had recently traded for. Her mother was very proud of it, with its un-marred glass-like surface and beautifully carved legs—by far her nicest piece of furniture. The rest of the house was sparsely furnished, and most items had seen better days.

After the main meal, her mother brought in the cake with fourteen lit candles. Everyone sang Happy Birthday while Meadow blew them out.

"What'd ya wish for?" Mike asked.

She narrowed her eyes, trying on a Mata Hari look. "I'll never tell."

As everyone dug into their cake and ice cream, her mother brought out a wrapped present. "Hope you like it, honey."

Meadow ripped open the package, revealing a sleeveless red sheath style dress with big white buttons at the shoulders.

"I love it, Mom!" She jumped up and pirouetted around the room holding up her new outfit.

Her mother laughed. "Good, I just finished sewing it this afternoon. You need some school clothes."

"Speaking of school, guess who I saw today?" Mike looked pointedly at Monty.

Monty raised his brows. "Who?"

"Cynthia Markowitz." Mike's smug expression was annoying. "She just transferred into my Biology class. She wanted to know when you're going to call her."

Monty concentrated on his cake. "Don't know if I will," he replied between mouthfuls. "After all, her father tried to sue us last summer."

"Well, anyway, she wants you to come watch her at the Pony Club horse show this Sunday." Mike smirked. "And she *is* kinda cute."

"You should get in that horse show, Meadow," her mother said. "I know you've been practicing with Foxy."

"I really can't. You need to have an English saddle to jump. They won't let you ride bareback."

"Hmm, an English saddle, you say?" Her father thoughtfully drummed on the table.

"Oh, Daddy!" Meadow squealed, knowing that look. "Where is it?"

He grinned. "Go check in our closet."

She ran to her parents' bedroom, found the saddle with a big yellow bow on it, and carried it out for the others to see.

"Look everyone, it's a Stubben. That's the very best. Thanks, Dad!" She pecked him on the cheek.

"Well, it's not new, but the fella I got it from took good care of it. His daughter used to ride, but lost interest."

"I'm glad it's not new. It's so much better to have one that's already broken in."

"Me and Monty have something for you, too," Mike said. "But you hafta come outside."

He retrieved a flashlight and led the way out to the old shed on the property. They followed the shining shaft of light to the building, and he shoved open the door. Meadow peeked in while he pulled out some rails and jump standards, painted white.

"Oh boy, jumps!" She grabbed one and helped him set them up.

Mike looked proudly at the array. "We built them for you, so you don't hafta use buckets and barrels anymore to practice."

"We used the old lumber that was stacked behind the barn," Monty said. "And tip money from last summer to buy the paint."

"Wow, this is a wonderful birthday," she said. "Thanks, guys, these are perfect."

Her mother put her arm around Meadow. "Now you don't have any excuse not to join Pony Club and enter horse shows."

"Yeah, that should be fun." She looked down and kicked at a rock, sending it skittering away. Her mother couldn't seem to understand—she would never fit in with that Pony Club crowd. Not only did they have fancy horses and trainers, but also expensive riding clothes and boots.

They admired the boys' handiwork for a few minutes, then trooped back to the house. After a while, Nueme stood to leave. Meadow walked him out to his pickup.

"I'm glad you came for my birthday."

"I have something for you, too." He opened the truck door, and pulled out a small halter. "It's hand-braided from horse hair. Should just fit Foxy's baby when it comes along in the spring."

She fingered the intricate pattern and didn't have the heart to tell him the foal was promised to Bill Bowman. "Thank you, it's beautiful. This must have been a lot of work."

He leaned against the pickup. "I have time on my hands in the evenings."

"Have you seen the wild herd lately?"

"No, not lately. I was in Hidden Valley just yesterday."

"Really? I wonder where they are?"

"You shouldn't worry. The stallion probably moved his mares to a lower range for winter."

"Oh. I hope they're all right."

"Arrow will take care of them." Nueme turned to go.

He was the only one, besides Colt, who referred to the stallion by the name she always called him. She was glad at least *some* people believed her.

Meadow waved as Nueme drove out of sight.

It was nearly ten o'clock that night when the phone rang. Meadow's parents had already gone to their room and her brothers were finishing up homework at the table. She sat alone in the living room reading, too keyed up to go to bed yet. A sudden jangling sound made her flinch and the book slipped to the floor. The phone had just been installed last week and they didn't get many calls. Who would be phoning this late?

She scurried to grab it.

"Hello?" There was no sound on the other end. She tried again. "Hello?"

A muffled voice came on. "Meadow?"

"Yes, this is Meadow." Another silence. "Hello?"

"Beware, I know where you live." The voice came across as a gravelly growl.

A shudder went down her back. "Who is this?"

The phone clicked and a dial tone came on. Meadow slammed down the receiver.

Who would do that? She racked her brain trying to think of all her classmates. Did she offend someone at school? Scott

Carter, the class clown, popped into her head. He was always teasing her. It *must* have been him.

Meadow stared at the phone for a moment and then headed for her room. She passed her mother in the hall.

"Who was that, honey?"

"Just some stupid guy from school, playing a prank." She walked into her room and flopped onto her bed. Dumb jerk! Why'd he do that? It was such a great birthday and he had to go and spoil it.

Like last week in school when Scott had shoved her into the large supply closet in the classroom and locked her in. She could hear the class laughing like hyenas while she banged on the door, yelling to be let out.

Finally the teacher, Mrs. Witherspoon, had come and unlocked the door. The teacher gave her a signature withering look, like it was Meadow's own fault. Yeah, like she asked to be locked in the closet.

She wondered if she would ever make any friends at school. The kids all seemed pretty lame compared to her friends last summer. She missed Linda and Brett Bowman, who were both older. Linda started Arizona State University this year and was studying archeology. And sixteen-year-old Brett was away in New York, at the miserable military academy.

The other person she really wanted to see was Colt. He was in Flagstaff going to college. Meadow thought of their shared secret when they found and hid the Indian Medicine Chest full of ancient artifacts. A treasure that the pot-hunters, led by the criminal master-mind Wendell, had lusted after—and nearly killed her for.

Meadow touched the amulet. It was strange she felt so connected to Colt, even when he wasn't near. As if she had known him forever.

Thinking about Colt always made her feel warm and safe inside—the same way she felt when touching the amulet. And whenever she thought of last summer at Brighten, it made her long to see Arrow, the Sky Horse.

Mom poked her head in the door. "School tomorrow. Time for lights out."

"Okay." Meadow was just crawling into bed, when she heard a screeching sound. She jumped like a frightened rabbit. Crap! What was that?

She sprang up to make sure the window was secured, and saw a wayward branch scraping against it. Meadow lay back in bed, her thoughts still churning.

The voice on the phone had said, *I know where you live.* That night she tossed and turned with an uneasy feeling in the back of her mind, and her dreams turned to nightmares before morning.

Chapter 2

Junior High

Meadow rolled out of bed, groggy from her restless night. Ugh, another school day. At least she doesn't have to try and come up with an outfit. The new red dress was waiting, calling to her impatiently. After fastening the big white buttons at her shoulders, she stared at her reflection in the mirror. Her mood lifted like the window shade. How did her mother know the latest style? She turned from side to side. Yep, it fit perfectly. Inspired by the new outfit, she brushed her thick, wavy hair until it glistened, tied it back with a red ribbon, and trotted out to the kitchen.

Her mother spooned out a bowl of oatmeal and placed it on the table. "You look nice today, honey."

"Thanks to my new dress."

Her father peered at her over the top of his newspaper. "You'd look good in a gunny sack."

Mike looked up from his breakfast. "Good idea, you should wear a gunny sack to school. It'll become all the rage, and then you'll be *really* popular."

"Shut up, Mike." Meadow eyed him. "And I see *you're* wearing a new shirt. Is that for Cynthia's benefit?"

Monty snorted and punched his brother in the arm. Mike punched him back. "Maybe I am interested in her. So what?"

"Well, you can have her." Monty put on his superior older brother look. "She's way too kooky for me."

Dad crinkled his paper. "I agree with you on that, Monty."

Mike frowned and concentrated on his oatmeal.

Meadow decided that classes at Scottsdale Junior High weren't much different than other schools. Boring teachers and dull subjects. Third period dragged on, and she gazed dreamily out the classroom window. The gray peaks in the distance contrasted sharply against the azure sky. Olive green Palo Verde trees and a few Mesquites decorated the background just beyond the school yard. When it cooled off, it would fun to explore those mountains. Late September and it was still in the nineties.

The large-faced clock above the blackboard ticked the seconds away with agonizing slowness. Her English teacher's voice droned on about sentence structure.

Meadow glanced around the classroom.

She knew a few kids from last year. Beth Cranston and Monica Flack—girls that belonged to the *in* crowd, were passing notes and giggling. It was a group Meadow didn't care to be part of. They were so snooty and self-absorbed.

Scott Carter, the class clown, was sitting right behind her. It *must* have been Scott calling last night, but it didn't make sense. He generally came up with something to make the other kids laugh. Why call her when she was the only one that knew about it?

The classroom door inched opened and the principal poked his head in. "Mrs. Witherspoon, may I interrupt? We have a new student."

"Certainly, Mr. Green. Come right in."

The new girl followed him in like a tall upright cat, hesitant and wary. The class that had been rustling like dry leaves became silent. Then the whispering started. The girl stared straight ahead and clamped her jaw. An aqua sweater set off her beautiful caramel-colored skin and deep chocolate eyes.

"Everyone, I want you to welcome Lisa Wilson. She just moved here from Dayton, Ohio. Mrs. Witherspoon, is this spot all right for Lisa?" Mr. Green indicated an empty desk at the back of the classroom.

"Yes, that's fine. I'm happy to have you in my class, Lisa." Mrs. Witherspoon stumped over to the new girl and handed her a copy of the novel they'd been reading. "Please take a seat and open to page two hundred thirty-eight."

Lisa sat down and opened her book, staring holes through it. The whispering continued. Meadow glared around the room. What a bunch of jerks.

"Quiet, class!" Mrs. Witherspoon waddled to her desk and picked up "Moby Dick," the literary selection of the month.

Meadow glanced at the clock again and squirmed in her seat. Who cares about some crazy old coot obsessed with killing a whale? She straightened her dress, tugging the skirt back down over her knees. The dress was fashionably shorter than she was used to.

The two weeks she'd been back in school seemed excruciatingly long. It was hard to settle down to school life and fit in after last summer. She tuned out Captain Ahab's ranting and lost herself in riding Arrow through the canyons of Sedona with the clean sweet scent of pine in the air. It was like a gentle roller coaster as they swooped and turned with cliffs on either side. She jerked in her seat when a raucous noise disturbed her musings.

"Meadow, Meadow Shepherd!" Mrs. Witherspoon called loudly and rapped on her desk with a pointer.

She turned her head toward the teacher and wondered where in the world she found those clothes—a flowered mid-calf dress finished with thick-heeled sensible shoes. To complete the look, her hair was pulled back into a granny bun. "Yes, Mrs. Witherspoon?"

"I asked you to read from our literary selection for the class. This is the second time I asked. You need to pay better attention, Miss Shepherd." Mrs. Witherspoon scowled like Captain Ahab when Moby bit off his leg.

Meadow ignored the titters of her classmates, stood, and read the ponderous prose. After an endless page of whale angst, she was allowed to sink down into her seat. While she busily rearranged her skirt, Scott reached forward and cleverly unfastened one of the big buttons at her shoulder. A collective hush fell over the class as the dress fell open and revealed her bra strap.

Then the giggling started.

She took a deep breath, re-buttoned her dress and stood up, swinging around at the same time. Meadow calmly leaned over and slapped Scott with a resounding whack square across his face. He gasped like an out of water guppy and his freckled face turned as red as his hair.

The rest of the students cheered and clapped, but Mrs. Witherspoon was not a happy woman. "Meadow, what is the meaning of disrupting my class? You're going straight to the principal's office this minute!" She scribbled out a hall pass.

Mrs. Witherspoon stomped over and handed her the pink slip. Meadow gathered her textbooks and started toward the door. As she passed Scott, his face still bearing a red mark from her hand, he winked at her. The new girl, Lisa, watched her pass by with a deadpan expression.

Mr. Green listened patiently to her side of the story, but still made her sit in his office until the lunch break. She slumped into the straight-backed chair with a sigh. At least she wouldn't have to hear any more whale woes.

The brightly lit cafeteria had the usual rows of tables and metal folding chairs. Meadow made her way to the far side, close to the windows. She saw Lisa sitting there, all by herself, with a tray in front of her.

"Hi, Lisa, do you mind if I sit here?"

"You actually want to sit by *me?*"

"Sure, why not?"

"If you hadn't noticed, I'm the only Negro in this school."

"So?"

"If you really want to, you can sit here." Lisa's tone was not inviting.

"Okay." Meadow plopped down and opened her lunch bag. She proceeded to lay everything out, an egg-salad sandwich, an apple and some chocolate chip cookies.

Lisa raised her eyebrows. "You make your own lunch?"

"Actually, my mother makes it. She's always worried the cafeteria lunches aren't nutritious enough."

"Your mom bakes, too?" Lisa ogled the cookies.

"Yeah, my mom's pretty much the all-American homemaker."

"I wish I didn't have to eat cafeteria food. Look at this stuff." Lisa indicated the unrecognizable meat with anemic looking sauce over the top.

"Pretty yucky. Would you like half of my lunch? I'm not really that hungry." Meadow held out part of her sandwich.

"I guess so." Lisa tentatively took a bite. "Mmmm, this is good. I'm going to start bringing my lunch, too."

Meadow smiled. "Good idea."

"I'll have to make it myself, though. My mother works long hours and wouldn't have time."

"What does your mom do?"

"She's a doctor, a heart surgeon."

"Wow, cool. She must be smart. And your father?"

Lisa hesitated and shifted like she was sitting atop a sharp rock. "Uh . . . I'm not sure. I don't know him, and my mother never talks about him."

Meadow knew when to drop the subject. She flashed on her own father. How would she feel if he weren't in the picture? Although lately, he *acted* sorta absent.

"Old Witherspoon shouldn't have sent you to the principal. That guy deserved a slap." Lisa stuffed a cookie into her mouth.

"Yeah, but it's okay. I was totally bored today, so Scott actually did me a favor." Meadow grinned. "Mr. Green let me work on my homework, so now I'll have more time to ride Foxy."

"Who's Foxy?"

"My horse. Her full name is Foxfire. She's an Arabian."

Lisa appeared to glow. "Wow, you have a horse? I love horses!"

"Why don't you come over to my house sometime? You can ride one of ours."

Her voice became wary. "Are you sure you want the stigma of having a dark-skinned person over to your house? And my mother is white. What will your parents think?"

"They won't care."

Lisa turned away. "No, I don't think so."

"Oh, come on. My parents aren't that way." Seeing Lisa was still hesitant, Meadow blurted out, "Besides, I'm part Indian."

The other girl faced her, eyes doubtful. "You just made that up."

It was Meadow's turn to be cautious. After all, it was still a secret. There must be some reason her father didn't want it known. "Forget I said that. But I still want you to come ride with me."

Lisa studied her for a moment. "Maybe."

The lunch bell rang and they exchanged phone numbers before heading out for their next class. Meadow figured Lisa's love of horses would win her over and if it didn't, at least she'd *tried* to make a friend. Nothing ventured, nothing gained.

Near the gym, she saw Scott coming toward her. Uh-oh.

"Why'd you have to hit me so hard?" He rubbed his jaw.

She gave him a drop-dead look. "I should have punched you. Especially after calling me last night."

"What'd ya mean? I didn't call you, I don't even have your phone number."

"Well, you must have put someone up to it then."

"No, I didn't."

"Yeah, sure. Like I'd believe anything you say." She shoved past him.

"Wait, Meadow. I didn't . . ."

After the bus deposited her at home, Meadow couldn't wait to set out her new jumps and try out the English saddle. She knew the basics of English riding from her avid reading of everything and anything horse-related. The posting was easy—just rise up when the horse's inside leg stepped out at a trot and sit on the next step. She practiced with Foxfire and before long they were in in perfect rhythm.

She trotted over low fences first and then urged her mare into a canter. Foxfire acted like she had been doing it all her life, so Meadow raised the bars higher.

"I think we'll be ready for the show on Sunday, Foxy." They rode for a while longer, and then Meadow sprayed Foxfire down with the hose before putting her away for the night.

After dinner, Meadow whizzed through her homework. She couldn't wait to call Lisa to invite her over for a ride on Saturday. The dude string was in pasture for the winter, but they had a new horse her father had just brought home. Lisa could ride him.

"I'm so glad you called." Lisa sounded almost giddy. "I wasn't sure if you were really serious about having me over."

"Of course I was serious. Will your mother let you come?"

"Sure, she's thrilled that I made a friend so fast. After we ride, she wants you to come to our house for a swim."

"You have a pool? That's neato. I'd love to."

They chatted about school for a few minutes, and said their goodbyes. Meadow had just put down the receiver when it rang again. She looked at it for a minute, then picked it up with some trepidation. "Hello?"

"I know where you live," the voice said.

"Scott, is that you?"

No answer from the other end. Just breathing.

"Scott, you'd better quit bugging me!"

Still no answer. What a creep. Meadow slammed down the phone and ran to her bedroom. She took a deep breath, refusing to let him bother her. She pulled out her latest Black Stallion book and began reading, but it took a while before she could concentrate on Alec and The Black.

Chapter 3

The Water Hole

Meadow rushed toward the cafeteria after being detained by Mrs. Witherspoon. The teacher had lectured her once again about paying better attention in class. Geez, whose mind wouldn't wander when presented with the dilemma of dangling participles?

She swerved to avoid a collision with Trudy Jones and ran smack into Scott Carter. Her textbooks flew in every direction. Scott smirked. "Why the hurry? Don't want to miss out on the yummy fish sticks?" He bent down and to help gather her things.

"Very funny. Why don't you watch where you're going? And quit calling me, for cripes sake!" Meadow grabbed the books from him and fled before he could answer.

Monica Flack and Beth Cranston saw her come in the lunchroom door and waved her over to their table. She eyed them suspiciously. They were leaders of the popular crowd—why were they bothering with her, the invisible girl?

Monica, surrounded by her entourage of sheep-like followers, smiled encouragingly. "Beth and I thought it was pretty cool how you slapped Scott right in front of everyone yesterday." Her nose was only slightly in the air. "You can sit with *us* today, right, Beth?"

Beth nodded, looking bored and clicking her short, hot pink nails on the tabletop. "Sure, sit with us." She pulled out a compact and checked her hot pink lipstick.

Meadow quickly firmed her slack jaw as a tingle of anticipation coursed through her veins. Had she heard correctly? Had Monica really just ask her to be part of their group, the ones that always seemed to be having such a good time, laughing and joking together? Was she finally being accepted? The strange girl without many friends, the girl who hung out mostly with a horse and a dog?

Monica pulled out a chair next to her own. She patted the seat, and Meadow, still dazed by her sudden acceptance, sank into it wordlessly. It was wonderful until she regained enough sense to remember Lisa.

She stole a glance at the table by the window, and there was her new friend, all alone. Lisa's dark eyes were watchful, accusing. Crap. Meadow squared her shoulders and stood, turning to Monica. "I would love to sit with you. I'll just go tell Lisa to come over."

Beth put a restraining hand on her arm. "Hold on, we're only inviting *you*, not Lisa. We don't want her kind at our table."

"No way!" Monica chimed in.

Meadow frowned. "What do you mean? What's wrong with her? She's a nice girl."

"Don't be silly. We can't be seen with a colored girl." Monica smiled and tugged at her arm. "C'mon, sit down."

Meadow felt as though her air was slowly leaking out, like a tire with a puncture. She knew exactly what it was like to sit alone. She drew in a deep breath. "Thanks for the offer, but I'm sitting with Lisa. See you guys around."

Shaking off Monica's hand, Meadow walked away, wondering why doing the right thing didn't feel better. She plopped down next to Lisa without speaking.

Lisa arched her brows. "What did the snoot-sisters want?"

"Oh, nothing important." Meadow concentrated on opening her sack lunch.

"They wanted you to sit with them. Why didn't you? Don't worry about me, I've sat by myself before. I'm used to it." Lisa raised her chin and her eyes flashed defiantly, like when Meadow had first met her.

"Oh, Lisa. Don't be like that. I want to sit with you, but it might have been fun to be popular for once in my life." Meadow grinned at her. "Oh well, with you as a best friend, guess I'll never know."

Lisa laughed and smiled back. "And me either, with *you* as a best friend."

Meadow lay in bed, feeling the first rays of sun kiss her face. Ahhh, Saturday. She rolled over to savor a few more minutes of delicious sleep, but her mind refused to cooperate. Like a sudden dust devil, her thoughts whirled back to the lunchroom scene last week.

After that incident, she'd been even more of a pariah. She sighed, what does it matter? Being popular isn't everything, and who cares about those snobby girls anyway?

With renewed resolve, Meadow bounced out of bed, determined to have a good weekend. Lisa was coming over today and they were going riding. And she hadn't gotten any more weird phone calls. Whoever had been playing pranks earlier in the week seemed to have given it up. Maybe she finally got through to Scott. She hadn't told her parents, they had enough worries of their own.

She frowned. It *had* to be Scott, but he'd so vehemently denied it, more than once . . . was it really him? But who else *could* it be?

She shook her head and went to her closet. After pulling on a tee-shirt and jeans, Meadow sprinted to the barn with Kelsey on her heels. Lisa was coming over early to avoid the heat, so she petted Foxfire, and then fed the all the horses.

Her mother was whipping up breakfast by the time Meadow got back to the house. Mom set a plate stacked with French toast in front of her. "Thanks, Mom."

"It's nice that you have a friend coming over today."

"I know. I have to hurry, they'll be here any minute."
She'd just swallowed her last bite, when Dr. Wilson pulled into
the driveway.

Meadow craned her neck and saw a slender woman with
dark blonde hair at the steering wheel. Lisa's mother was pretty in
a different sort of way from her own mom. More fragile looking.
Better quit gawking, and get out there. She banged out of the
house and ran to the car.

"Hi, Dr. Wilson, I'm so glad Lisa could come over
today."

Dr. Wilson offered a warm smile. "You must be Meadow.
Lisa has told me all about you."

Mom came out of the house and joined them.

"Hello, I'm Rose Shepherd." She extended her hand
through the open car window.

"Pleased to meet you, I'm Laura Wilson. Thank you for
having Lisa over today."

"Of course. It will be fun for Meadow to have someone to
ride with. I understand that Lisa had some riding lessons in
Ohio?"

"Yes, she was making good progress, too."

"Until they decided it was a 'white only' riding club." Lisa
grimaced and her words sounded bitter.

Dr. Wilson's lips became a thin line. "Yes, we've had to
deal with some of that. I hope it's better out here in the West.
That's why I decided to take the job at Scottsdale General."

"We're happy you did. Aren't we, Meadow?" Without
waiting for a reply, her mother went on, "Would you like to come
in for a cup of coffee, Laura?"

"Sorry, I have to get to the hospital and do my rounds this
morning, but I'll take a rain check."

"Anytime. And don't worry about Lisa, I'll get her home
after lunch."

"Thank you, that's perfect. I should be home by noon."
Dr. Wilson smiled. "Lisa would love it if Meadow could spend
the night."

"That will be all right, but she'll have to be home early to
get ready for the horse show tomorrow."

"No problem. Make sure you bring your swim suit,
Meadow," Dr. Wilson said. "And bring yours, too, Rose, if you'd
like an afternoon swim."

Mom nodded. "That does sound nice."

Dr. Wilson started the car, waving out the window as she
drove away.

Meadow led Lisa to the barn, where Foxfire nickered a
welcome. "This is Foxy."

"Wow, she's gorgeous!" Lisa stroked her neck. "Which
one is mine?"

"Over here." Meadow walked toward a bay gelding
poking his head over the stall door. "Dad just got him from Turf
Paradise. You know, the racetrack."

"Was he a racehorse?" Lisa petted the bay.

"No, he was a pony horse."

"What's that?"

"That's what they call the horses they use to lead the
racehorses onto the track." She handed Lisa a halter. "He's really
a good boy, and I think you'll like him. His name is Major."

"I like him already." Lisa giggled as Major nuzzled her
over the gate.

After they groomed the horses, Meadow asked what kind
of tack Lisa preferred.

"What are you using?"

"I always ride bareback, but you can use my Stubben or a
western saddle . . ."

Lisa patted Major's broad back. "He's perfect for
bareback."

Meadow hesitated. She remembered all too well Cynthia's fall off Foxfire last summer, and the threat of an ensuing lawsuit. "Maybe you should try him out first." She gave Lisa a leg up.

Meadow breathed easier as Lisa trotted Major around the yard, sitting the trot. "You're a natural, Lisa."

"Thanks, I love riding. It was crushing when they banned me from the riding club. Some of the kids were really jealous that I was doing so well in the shows."

"That's too bad. I'm showing Foxy tomorrow at pony club. Want to come watch?"

"Sure."

Meadow hopped on Foxfire. "Let's go ride."

The desert spread out before them like a western canvas, sprinkled with greasewood bushes and the occasional cholla cactus. They laughed when Kelsey flushed out a jackrabbit and went ripping across the sand determined to catch it. It darted down a burrow and she began digging, unable to admit defeat.

Meadow called to her. "C'mon, Kelsey. Let it be." Her dog came trotting over, tongue lolling. "I know, let's go to the water hole."

Lisa knitted her brow. "What's a water hole?"

"It's a dirt tank to water the range cattle. Sorta like a big pond with dikes around it."

"How does it stay full when it's so hot?"

"There's a creaky old windmill attached to it. You'll see."

Major matched Foxfire's quick pace, and before long, the embankments of the water hole were visible in the distance. Large mesquite trees intermingled with shady cottonwoods made it seem like a desert oasis.

They drew near and then scrambled to the top of the bank, looking down into surprisingly clear water. The large pond had reeds around the edges and was about a hundred feet across.

Meadow knew from experience that it was pretty deep in the center. Startled frogs suddenly quit their hoarse croaking and leapt with large plops into the pond. Kelsey charged at a few casually swimming ducks that flapped their wings and swam to the middle.

Lisa's eyes widened. "This is great! I had no idea something like this existed in the desert."

Meadow laughed. "Pretty neat, huh? It's hot, let's take off our pants and swim the horses."

After they hung their jeans in one of the trees, Meadow waded Foxfire into the pond. When Lisa followed on Major, he started pawing the water and splashing it up on them.

Meadow knew what was coming. "Careful, Lisa . . ."

Major lay down with a big splash, cooling his whole body.

"What the heck!" Lisa bailed off into the pond, then came up sputtering. She dissolved into laughter when Meadow jumped in to join her. Kelsey started swimming laps around them. Major clambered to his feet and both horses stood belly deep in the water, watching, and no doubt wondering why Meadow and Lisa were giggling uncontrollably as if they'd lost their senses.

After regaining their composure, they remounted and swam the horses across the water hole, where they played and splashed each other. Finally, out of breath, they climbed the far bank, dismounted, and lay back in the shade.

Lisa was saying what a great place it was when Kelsey gave a low woof, staring out into the desert. Meadow swiveled her head just in time to see two riders approaching at a canter.

"Someone's coming. I can see red hair—must be Scott Carter. And that's Jack Dawson with him. I recognize his horse."

"Oh no, we're in our underwear and our jeans are on the other side of the water hole!" Lisa squeaked. "C'mon, quick. Let's ride around and get them on."

Meadow boosted Lisa and then swung up onto Foxfire. But it was too late, the boys spotted them.

Scott called, "Wait up. Where are you guys going? We want to talk to you."

Meadow and Lisa quickly rode into the trees, then looked at each other and tried to stifle giggles. They could hear the boys crashing through the brush trying to find them.

Jack bellowed out, "Wait up."

Meadow motioned for Lisa to follow her, and they weaved in and out of the trees as fast as they could, trying to keep away from their pursuers.

The boys abruptly turned to go the opposite way around the dike, galloping. It was easier traveling that way and they came upon the hanging pants. Meadow and Lisa reined in behind a tree and watched as Scott grabbed the jeans.

He held them aloft, laughing hysterically. "Now we know why you were hiding." Scott began to tuck the pants into his saddlebag. "I think we'll just take these with us."

Meadow stuck out her nose and yelled, "Scott Carter, don't you dare! Put them back and just go away."

"Maybe I will . . . but you have to make a deal first. If I put them back, you guys have to ride with us. Deal?"

"Deal." Lisa burst out, before Meadow could say anything. "Hang them where they were, then ride to the other side while we put them on."

Scott returned the jeans to the branch and they rode slowly to the other side of the water hole, sneaking back looks every once in a while.

Meadow fumed when they were gone. "Why'd you make a deal with that jerk?"

Lisa pursed her lips. "Actually, I think Jack is kinda cute. It won't be so bad riding with them."

"Are you kidding? My brothers and I call him 'Runnin' Jack' because he's always galloping that poor horse of his everywhere. He thinks it only has one gear."

"I still think he's cute. You don't mind too much, do you?"

Meadow huffed. "Guess I don't have much choice."

Lisa smiled and pulled on her jeans.

After getting dressed, they joined the boys on the far side of the dike and they all started for home. In deference to them, Jack was keeping his lean, flea-bitten gray gelding to a walk next to the other horses. Scott rode a pale palomino mare.

Scott eyed Lisa. "Who is the lady that picks you up after school sometimes?"

Lisa shot him a drop-dead look. "It's my mother."

Scott stared back at her. "But, she's uh, you know, white. Are you adopted?"

Jack kicked at Scott's stirrup. "Shut up, Scott, you're a dope."

"It's okay." Lisa ignored Scott and focused on Jack. "My father is Negro, so I'm Mulatto. You know, half white and half black."

"Oh, that's why you have such pretty skin." A slow flush crept up Jack's face when he realized what he'd said.

Lisa flashed him a smile.

They rode on for a while, and Scott maneuvered closer to Meadow. She looked straight ahead, refusing to acknowledge him.

He finally spewed out, "I'm sorry I unbuttoned your dress in class. Maybe I went a little too far."

Meadow glared. "That was bad enough, but then you call and threaten me. Why've you been doing that?"

"I told you, I've never called you!"

"Really? You're telling the truth?"

"Cross my heart, hope to die." Scott steered his mare closer and leaned over. "Can't we be friends?"

Meadow recoiled from him. "Well, I guess so—if you promise to stop teasing me in school."

"I promise. Will you be at the horse show tomorrow? I'm entering."

"Yeah, I'll be there." By that time, they were in front of her house. She reined Foxfire to a halt. No way was she inviting them in. "See you."

Scott and Jack hesitated, but got the hint and rode on. Lisa gazed after them.

"C'mon, Lisa." Meadow headed toward the barn, hoping the irritation wasn't too apparent in her voice. She was feeling a little edgy knowing Scott hadn't phoned her after all. Who was it then? She tried to shrug it off and they went into the house where her mother had sandwiches waiting, but Meadow didn't have much appetite.

After lunch, her mother drove them to Lisa's house, which wasn't far. To get into the subdivision, they passed through a gate. Houses were scattered here and there, surrounded by a golf course. All of the upscale homes looked similar with stucco exteriors, tile roofs and desert landscaping. Her mother pulled into the driveway that Lisa pointed out and they all piled out of the Ranch Wagon.

The house was quite luxurious. It had formal living and dining rooms with the latest modern style furnishings and pretty art objects. The wall-to-wall carpet was light beige, almost white, and Meadow wondered how it stayed so clean.

Lisa led them through the house to the back patio and pool. Beyond the pool was a green expanse of golf course with a small lake in the middle. Meadow gaped at the view until she noticed Lisa's mother sitting in the shade of an umbrella, reading *Ladies Home Journal.* She looked like she had just stepped out of the magazine, very stylish in a white two piece swim suit. Dr. Wilson glanced up as they came through the glass door.

"Hello, everyone. I was just about to make some iced tea. Would you all like a glass?"

"Mmm, sounds good," Mom said.

"Meanwhile, Rose, you can get changed over there." Dr. Wilson nodded toward the poolside cabana. "Lisa probably wants to show Meadow her room."

Mom went to change and Lisa grabbed Meadow's hand and pulled her down the hall. As they stepped through the door to her room, Meadow stopped short. Instead of a typical frilly girl's bedroom, she was surprised by a shadowy interior with all the curtains drawn. The walls were painted deep blue, almost black, and the only decorations were Elvis and Ricky Nelson posters along with some pop bands Meadow didn't recognize.

Lisa flipped a lamp switch. "Pretty weird, huh?"

"Well, it's kinda dark, don't ya think?"

"Yeah, when we moved here, I was feeling dark, so I painted the walls like this. Now that I met you, I might repaint. C'mon, let's get changed and go swim."

"Okay." Meadow began to undress and revealed the amulet, gleaming in the soft light.

"What's that? It's really pretty." Lisa peered at the necklace.

"It's just something an Indian gave me." Meadow carefully placed it in her bag.

Lisa stared for a second. "So you really *are* part Indian?"

"Yeah . . . but don't say anything, it's a secret."

"Why?"

"Don't ask, okay?"

"Whatever you say," Lisa said, shrugging. "It's not like *my* family's normal."

Meadow and Lisa came out to the patio, then ran past their mothers to dive into the pool. They swam and goofed off for an hour before getting out and lying on towels to sun themselves.

After a while, Lisa went to her bedroom to shower and Meadow could hear Mom's conversation with Dr. Wilson. She didn't mean to listen, but it was hard not to.

"Your home is beautiful, especially this view," Mom said.

"Thanks. I picked this house because looking out at the golf course reminds me of Ohio."

"It's a little like where we came from in Oregon, too."

"I wanted to tell you that I'm so grateful that Meadow made an effort to befriend Lisa." Dr. Wilson sniffed and put a tissue to her nose. "When we first moved here, she didn't want to start school, so I kept her out for a while. I even let her decorate her own room. It's hasn't been easy for her, you know, being bi-racial."

Mom covered Dr. Wilson's hand with her own.

"Lisa has been very important to Meadow as well. She tends to be kind of a loner and I worry sometimes."

Meadow squirmed. Geez, what's Mom worried about, she had friends now. Well, *one* friend, anyway.

The afternoon sun was dipping low in the horizon before Mom prepared to leave. It was nice that she had made a friend, too.

Later that evening, Lisa's mother called to have a pizza delivered. Meadow's mouth watered. Eating out was a rare treat for her family, and pizza was almost unheard of.

After chowing down until ready to burst, her eyes began to droop. Lisa laughed at her and they got ready for bed early.

She lay in bed next to Lisa, tired but happy, knowing that the next day would be full of excitement with the horse show. A good friend and new experiences to look forward to. Finally, things were going right.

Chapter 4

The Horse Show

Meadow sank lower in the seat as they pulled into the Pony Club grounds the next morning. The old truck stood out like an Okie wagon among all the fancy rigs in the parking lot. Horses and riders were warming up in the large arena, and Foxfire peered out of the truck bed with her nostrils flaring. Alongside her, Major stood calmly, used to the hubbub of the race track. Her father had agreed to bring the extra horse for Lisa so they could ride together between events.

Mom and her brothers would be coming a little later in the Ford, so if she messed up, the whole family would witness her humiliation.

"Dad, do you really think Foxy and I have a chance with all these expensive horses?" She watched a competitor trot by. "And these kids have lessons every week."

Her father patted her arm. "Don't worry. You're every bit as good a rider, and Foxy can compete with any horse in the world."

She wasn't at all convinced, and glanced down at her jeans and cowboy boots. Except for the western riders, everyone else had on hunt coats, tall English riding boots and helmets. Darn, maybe a hard hat was required. She didn't own one and hadn't thought to check the rules.

They unloaded the horses and Dad ambled off, no doubt to make some horse trading contacts. Meadow was brushing out Foxfire's long red tail, with Lisa nearby working on Major, when she heard a familiar voice behind her.

"Hi, Meadow, where are your brothers? I've looked all over the place and haven't seen them. They *are* coming, aren't they?"

She turned to see Cynthia Markowitz on the back of a tall, seal brown Thoroughbred. A few blonde strands curled up from under her black hunt cap. She was beautifully turned out in a maroon hunt coat. Her obviously well-bred horse acted like a veteran, unfazed by the commotion.

"Hi Cynthia. They'll be here a little later. Nice horse."

"Thanks, he *should* be nice, Daddy paid an absolute *fortune* for him. Daddy says if I don't win absolutely *everything* with this horse, then he'll sell him and I'll never get to ride again. Of course, I would be just *devastated.*"

"Oh." She was *so* annoying.

"I'm terribly glad your brothers are coming. I can't wait to see Monty again. Of course, I see Mike all the time in school. He's pretty cute, but I still like Monty best. You know, an *older* man." Cynthia eyed Lisa. "Did you bring a groom with you?"

Meadow felt a slow burn. "No, this is my *best friend.*" She grabbed Lisa by the hand. "Lisa Wilson—Cynthia Markowitz."

Cynthia's nose wrinkled. "Oh, hello."

Lisa didn't answer, just turned and went back to grooming Major. Cynthia yanked her horse around and rode off without another word.

"What a ditz! Who is she?" Lisa clenched the curry comb and her jaw tightly.

"We met her at our riding stable last summer. She fell off Foxy, and then her father tried to sue us." Meadow rolled her eyes. "She thinks she's in love with Monty."

Lisa snorted. "I knew plenty of her type back in Ohio and can do without them. Let's go warm-up."

They hopped on the horses bareback and rode to where other riders were practicing. Meadow saw the Ranch Wagon pull up with the rest of her family and waved. Her brothers were immediately spotted by Cynthia, who dismounted and began talking a mile a minute. Scott Carter, on his pretty palomino, spied Meadow and cantered over.

"Hi, Scott, what are you entered in?" she asked.

"I'm in the all-breed halter class and the western events. You?"

"Halter, bareback, trail horse and jumping." She ticked them off on her fingers. "Oh yeah, horsemanship, too."

Scott chuckled. "You must be going for the high point medal at the end of the season."

She nodded. "I thought if I was going to show, no use going half-way."

Lisa edged Major closer. "Hey Scott, is Jack here?"

"Yeah, I saw him over by the grandstand talking to Cynthia . . . before Meadow's brothers arrived."

"I'm going to find him, okay, Meadow?" Lisa started to ride away.

"Sure." Meadow turned back to Scott. "Want to ride with me to warm up? Foxy's a little spooky with all these strange horses."

Scott grinned. "I'd like that."

They rode around the ring, and after a while, Cynthia joined them.

"Meadow, I saw your friend talking to Jack Dawson. I just want to warn you he's got a bad reputation."

"Why were you talking to him then?"

Cynthia's Carnation pink lips pouted. "I *wouldn't* have talked to him at all, except he accosted me. He's *always* pestering me to go out. But I happen to know he's *not* a nice boy. He's part of a wild gang and they get into all *sorts* of trouble. Just wanted to tell you because Lisa is new here. I'm *trying* to be a good friend."

Without waiting for a response, she turned her horse and rode the opposite direction.

Meadow saw Scott raise his eyebrows a little. "What do you think, Scott? Is Cynthia just being Cynthia? You know Jack pretty well, don't you?"

"Not really. Yesterday at the water hole was the first time I rode with him. He came galloping up to me and we just hooked up. I haven't heard anything about him, one way or the other."

The loudspeaker came on announcing the first class was beginning, which was the all-breed halter category. Scott left to take off his saddle, and Meadow trotted back to the truck to get Foxfire's halter on. Her mare was still a little skittish, playfully shying and snorting at imagined boogie-men. Meadow laughed at her antics. "You'd better settle down, Foxy, and save your energy for the show ring."

She gave her one last brushing, grabbed the lead, and headed for the arena. The halter horses were all lined up, ready to go, and Meadow followed Scott into the ring. Cynthia with her fancy Thoroughbred was just ahead of them.

There were several other Quarter Horses, Thoroughbreds, and Arabians in the class, and a few other breeds, including a high stepping American Saddlebred. It was a large class with more than thirty entrants, and the best representation of the breed would win the blue ribbon.

The horses walked around the ring, then lined up in the center, with the judge looking them over. When Cynthia's turn came, Meadow had to admit, her horse was handsome and stood and moved flawlessly. Next it was Scott's turn, and his horse also performed very well.

Meadow held her breath as the judge walked over to her. Foxfire moved up and butted her from behind and she nearly fell into the judge's arms. He did not look amused. "Uh, sorry." She could hear a titter nearby and figured it was Cynthia. She straightened up, put Foxfire back into position, but not before the judge made a notation on his pad.

The ring steward nodded for her to trot out, and she led Foxfire, prancing at first, then settling into her floating, effortless gait. A few people clapped at the spectacle Foxfire made, with her burnished copper coat, long dark red mane and her tail flowing like a banner behind her.

The judge handed his assistant the results, and he sped to the announcer's booth.

"Third place goes to number twenty-three, Meadow Shepherd and Foxfire."

Meadow patted Foxfire and made her way over to the ring steward to receive her yellow ribbon. Scott Carter and Blondie won second place, with Cynthia and Majesty taking the blue.

Outside of the arena, Meadow's family surrounded her with congratulations.

"You did great, honey." Her mother beamed and gave her a hug.

Her father stroked Foxfire. "Foxy was the best, but she moved a little when the judge was looking at her. She'll win the blue next time."

"You'd better get ready for Hunter under Saddle," Mom said.

Meadow headed back to the truck, leading Foxfire to get her tack on. The Stubben saddle was perfect, but her clothes were not right—like she showed up at the prom wearing jeans and sneakers. She rode into the ring behind Cynthia so wrought up and nervous that Foxfire started prancing. Crap, her nerves were making her mare flighty, too. She *had* to calm down.

She took a deep breath and Foxfire began behaving herself. Just as Meadow was starting to feel more confident, the judge signaled her over. Her jitters came back in full force when she saw his sour face.

"I'm sorry, Miss. Your clothing is a little . . . shall we say, unorthodox? You must have proper attire for this class, including a hunt coat. You are dismissed from the ring." He gestured for her to exit.

She rode out of the arena with hot tears streaking her face. Scott was waiting at the gate and she tried to turn away from him.

He followed her, coming up close. "What happened, Meadow?"

She sniffed and peeked at him through watery eyes. "My clothes are all wrong. I didn't think they'd be so strict at a Pony Club show."

Scott frowned. "Well remember, it *is* Scottsdale." Then he brightened. "But you can still ride in Bareback, Horsemanship, Trail Horse, and Open Jumpers. You can wear anything in those."

She wiped the back of her hand across her face. "That's true."

"But you need a helmet for jumping. Maybe you can borrow one."

"From who?"

"Don't worry, I'll go find one for you." Scott firmed his chin and rode away.

Meadow watched him go, surprised that her former tormentor was becoming her champion. Then she started wondering where Lisa was. She hadn't seen her since the warm-up ring when she had gone to find Jack Dawson. She sighed. No use worrying about that right now, the next class was about to start.

She squared her shoulders and rode into the ring with renewed resolve. No hard hat or special clothes were required, thank goodness. Foxfire settled down and they rode in perfect harmony. So well that they won two firsts and a second in the next three classes. It was a different judge, who was apparently impressed with their teamwork.

Meadow grinned when she beat Cynthia in horsemanship. So much for private riding lessons. Cynthia was doing pretty well, though, winning four classes and taking third in another one. The last event, Open Jumping, would determine who would be high point for the day, since it was worth more than the others.

Scott came over to her during the lunch break, with a long face, dragging his feet.

"What's wrong, Scott?"

"I really tried to borrow a helmet for you. Trudy Jones doesn't even need hers since her horse came up lame, but when I told her it was for you . . ."

"I know, she's Cynthia's best friend. Of course she didn't want me in the class. Guess I'll have to scratch." She turned to go.

"Sorry, I tried . . . ." She could hear the hurt in his voice, but kept walking. With her head down she almost ran into a strange man.

He held out his hand. "Hello, I'm Joel Adams, a reporter with the Phoenix Gazette. You're Meadow Shepherd. I heard your name announced and came to find you."

Meadow frowned and looked him over. He seemed harmless enough—young, with sandy-colored hair that stood straight up in a short crew-cut. He put her in the mind of someone playing Jimmy Olsen in a Superman comic, complete with baggy pants, a rumpled shirt, and a pencil stuck behind one ear. He pulled out a pad from his breast pocket.

Meadow took a step back. "What do you want?"

"I'm covering the show for the sports section today. I'm a cub reporter and get stuck with some dumb assignments . . . I mean . . . you know—human interest stuff. All the snooty parents here like this kind of story . . . if their rich brat wins." Joel shuffled his feet.

"But why talk to me? I don't have any snooty parents to impress. You should interview Cynthia Markowitz." She started to walk away.

He grabbed her arm. "Wait. I'm interested in you because you're the one that foiled the band of Indian cave robbers last summer." Joel looked at her intently. "I was the one who broke that story. You were almost killed. That's much more interesting than covering this show."

"Oh." Her heart started fluttering and she felt the pendant under her shirt. Why couldn't everyone just forget about that?

He took the pencil down from behind his ear. "Do you know if they have any new information on the ringleader, Wendell Halstead?"

She shook her head and was about to flee when they were distracted by a powder blue Cadillac driving into the parking lot. A stunning blonde girl stepped out and waved. Meadow ran over. "Linda, I'm so happy you're here!" She hugged her. "I've really missed you."

Linda smiled. "Hi, sweetie, me too. Your mother phoned last night to tell me about the show, but I couldn't make it any earlier."

Joel had followed Meadow over to the car, and now stuck his hand out to Linda.

"Hello, Miss Bowman. Remember me? I interviewed you and Sheriff Dave Redland about the artifact thieves last summer."

"Of course I remember you, Joel. I told you I'd let you know if there were any more breaks in the story. Nothing so far." Linda put her arm around Meadow. "And I don't think Meadow wants to talk about it right now."

Joel backed away. "Okay, but be sure to let me know if the sheriff gets a lead on Wendell Halstead's whereabouts. You still have my card?"

"Yes, don't worry, we'll let you know."

Linda took Meadow's hand, led her over to the trunk of her car, and opened it. There was a large box full of English riding clothes, including a hard hat and tall boots.

"I thought you might be able to wear these. I was an avid Clubber when I was your age," Linda said. "Just thought I would pass them on to my 'little sister'."

"Oh, thank you! You're the best!" Meadow hugged her again.

"The boots may be a little big, but I think the rest will fit all right." Linda pulled the box out. "Go try them on."

Everything fit perfectly, except the boots were one size too big. Undeterred, Meadow poked some tissue into the toes. When she came out of the dressing room, she was transformed into the quintessential Pony Clubber.

Linda grinned. "You look fabulous. Let's get some lunch."

They made their way over to the lunch counter and ordered burgers, fries and Root Beers. Meadow peered over where her brothers were sitting and saw Lisa with them, thank goodness. On the other side of the pavilion, her mom sat with Dr. Wilson, but Dad was not there. Probably doing a horse trade.

Meadow sat down next to Lisa.

Lisa ogled her new outfit. "You look great. Where'd you get the clothes?"

"My 'big sister'." She nodded toward Linda, who was sitting next to Monty. "Remember, I told you about the Bowmans?"

"Yeah, she has nice togs."

Meadow leaned toward Lisa and whispered. "Where have you been? I was getting worried."

"With Jack." Lisa sighed. "He's dreamy."

"Just be careful, we don't know him very well."

"I will. But it's so exciting. I never thought a cute boy like Jack would ever even look at me." Her face glowed.

"Why not? You're smart as a whip and gorgeous to boot! Just be careful." Lisa looked at her curiously, but Meadow didn't have the heart to tell her what Cynthia had said. Besides, knowing Cynthia, it might not be true.

Meadow turned her attention to Linda, who was still speaking with Monty and Mike, updating them on her family. Linda's mother was in New York, running her galleries, and her father, Bill, was away in Mexico on business.

"What's Brett up to?" Mike asked.

"He's finally settling in and has found some new friends, I'm happy to say." Linda smiled. "He's even taking a girl to the Harvest Ball at Eaton."

Meadow felt her breath catch. He was dating some girl back East? Even though she had written several times, she had only received the one short letter from Brett. And now it seemed he had a new girl. Well, forget him, then! But it wasn't so easy when her mind flashed on his devastating blue eyes and how good it felt with her hand in his during the Bowmans' party last summer.

She sprang up when the announcer blared it was time to saddle for the Open Jumping class, and sprinted to retrieve Foxfire. When Meadow approached the arena, she saw all the various fences arranged for the competition. There were different types of obstacles—a picket fence, a chicken coop and a brick wall among others. She wasn't worried. Foxfire would jump anything she was pointed at.

A diagram was posted showing the required jumping pattern. In this class all that mattered was to have a clear round, in the right order. There would be a jump-off for horses without knocked down poles.

The first horse went onto the course and Meadow watched it bump two fences down. The next rider was excused for not following the pattern. Then it was Cynthia's turn. Her horse was a real pro and had a perfect round, in spite of the fact that Cynthia was a little off balance at times.

"Next up, number twenty-three, Meadow Shepherd aboard Foxfire."

Her stomach got tight cantering toward the first jump, but Foxfire settled in and jumped beautifully, clearing each obstacle with room to spare. Meadow let out her breath and smiled at her family, who were clapping wildly.

The rest of the class had fences down and then it was between her and Cynthia.

The loudspeaker came on. "Since there are two rounds with no faults, a jump-off will be held between number twenty-six, Cynthia Markowitz and number twenty-three, Meadow Shepherd. Some fences will be eliminated and the rest will be raised six inches higher. Please check the diagram for the new pattern."

This time Meadow was up first. She trotted into the arena, confident that Foxfire couldn't be beaten. Her mare proved true to form and cleared all the jumps cleanly. Cynthia clutched her reins tightly, and almost got her horse into trouble at the brick wall by getting behind his rhythm, but Majesty compensated well and they had a clear round.

"This is turning into a real duel, ladies and gentlemen," the announcer boomed. "Another jump-off between two beautiful horses, Foxfire and Majesty. The jumps will be raised another six inches and the best clear round with the fastest time will take home the trophy."

Meadow grinned. It was going to be timed and Foxfire was much handier than Majesty. She could cut corners and still jump cleanly. Cynthia wasn't a good enough rider to maneuver her larger horse around the course faster than Foxfire.

She looked over and saw Cynthia and Trudy talking near the gate. Trudy turned and walked toward her. What did she want?

Trudy offered a friendly smile. "Hope you understand about the helmet—my parents don't allow me to loan it out. I'm glad you found one."

"Yeah, it worked out."

"And I wanted to let you know the ring steward told us number five, the picket fence, is eliminated. They didn't mark if off the pattern yet. He said to tell you. It's pretty important, since you're going first."

"Thanks for letting me know, Trudy." She headed for the gate.

Meadow rode in and Foxfire flew over the brick wall and took the 'in and out' handily. She quickly dodged around the picket fence and galloped towards the large double oxer, clearing it with room to spare. Meadow felt a heady rush, knowing Foxfire was making good time. Only two more to go.

Uh-oh, the ring steward was signaling to her and then she heard the loudspeaker come on. "Number twenty-three is excused from the ring for breaking the pattern."

Meadow, fuming like a steam engine, heard some groans from the crowd as she rode out of the ring. Cynthia must have put Trudy up to it. Trudy had purposely given her false information about the change in pattern. How could Cynthia want to win bad enough to cheat?

Without any competition left, Cynthia took her time and cleared all the fences. When it was announced she won, the blonde ditz waved to everyone like a rodeo queen as she rode in and accepted high point trophy for the day. Then Cynthia had the nerve to put on a syrupy sweet smile for the photographer. Ugh.

Meadow was still seething as she removed Foxfire's tack. Her father came striding up.

"What happened, Meadow?"

She turned to him, her fist clenched. "Cynthia's friend told me the wrong pattern on purpose, so she would win."

"Why that little bi. . . brat! You were about to beat her, too. Oh well, anyone with a brain knows you could outride Cynthia with one arm tied behind your back." He shrugged. "You'll make up the points at the next show, don't worry."

"I hope so."

Her father smiled. "I made a deal with the director of the Pony Club to host some of the group on a hay ride for Halloween. You know I just traded for that nice team of Percherons. Should be fun for you kids, you're all too old for trick or treating."

"Sure, I guess." Oh boy, a hay ride with these snobs.

The rest of her family, along with Linda and Lisa, walked up. After saying goodbye to Linda, they loaded the horses for the ride home. Her spirits lifted with Lisa chattering and saying how good Meadow looked in her new clothes.

Her lips curved up. "Cynthia better watch out. I won't be fooled again."

Meadow caught a glimpse of the reporter, Joel Adams, as they left. He waved at her and she nodded. Why did he have to bring up Wendell Halstead—she hadn't thought of him in months. What if he had something to do with the creepy phone calls? A chill ran down her back, and she reached for the amulet.

Chapter 5

The Hayride

The fall day was warm and Meadow rolled up her sleeves to help her father load the pretty Percheron mares, Babe and Belle, for the Halloween hayride. When her father first told her about his plan, it sounded like a terrible bore, but now she was tingling with anticipation. Especially after she found out it would take place at the site of an old western movie set near Apache Junction. It even had a spooky boot hill cemetery to scare everyone. Cool.

"Really, Dad? They made movies there? Why didn't you tell me before?"

Her father grinned. "I wanted to surprise you. Besides, Bill was still finalizing the Fort Apache purchase until a few days ago. If it hadn't gone through, I would have taken you kids to a scary cemetery here in Scottsdale."

Meadow rolled her eyes. "I can just picture that, driving a wagon full of kids down Scottsdale Road to some fancy place where all the rich folks are buried. They'd throw us all in the slammer."

"Yeah, probably just as well we're going to Fort Apache. It hasn't been used in years and the buildings are fairly ghostly. Just right for Halloween."

"But why is Mr. Bowman buying it?"

"He's going to fix it up for guests. Sort of a Brighten South without the hot springs. In the early fifties they used it for filming westerns. You know Bill, he loves everything about the Old West."

This interaction with her father seemed almost normal for a change, so Meadow was sorry when their discussion was interrupted by a car pulling up. Monty parked the '49 Chevy sedan he'd purchased with some financial aid from Dad. Her big brother had landed a job at Turf Paradise, and Meadow was green with envy. Initially, he was only working after school cleaning the stalls, but had already been promoted to exercise boy on the weekends. How neat to be able to ride those gorgeous race horses and actually get paid for it.

Dad eyed Monty as he climbed out of the car. "I hear you have a hot date for the school dance tonight."

A slow flush suffused Monty's face. "Yeah, I'm taking a girl in my class, Susan Hart."

Meadow smirked. "Cynthia will be crushed."

Dad snorted. "That silly blonde will have to make do with Mike. He's coming along to help hitch up. Meadow, go get him. It's time to leave."

She left her father and Monty talking and went into the barn, where Mike was feeding the horses. Foxfire stuck her head over the gate, chewing a mouthful of sweet Bermuda hay, and Meadow petted her. Mike twisted the faucet to fill the water buckets.

"I'll finish up, Dad's ready to go." She took the hose from him. "You'll have Cynthia all to yourself tonight."

"She likes me anyway." A furrow appeared between his eyes. "Don't you think?"

"Sure, she likes any boy that pays attention to her. She's totally self-centered, you know, and will probably break your heart."

"I'm smarter than that."

"Are you going to wear a costume?"

"Nah, that's kid stuff." He gathered a couple of flakes of hay for Babe and Belle and headed to the truck.

Meadow turned back to Foxfire. She smiled while fingering the ribbons displayed on the front of the stall. She had done much better in the October horse show with no one cheating, and had easily won high point for the day. Cynthia hadn't even been much competition, falling off during the final jumping round. Meadow had laughed at her red face, but later felt a little bad when she saw Cynthia's father yell at her for not winning. What a jerk.

There would be another one-day show in November and then a two-day finale for the season in December. Meadow found she loved competing, but it was pretty annoying that some of the judges were obviously partial to the more well-connected kids.

She stroked Foxfire once more and gave Kelsey a scratch behind her ear, before heading back to the house. The sun was getting low in the sky and she needed to get into her Halloween costume. Meadow was going as an Indian princess and Lisa would be dressed as a dance hall girl. Her mother had spent hours sewing the outfits.

As Meadow came through the door, Mom looked up from last minute alterations. "I just finished the hemming. Here, try it on."

"Oh, Mom, this is wonderful." She rubbed the soft material against her cheek. "It feels just like deer skin. Where'd you get it?"

"Lisa's mother bought the material for both costumes at a fabric store in town. Then she found these moccasins to match. And look at how Lisa's costume turned out."

It was a flouncy sequined red dress featuring a low neckline with a feather boa to go with it. Meadow laughed, and wrapping the boa around her neck, danced around the room.

"She'll love it! All the boys will, too."

"It's what she asked for." Mom put on her stern face. "I wouldn't let *you* wear it, though."

"Oh, Mom, Lisa's a year older than me. It'll be okay."

Her mother held out the Indian dress. "Get into your outfit. Laura will soon be here to pick us up. I'm looking forward to a night out with her."

Meadow went into her bedroom and slipped on the dress, leaving the amulet on the outside for a change. After wriggling her feet into the moccasins, she went to the mirror to fasten the beaded red headband. She sucked in her breath and took a step back. The resemblance to the real Indian princess, Meda, was uncanny. In this outfit, she should be riding Arrow through the canyons with Colt by her side. But as soon as the thought popped into her head, her brow puckered. Why had she thought of Colt along with Meda and Arrow? It must be because he was dressed in buckskins when she first saw him, so beautiful and mystical.

She hadn't heard from him since they moved down to Scottsdale, but then she hadn't expected to. His father, Chief White Horse, said Colt was busy with his college studies in Flagstaff. She was pretty sure he didn't have time for a mere girl he had only met a couple of times. They did have a special connection though, she was positive of it.

Meadow was brought out of her reverie when Lisa threw open the door and flew into her room, clutching the dance hall costume. She quickly stripped down and got the dress on.

"Your mother is a genius! This is perfect, absolutely perfect." She turned before the mirror. "Yours is great, too. I'm glad you're wearing the necklace—just the right touch."

"We'll have the best costumes of anyone, I'll bet. Let's go. We don't want to miss the hayride."

They came out of the bedroom arm in arm, and then did a few pirouettes in front of their mothers.

"Very nice, girls. But Lisa, don't you think it's a little low cut?" Worry lines creased Dr. Wilson's forehead.

"No, Mom, I'll wear the scarf around my front. Nothing will show." Lisa demonstrated by draping the boa so she had full coverage.

Her mother heaved a sigh. "Okay, I guess you're right. We'd better leave now."

They drove out the road called Apache Trail, winding through the heart of the Sonoran desert east of Scottsdale. Large Saguaros were intermingled with Ocotillos, their long tendrils reaching out like tipped over daddy longlegs. In the distance, the Superstition Mountains rose majestically to reign over the land.

Apache Junction was hardly a town at all—really just a wide spot in the road, boasting a gas station, post office, and small store. The peaks of the Superstitions loomed darkly above them as they got closer. Near the base of the mountains, a stockade came into view, effectively blocking the buildings inside. A sign above the enormous entrance said "Fort Apache."

As they approached the gate, it creaked open a little, just wide enough for a single person. A hooded man with sunglasses appeared out of nowhere and slouched over to their car. Creepy. He must have been watching through a peep hole. Dr. Wilson lowered the window of the Lincoln and he scowled.

"Whataya want?" he asked.

Dr. Wilson drew back. "Is this the right place for the Pony Club Hay Ride?"

"I'll get the gate. Drive in to the left and park near the stables."

The man shoved his dark glasses up and his hood fell back. Meadow got instant goose bumps, wondering if he was a prop for the Halloween party. His nearly colorless eyes, and white hair cropped short reminded her of a zombie—all he needed was rags hanging from his limbs to complete the effect.

Her attention was drawn back to the surroundings by Lisa's excited voice. "Wow, this is neat. I feel like I'm in a movie."

Lisa was right. Dozens of log buildings were arranged like a frontier fort—so realistic that Meadow expected blue coated cavalrymen to materialize at any moment and escort them around.

The big wagon with straw bales was parked in front of a maze of rickety corrals, and behind them stood a cavernous barn. Babe and Belle were already hitched to the wagon and a few of the kids were petting them. Her father stood nearby, patiently answering endless questions about the team. When he saw Meadow, he stopped mid-sentence, staring at her.

"Don't you like my costume, Dad?"

"I wished you picked something else." His voice had a sharp cutting edge. Then he ignored her and went back to answering questions.

Her mood plummeted at his reaction. She knew from Colt that they were part Indian, why was Dad so negative about it?

Lisa had disappeared. She wasn't with the chatty group that included Cynthia, Trudy Jones and Scott Carter. Cynthia was dressed as Glinda from the Wizard of Oz, Trudy seemed appropriate as the Wicked Witch and Scott looked dashing in his Texas Ranger outfit. Jack Dawson and Mike were a little apart talking to each other. Jack wasn't wearing a costume either and had on a tight tee-shirt with a pack of cigarettes rolled into one sleeve.

Lisa came out from behind the wagon and Meadow touched her arm. "I didn't know Jack was coming, he's not part of the Club."

"I invited him. I hope that's okay."

"Too late now."

Mom and Dr. Wilson waved goodbye to them before turning the car around, on their way to a ladies' night out. A couple more carloads of clubbers had arrived by this time to complete the group and her father started organizing them.

"Okay everyone, gather around," he said, and they all moved closer to the wagon. "There's a surprise for you. Not only are we having a hayride to the cookout, but afterwards, when it's totally dark, you'll have a ghost fort to explore, complete with some surprises of its own."

Everyone clapped and cheered at the news. This would be more fun than they originally thought. The Pony Clubbers all seemed appreciative of Dad's efforts to put together a good time for them. At his direction everyone started climbing onto the wagon, jostling for position. There were around twenty-five kids crowded together, but nobody seemed to mind the close quarters; in fact, they seemed to like being crushed together.

Cynthia squeezed in next to Mike, smiled, and took his arm. If she was disappointed that Monty didn't come, she didn't let on. Jack sat down by Lisa, eyeing her neckline.

Meadow climbed up on the driver's seat with her father. Being squished in next to a bunch of pimply teenagers didn't seem very appealing. Scott poked his head up from the back.

"Okay if I ride up there, too, Mr. Shepherd? I'd like to see how you manage the team. I've always wanted to learn to drive."

"Sure, young fella. I might let you try. What's yer name?"

"Scott Carter, sir."

"Okay, Scott. Watch me." Her father took up the reins, released the brake, and clucked to the mares.

Babe and Belle moved off smoothly on a dirt track that went through the back gate of the fort and were soon in a trot. The cheerful jingle of their harnesses contrasted with painful creaks of the loaded wagon. As the sun lowered below the horizon, the filtered light of dusk quickly waned into darkness. Someone had thoughtfully placed lanterns alongside the road in intervals to show the way.

Scott grinned at Meadow, and then scooted closer, so they were touching. She tightened her lips and slid up against her father, linking his arm with hers. Dad shoved back his hat and looked over at Scott.

"Hold on there, young man. You just slide your butt back over where it belongs or you'll soon be afoot."

Scott gulped and did as he was told, red creeping up his neck. Her father turned to the kids in the back of the wagon.

"If anyone gets any bright notions about some hanky-panky, just get it out of your heads right now. It's a long hike back to the fort from the chuck wagon."

There was nervous tittering from the back, and some of the boys removed their arms from around the girl next to them.

They finally arrived at the cookout site, where the weird gatekeeper had the campfire going. The delicious aroma of hotdogs and hamburgers on the grill caused a stir from the hungry crowd. An ancient army jeep was parked nearby. It must belong to the creepy white-haired guy.

"Who is he, Dad?"

"He's the caretaker, Clay somebody. Apparently, he's been living at Fort Apache since they quit making movies here."

"He seems sorta . . . different."

Her father nodded. "He *is* a little odd. Acts like he doesn't want anyone around here. But he cooperated about this party. I couldn't have put it together without him."

Everyone grabbed napkins and paper plates, standing in line while deadpan Clay doled out food. After they got hotdogs, Scott sat down next to Meadow near the fire. The burning wood crackled and popped while they ate. Lisa and Jack huddled together in the shadows with their heads close together. Scott finally broke the silence.

"Do you think your father's mad at me?" His face was pinched.

"Nah, don't worry about it."

A smile broke out. "Whew, that's good. I thought I really blew it. By the way, you look great as an Indian princess. Pretty necklace."

"Thanks. I like your outfit, too. Especially that ten gallon hat." She playfully pulled it down to cover his eyes.

"Hey, knock it off."

"Okay." She flipped the hat off his head and giggled when he scrambled to retrieve it from the dirt.

"Darn, now it's dusty." His shoulders sagged as he plopped down.

She took the hat, dusted it off, and handed it to him. "Just payback for teasing me so much at school."

"You know I did that because I like you." His expression turned serious. "Um . . . I want to ask you something."

"Sure, what?"

Scott hesitated, swallowing.

"What is it?"

"Will you go steady with me?" The words tumbled out and fell flat at her feet.

Meadow blinked. "*What?*"

"You know, steady. Like you wear my ring."

"I *know* what it means, Scott." She shook her head. "I'm sorry, I don't think of you that way. I thought we were friends."

"We are, and I don't want that to change. I just thought maybe . . ." his voice trailed off and he stared at the fire.

Meadow knew his feelings were hurt, but the last thing she wanted to do was encourage him romantically. Not knowing what else to say, she just sat there, listening to the night.

After they finished eating, everyone piled back into the wagon, shoving each other and giggling. This time, her father directed Scott to sit in the driver's seat and he sat in the middle with Meadow on the outside. He handed Scott the reins for the drive back to the ghost fort, and then leaned back and pulled his Stetson low on his head. Scott clucked to the mares and for the first time since Meadow rejected his offer, he smiled.

By the time they got to the Fort, it was pitch black. Jack-o-lanterns were placed to indicate a route for a ghostly walk past the boarded up buildings. On a rise outside of the stockade, the trail led to Boot Hill Cemetery. When the kids broke into groups of their friends for the walk, Scott pushed past Meadow, and joined Trudy, who was with Cynthia and Mike.

All alone, and watching Lisa and Jack start out holding hands, Meadow slunk along behind the others. This was just great, no one wanted to walk with her. She allowed the others a good lead, hoping nobody would notice she was some kind of outcast.

The path revealed various scary Halloween figures, like Dracula, Frankenstein and the Werewolf. Once in a while a moan, howl or hair-raising laugh would escape one of the creatures, making the girls jump and scream. Meadow peered into the only open window on the way, and saw a ghost float by. How'd they do that?

She was the last person to reach the burial ground. The rest of the kids had already started back down the trail, laughing and talking about the mummy they'd found there. She wandered around for a few minutes, reading some of the tombstones. It seemed amazing that Wyatt Earp, Billie the Kid and Annie Oakley were all buried in the same graveyard. Likely story. In no hurry to get back to the others, she sat down on one of the stones, absently fingering her amulet, when she heard something sounding like the snort of a horse.

Meadow swung around, and could barely make out the ghostly form of a horse on the hill above her. The horse snorted again, reared onto his hind legs, and galloped out of sight in a flash of silver light.

Excitement coursed through her. *Arrow.*

Meadow ran up the hill, stumbling on the rocks in the darkness. She reached the top, with her breath coming in short gasps, and searched in vain for the stallion. She looked down to try and find his hoof prints, but it was too dark. It must have been him, though.

Frowning, she slowly made her way down to the cemetery. Maybe she wanted to see him so badly, she'd imagined the whole thing. After all, what would he be doing in the Superstition Mountains?

She hiked back toward the group and reached the fort's outermost building, marked "Guardhouse." It had bars on the windows and the doorway was indented from the walkway, with the door slightly ajar. Curious to see inside, she started forward when suddenly a ghost materialized on the threshold. Startled, she jumped back, but then smiled. It was just another prop for Halloween.

But instead of moaning, it talked.

"You'll be sorry for what you did," said the low menacing voice, and then it came forward, reaching out for her.

Meadow turned and fled to where the others were gathered. She panted to a stop next to Lisa, her heart thudding. Lisa took her arm. "You're white as the ghosts out there. What's wrong?"

"A ghost is what's wrong. It talked and tried to grab me!" Meadow stared back up the street. "There, in the old jail."

Lisa laughed. "Is that all? Probably someone goofing off. Look at all the 'ghosts' here."

Meadow peered around at the costumes. There were at least three in the group. For some reason, she hadn't noticed them before.

"I guess you're right." How embarrassing. "I've been a little jumpy lately."

"Guess so. C'mon, my mother's here to pick us up." Lisa led the way to the car and clambered in the back seat.

After settling next to her friend, Meadow wrinkled her nose. She whispered, "Lisa, have you been smoking?"

"Shhh, just a couple of puffs. It's nothing, don't worry about it."

Meadow sighed. She *was* worried, not only about Lisa, but also the strange events that night at Fort Apache. She wasn't totally convinced that the ghost had been a harmless prankster. What if it was one of Wendell's schemes?

Shoot, it *could* have been Wendell himself!

Chapter 6

Ladies Night Out

Rose heard the girls whispering after they bounced into the back seat. At first she smiled, thinking how nice to be so young and have all those teenage secrets. But as the door closed, a rush of air wafted the acrid odor of cigarette smoke to her sensitive nose. Rose glanced at Laura. She didn't seem to notice the smell, and was concentrating on backing the car out of the parking lot with dozens of other parents doing the same.

Meadow would never smoke—her asthma problems had taken care of that. In fact, she'd moved as far as possible from Lisa and they were not talking anymore. Maybe Lisa was getting in with the wrong crowd.

Laura had confided that her daughter could be a bit of a handful, willful and headstrong at times. Rose's thoughts drifted back to their earlier dinner conversation.

The evening had begun with them getting to know each other better. It didn't take long. Laura seemed as starved as she was for a female friend. Rose had been a little lonely since they'd left Oregon. She kept reminding herself how blessed she was to have Shep and such great kids, but there's nothing quite like a girlfriend. A night out with another woman was a real treat.

Neither of them knew the area, so when a sign for the *Lost Dutchman Steakhouse* popped up, they looked at each other and grinned. It was a cutesy type place fashioned after a mining claim, complete with an antique ore car on tracks, heading toward a faux mine adit.

After entering through heavy wooden doors, they crossed a sawdust strewn floor, and settled into a booth. Rose sank into the overstuffed cushions with a satisfied smile, while Laura perused the drink selection. "How about a glass of wine?" she asked.

"Sure. I like a good cabernet with my steak."

The waiter, all decked out in miner's garb entertained them by saying, "Y'all must be mighty hungry after a day of prospectin' but this is the right place, cuz the grub is mighty good here." After a few more clever comments, he hobbled away like Howard in "Treasure of the Sierra Madre."

When Rose looked at Laura they both dissolved into giggles. "I didn't realize we would get a comedy routine along with dinner."

After recovering her composure, Laura eyed her. "I'm envious of your sewing talent. The girls' costumes turned out beautifully, and aren't you wearing a new outfit? Very flattering."

Rose smiled and adjusted her skirt. "Yes, I decided to sew one for myself for our special occasion tonight."

"Love the pale yellow on you, it's quite attractive. Meadow looks a lot like you." Laura sighed. "I wish Lisa resembled me more. She's got a sultry air about her. I'm afraid she's going to turn into a real bombshell."

"She's a beautiful girl."

"I'll tell you, it's no picnic raising a teenager alone."

"It can't be easy, but you're a doctor. What a great career."

"I do enjoy my work. It's just that you and your family seem to have it all. I'd love to have a relationship like you have with your kids . . . and with Shep for that matter."

"Well, we don't have a lot of extras. But you're right about our family, we're very close." Rose wondered if something else was bothering Laura, but they were interrupted by the waiter. He pulled the cork, then filled their glasses with red wine. After taking their T-bone orders, he hobbled away.

Laura waited until he was out of sight. "I've been worried about Lisa. She seems happier lately, but kind of secretive. I'm afraid it might be a boy."

"She *is* that age. Just make sure she knows the boundaries."

"It's very hard for me to say no to her. Being from a broken home, plus bi-racial has made it difficult for her to fit in. If she has a boyfriend, is that so bad? Isn't it good for her self-esteem?"

Rose answered slowly. "She's pretty young. Really too young to date. I guess if they're always in a group it might be all right."

A cloud passed over Laura's face. "Oh, I wish Perry was still with us."

"Perry?"

"He's my ex-husband. We were very much in love." Laura hastily wiped a tear away. "Sorry to be so emotional."

Rose covered Laura's hand with her own. "What happened to him?"

"It was all too much pressure, having a mixed race family. He left when Lisa was less than a year old, saying we'd be better off without him." Her voice broke. "I've never told anyone this story."

"How did you meet?"

"We met at college, he was working his way through." Laura began hesitantly, then gathered momentum. "Tall, good-looking and always happy. He had this wonderful way of speaking. From Jamaica. Came here to make his fortune, and then found out it wasn't that easy for someone different."

Rose squeezed Laura's hand in sympathy. After a pause she continued her story.

"While I interned, Perry got a job as an orderly at the same hospital. He was always helping everyone, doing all the jobs no one else wanted to do. I admired him for being so strong and not caring what others thought. We fell in love and eloped without telling my parents."

"Oh."

"My parents were shocked at first, but when they got to know Perry, they adored him. But they were the only ones that accepted us. When I finished my residency, the hospital refused to give me a job, and they let Perry go, too. By then I was pregnant."

"It must have been hard with no income and a baby on the way."

Laura looked down at the table. "We had to move in with my parents. Perry's pride was injured, and finally he decided to leave us, saying we'd be better off without him and to forget he ever existed. He made me promise to never tell Lisa anything about him."

"Where did he go?"

"I suspect he joined the military, but I don't know for sure. I never heard from him again." Another tear escaped. "I should never have let him go."

By that time, their waiter had arrived with the steaks, and Laura abruptly changed the subject. Rose could tell she was done talking about her past life.

Laura took a bite and chewed slowly. She put down her fork and smiled at Rose. "Anyway, I know that Lisa is very fond of Major. I'd like to buy him from you, to give her something else to focus on besides boys. Maybe she could even show him in Pony Club."

"I think that's a great idea. He's a very nice horse for her."

"Can we keep him at your place? Of course, I'll pay for his upkeep. Whatever you feel is fair."

"Meadow would love that! We have plenty of room to board him."

The band started to play while the women finished their meal, and they fell quiet watching dancers step to the country swing. After a bit, they paid the bill and were on the way to pick up the girls.

Rose peeked over to the back seat. The girls were still sitting far apart, not speaking.

Something was really wrong.

Chapter 7

A Lost Soul

Meadow sat in the backseat and fumed. She glared over at Lisa, then out the window. The stony silence had become an insurmountable wall. How could her friend be so *stupid* to like that awful Jack? And to *smoke* with him! Lisa *knew* how Meadow had suffered with asthma. How could she deliberately take smoke into her lungs?

The only gas station in Apache Junction came into view and Lisa spoke up. "Mom, can we stop? I need to use to the restroom."

Meadow raised one eyebrow. Probably wanted to rinse her mouth out and wash her hands.

"Yes, dear." Dr. Wilson glanced into her rear view mirror. "You two are awfully quiet. Everything okay?"

"Yeah, fine." Lisa stared out the side window.

Dr. Wilson and her mother exchanged a look, but they didn't say anything. The Lincoln wheeled into the gravel parking lot of the sad looking station. The forlorn pump had an old fashioned round sign on top with a red star reading "Texaco." A greasy gas attendant shuffled out and Dr. Wilson asked him to fill it up.

Lisa pushed open the door and sprinted toward the Ladies room without a backward glance. Meadow got out more slowly and walked around the other side of the building to get away from the gas odor. She sucked in a cleansing breath of night air.

As she turned the corner, Meadow was startled to see a guy sitting hunched against the outside wall. It was nearly

11:00 p.m. and the temperature was dropping. The man, wearing only a thin jacket, shivered in the chill.

Meadow hurried to get past him, but then he looked up at her, eyes dull, like an animal that has been abused. As he stared at her vacantly, the hurt, bewildered look stirred a memory.

She peered at him more closely. "Wally, is that you?"

Was it the same guy from last summer? The one that had risked his life to save her from his crazed brother? She wasn't sure because this person appeared frail and boney, very different from the beefy guy that had been part of the pot hunter gang. But there was something about his eyes . . . she had to try again.

"Wally, it's me. Remember last summer at Brighten?"

He looked at her numbly with his mouth slack. She put her hands on his shoulders and gave him a little shake.

"Wally, can you hear me? It's Meadow."

Finally, some recognition filtered through and he seemed to become aware of her. A smile slowly replaced the drooping lips and his countenance brightened.

"Meadow? Is it really you? I thought . . . I thought I was dreaming—about an Indian princess."

"It's me. This is a Halloween costume. But what happened? You look terrible."

Wally sniffed, then wiped his nose on his sleeve. "I haven't been able to get a regular job since Rick died." He gazed at her with frightened puppy-dog eyes. "You know he always took care of me."

"But how are you making it? Where do you stay?"

"I wash windshields here, and sometimes people give me money for it. The owner is nice. Sometimes he gives me a dollar for helping out, and he lets me sleep inside when he closes. He's open late tonight because of Halloween."

"You mean, you have nowhere to go? Don't you have any other relatives?"

Wally blinked away tears. "Rick was my only family. I'm so glad to see you, Meadow. I've been so . . . alone."

Meadow swallowed. Wally wasn't exactly a friend, but he *had* helped her when she needed it. She took hold of his arm. "C'mon, Wally. You can come home with us." He stood, wobbly on weak legs, and she guided him toward the car.

Her mother rushed over when she saw them. "Meadow, what in the world? Who is that?"

"It's Wally, Mom. He needs a place to stay. He's been sleeping here."

"Heavens, he's skin and bones! At least we can offer him a warm barn." Her mother took his other arm. "Laura, is it all right if he rides back with us? We know him."

Dr. Wilson frowned. "Are you sure you want to take on a homeless person? We could just call the authorities."

"No, I'm afraid of what they would do with him. He fought to save Meadow's life. I think we owe him."

"Oh, that's different. Of course he can ride with us."

Wally climbed into the back seat, on the driver's side. Meadow cracked the window before she closed the door on him. She went around the car and scooted into the middle and Lisa scrambled in next to her, now smelling of cologne. Lisa stared at Wally and elbowed Meadow. "Who's that?" she mouthed.

"Someone we knew last summer. He needs a little help."

Lisa shrugged and turned away.

Dr. Wilson started the car and glanced over at Mom. "Will Shep be okay with this?"

Her mother chuckled. "Shep's famous for bringing home strays and Meadow seems to be following in his footsteps. I'm used to it." She looked at Wally and sighed. "He needs to be fed up. Believe it or not, he used to be a big guy."

They arrived back at the adobe house, and Meadow helped Wally out of the car. Her father had beat them home and shook his head when he saw the sad state Wally was in. "Okay, young fella, let's get you a bite to eat."

Monty got home from his date, walking in with a silly lovesick grin, just as Wally polished off the last of the leftovers. His expression changed when he saw a scruffy ragamuffin at the table. "Who's that? Is he going to sleep here?"

Mom patted his arm. "Remember Wally? And don't worry, Monty. He's not staying in your room. We'll fix up a spot in the barn, after he's had a shower."

"Good," Monty said. "It's bad enough sharing with Mike."

"Hey, I'd like to sleep out in the barn. It sounds more fun than rooming with a total bore bookworm." Mike slapped Wally on the back. "C'mon, Wally. I'll show you the bathroom."

Wally followed Mike, steadier on his feet after his meal. Mom bustled around gathering clothes and a toothbrush, while Meadow found her cot from Brighten and carried it to the tack room. Dad was already there, clearing out a place for Wally. An electric heater whirred softly in the background.

Meadow looked around. "This is a lot better than a gas station. Poor Wally, what will we do with him?"

"Don't worry. I have some plans coming up where Wally might fit in. I've been talking to Bill Bowman about a deal."

"What deal?"

"Bill and I are cooking something up, but I can't talk about it just yet. Nothing will happen until after the first of the year. By then, Wally will be healthy again and ready to earn his keep."

"Oh, Dad, can't you tell me anything?"

"Not right now, but soon." Her father turned from her to show the conversation was at an end.

Meadow sighed and left the tack room. She wandered over to tell Foxfire goodnight. After kissing her horse, she plopped onto a hay bale and Kelsey jumped up beside her. A possibility started dancing around in her head.

Hmmm, someplace where Wally could earn his keep . . . maybe they were going back to Brighten early!

Chapter 8

Double Date

Meadow brushed Major until his bay coat glistened, then tied a big red bow to his forelock. She led him out when Lisa's mother pull into the driveway. It was Saturday, a week after the hayride, and Lisa had been absent from school ever since. They hadn't even yakked on the phone.

Lisa crawled out of the car, her face an inscrutable mask. "Mom said we're riding today." She petted Major. "He looks pretty, what's up with the bow?"

Dr. Wilson joined her daughter and grinned. "He's yours now. I bought him for you, dear."

"Wow, Really?" Lisa's eyes brightened and she gave her mother a peck on the cheek. "What a neat present! I love him!" She hugged Major's neck. "Thanks, Mom."

Meadow stroked the gelding. "I'm glad you got him. Sometimes I worry about where the horses end up." Lisa didn't respond and wouldn't look at her. Meadow plunged on. "We can practice on my jumps, and then you'll be able to show him in Pony Club. You can use my English saddle."

"Okay." Lisa still hadn't faced her.

"Great idea, Meadow." Dr. Wilson climbed in her car and called out the window, "I'll pick you up after I get done with my rounds."

"Bye, Mom. Thanks again, you're the best!" Lisa led Major to the hitching rail and began tacking up.

Meadow went to the barn, retrieved Foxfire, and tied her next to the gelding. "Why haven't you been in school?"

"Uh . . . I've been sick," Lisa mumbled, busily tightening the girth.

"What was wrong?"

"I had cramps, you know, the curse." Lisa still had her back to her.

"Oh." Meadow scowled. Okay fine, be that way.

She left Foxfire tied, and set out ground poles for Lisa to teach Major some jumping basics. Before long they progressed to low fences. It turned out the gelding was game for learning a new skill and once he got the hang of it, jumped with beautiful form.

"You'll do great in the hunter classes. Major is so calm and really tucks his legs." Meadow wrinkled her nose. "Some of the judges don't think Foxy has the right appearance for a hunter, she's too forward and Arabian looking."

Lisa patted her new horse. "Yeah, Major won't do as well as Foxy in open jumping, but he's so quiet and steady, just what they like in the hunters."

Meadow hopped on Foxfire bareback and they practiced together most of the morning. Afterwards, they washed the horses down and put them in their stalls with some oats to snack on.

Tired from changing jump heights and working the horses, they dropped down side by side on a bale of hay in the barn to await Lisa's mother. Kelsey jumped up with them to get some attention.

Wally made his way out of a stall, shoving a wheelbarrow piled high with manure. He looked much better with a week's worth of steady meals under his belt, but he still wasn't back to his normal ox-like strength. He groaned and puffed with the effort of pushing the load.

"You're doing a good job keeping the stalls mucked out. The barn has never looked cleaner." Meadow grinned at him. "Glad I don't have to do it anymore."

He smiled. "I love doing this and being with the horses." He kept going without stopping to chat. Wally took his work seriously, and once he learned a task, doggedly kept at it until it was done. He was slow, but time didn't seem to have much meaning for him. Her father was teaching him to handle some of the gentle horses, letting him groom and pick out their hooves.

Lisa watched Wally roll his load away, and then turned to Meadow. "I'm glad you're not still mad at me." It was the first time she really looked at Meadow that day.

"I hope you don't pull something dumb like smoking again."

"I won't. Are you going to the dance tonight?"

The community center held teen dances every Saturday night, but Meadow had never attended one. Scott was trying again and asked her to come that night, but she put him off. "Are you going?" she asked.

"Yeah, I'm going with Jack. Mom said it was okay as long as we stayed with the group. Why don't you come? You won't need a date. There'll be tons of guys to dance with."

"Well, maybe. I *do* like to dance."

"Come on." Lisa donned her most charming face. "I'm double dating with Mike and Cynthia, and you can ride with us."

Meadow knitted her brows. "Who's driving? None of you have a license."

"Monty's dropping us off at the dance, then taking Susan to the movies. He'll pick us up after."

Meadow's head swam. When had they cooked all this up? "Okay, I guess I'll come." Better than sitting home alone.

"Oh good, it'll be fun." Lisa stood as her mother drove up and braked in front of the barn with the motor running. "Bye, see you tonight."

"See ya." Meadow heaved a sigh that they were on speaking terms again. She'd missed her friend. The Lincoln purred out of the driveway, and she took a mental inventory of her clothes while walking to the house.

Mom noticed she looked down in the mouth. "What's the matter, honey?"

"I said I'd go to the dance with Lisa tonight, but I have nothing to wear."

"Don't worry, I have just the thing." She brought out her new yellow dress. "I'm pretty sure this will fit you just fine."

"Oh, Mom, I love it!" She was an inch taller than her mother now, but about the same otherwise. The waist was a little too big, but her mother had a solution for that.

"I made this to go with the dress, but then thought it was a little too young for me." Her mother cinched a yellow sash with blue periwinkles around her slim middle. "It looks just right on you."

The rest of the day, Meadow busied herself with washing her hair and buffing her nails, carefully scraping out the barn dirt.

Her father arrived home after delivering one of the Navajo ponies he'd sold. "What's going on here? Everyone's rushing around like a bunch of scalded apes."

Mom laughed. "Monty's taking Susan out and dropping Meadow and Mike at the community center dance. No kids tonight."

"Yeehaw!" He grabbed her mother and started whirling her around the room. "Get your dancin' shoes on, darlin', I'm taking you out on the town tonight. We're overdue for a date." He gave her a big smooch on the lips right in front of everyone.

When Mom recovered her breath, she asked, "What about Wally?"

"He can fend for himself for one night. Now go get ready." He spanked her on the bottom as she walked away, giggling.

Mom couldn't help herself and left Wally a plate warming in the oven, worried that he wouldn't eat something nutritious on his own.

On the way to pick up the other teens, Meadow fidgeted in the back seat, irritated that everyone seemed to be in the loop except her. "Mike, why are you double dating with Jack and Lisa? I didn't know you were friends with him."

"Sure, Jack and I are pals. We hang out all the time at school. He really likes Lisa. Cynthia wasn't crazy about the idea of double dating with them, but I talked her into it."

Monty chuckled. "Sounds like Cynthia's obsessed with you now instead of me."

"Yeah, she's crazy about me."

"Better you than me."

Meadow broke in. "Well, I'm not crazy about Jack. I heard he has a bad reputation, like gang stuff."

Mike turned and looked at her. "Nah, that's not true. Don't believe everything you hear."

After picking up the rest of the group, Monty dropped them off at the dance. He sped away, apparently anxious to get to his new love.

The community center was jammed with kids of all descriptions and had a local teen band playing pop favorites for the crowd. Mike and Jack immediately escorted their dates onto the dance floor, leaving Meadow like the proverbial wallflower among some other single girls, just waiting. She wasn't alone for long, though.

Scott spotted her, and leaving Trudy behind, made his way over. He acted a little peevish. "Thought you weren't coming tonight."

She shrugged. "I changed my mind."

"You look nice. Wanna dance?"

"What about Trudy? Aren't you with her?"

"Yeah, but we're just friends. She won't care."

Meadow only hesitated a moment—the lure of the dance floor was too strong. She took his proffered hand. Out of the corner of her eye, she saw Trudy glaring at them, and wasn't so sure Scott was right about the "just friends" assessment.

From then on, Scott tried to monopolize her time, but Meadow managed to evade him and dance with other boys. She had just finished partnering with a good-looking sophomore who was on the football team, when Scott tracked her down once again. He scowled at the football player and when the big guy got the hint and left, Scott turned to her. "I just found out, there's going to be a party at Jack's house tonight. Wanna come with me?"

"No, I'm here with my brother and Lisa. I can't go."

"Mike and Lisa are going to the party. Now you *have* to come." Scott's smug look was annoying.

"My brother's going? I'll just see about that." Meadow scanned the room to find him.

She spotted Mike with Cynthia draped around him on the far side of the room. Jack and Lisa stood close by, and they were all talking. Meadow made her way through the crowded room, with Scott trailing along. "Mike, we can't leave. Monty is picking us up *here*, remember?"

Mike patted her shoulder. "It's okay, Med. We'll only be gone for a little while, then come back."

She lifted her chin. "I don't like it. I think we should stay here."

Jack got an ugly look. "Oh, Meadow, don't be such a prude."

"Yeah, don't be a stick in the mud." Cynthia had to add her two cents worth.

Scott took her arm. "Oh come on, it'll be fun."

Meadow, surrounded by the intense face of her brother and friends, wavered. She didn't want to be a complete square. "Okay, but we can't stay too long."

Mike grinned. "We'll be back in plenty of time to meet Monty."

An older friend of Jack's just happened to have a car, so they all piled into it. It was pretty tight, with seven of them in the small Ford coupe. The double daters squeezed in the back seat, and Meadow was crammed between Scott and Jack's friend. She stole an uneasy look at the driver, a guy who appeared to be in his late teens or early twenties. He had long greasy hair, slicked back with pomade and a tattoo of a rattlesnake coiled around his bicep.

He caught her looking at him and leered. "I'm Frankie. You're pretty cute. Why don't you ditch Scott and hang out with me?"

"No thanks." She scooted a little closer to Scott.

Scott beamed and put his arm around her. Meadow squirmed. Oh brother, this was working out great.

Thankfully, it wasn't far to Jack's place and as soon as they arrived, Meadow shook off Scott's arm and marched into the rambling ranch style house where Mike and the others had already disappeared. Then she overheard someone saying how cool it was that Jack's parents were out of town.

A group of guys with girls hanging on behind, roared up on motorcycles with a deafening din. Soon the house was bursting with rambunctious party goers. Many showed up with six-packs in hand. Most of the new arrivals were Frankie's friends and seemed to be around the same age. Meadow was almost sure she was the youngest one there.

Jack turned the hi-fi on full blast and started handing out drinks he'd mixed. Meadow, parched from all the dancing, gratefully took one of the punch-flavored concoctions. She took a long swig, downing half the glass. It tasted a little funny to her, but pretty good. After a couple more swallows though, she began to feel light-headed. The room swayed precariously and she sank against a wall, trying to focus her eyes. She squinted up and saw Mike approach with a glare. He grabbed the drink away.

"Hey, give that back." She swung at him but missed.

"Don't drink any more of this." He pulled her toward the kitchen.

She stumbled after him. "Why not?"

"It's spiked." He filled a glass with water and handed it to her. "Drink this. All of it." He watched her drink, refilled the tumbler, and then sat her down at the kitchen table.

"Stay here, I'm going to find Cynthia and Lisa, and we're getting out of here."

Meadow sat and gulped water, and finally the haze started to lift from her brain. She was a little queasy and worry about Lisa didn't help matters. What if she drank too much of the punch with the deadly punch? Her legs were steadier now and Meadow got up to find her friend. She made her way to the living room, and peered through the crush of people. Some of them were dancing, but many couples were lolling about on various seats, or sitting on the floor. They all seemed to be drinking beer or Jack's brew.

Frankie sidled over to Meadow's side, ogling her with hooded eyes.

"I'd like to take you for a ride on my motorcycle, pretty girl. How would that be?"

"You don't even have a motorcycle." She edged away from him.

"Oh, yes I do. I borrowed that car we came in, but my motorcycle is right outside now."

"No, I'm with Scott." She made a beeline across the room.

Scott was on the couch next to Trudy, who apparently hitched a ride to the party with someone else. They were both holding glasses of punch, giggling and looking generally goofy.

Meadow stood in front of them. "Be careful of that drink. It's spiked."

Trudy rolled her eyes. "Go away, Miss Prissy Pants. We know what we're doing."

With a lopsided grin Scott patted the couch for her to sit next to him. Meadow shook her head and went on searching for Lisa. She saw Mike talking to Cynthia in the dining room. When Meadow peeked out to the backyard, she found it was layered with people sprawling all over the grass. She started down a long hallway with bedrooms on both sides and glanced into each one in passing. The rooms all contained couples kissing and fondling each other.

As she approached the master bedroom at the end of the hall, Meadow heard voices inside and one sounded like Lisa. She cracked open the door, and poked her head in.

She saw Jack and Lisa lying on the double bed. Lisa's dress was partially unzipped and pulled down. She was trapped under him. Meadow stood frozen, not sure what to do.

"Come on, baby. You know you want it," Jack was saying.

"No, Jack, please stop."

"Don't be a tease, baby." He kissed her neck.

"Jack, please, no." Lisa struggled to pull away from him, but he held her down with a strong grip.

Without thinking, Meadow rushed into the room, grabbing Jack's arm. "Let her go!"

"Get away from me." He violently elbowed her and she fell onto the carpeted floor.

The door banged open and Mike barged in. He pulled Meadow to her feet. "You okay?"

She nodded, rubbing her side.

Mike turned to Jack. "Leave Lisa alone."

Jack's face turned purple and he leapt off the bed, lunging toward Mike. Mike sidestepped and grabbed his arms, wrestling him to the floor. They rolled over and Mike pinned him, sitting on his chest and holding his head between his hands.

"You've had too much to drink. When a girl says no, you need to listen. You understand?" He squeezed Jack's face. "Understand?"

Jack gasped and nodded; then Mike released him, allowing him to get up. Meadow went over to Lisa, who was sobbing and trying to zip up her dress.

"I'm so sorry. You must think I'm awful."

Meadow tightened her lips and helped with Lisa's dress.

"Please don't tell my mom."

"I won't."

"You're the best friend ever, and I've been just horrible." Lisa hugged her tight.

Mike stepped over to them. "Come on, girls. We need to get out of here. This party is going downhill fast."

The music was blaring louder than ever, and even more people had arrived. They located Cynthia sitting in a corner of the living room, looking worse for wear. She was sipping daintily out of a paper cup.

Mike went to her and snatched the drink away. "Cynthia, I told you not to drink that stuff. And I told you to wait in the dining room until I found the girls."

She looked up at him, started tittering, and then hiccupping. Mike groaned, brought her some water, and watched as she drank it down. He pulled her up, and walked her back and forth.

"Uh, I don't feel so good." Cynthia held her hand to her mouth.

Mike led her over to the bathroom, shoved her in, and closed the door.

They could hear retching and after a few endless minutes, Cynthia stumbled out smelling bad, with mascara smeared down her face. Mike gave her more water and just as she started to perk up, they all heard a short blast of a siren.

Meadow's stomach did flip-flops when flashing lights began making eerie patterns on the walls of the living room.

"Oh crap! A neighbor must've called the cops." Mike latched onto Cynthia and towed her toward the back door. "C'mon, let's get out of here."

Meadow and Lisa raced after him, across the body-strewn lawn and into the alley. Lisa turned at the last minute and waved to Jack, standing in the doorway, watching them. Meadow grabbed Lisa's arm and gave it a yank. How could she still *like* that guy?

It was only a couple of blocks back to the Community Center, but Cynthia started moaning immediately. "My feet hurt. Slow down."

Meadow looked down at her spike heels. "Maybe you shouldn't have worn such dumb shoes."

Cynthia's face crumpled. "Oh, just shut-up, Meadow."

"You shut-up, you mealy mouthed whiner. We save you from the cops and all you can do is whimper about your stupid feet!"

Cynthia didn't say anything else, but laid her head on Mike's shoulder, looking wounded, and occasionally sniffling.

By the time they approached the center, the dance was winding down, and they could see Monty's Chevy parked in the lot. He came striding out of the building, his mouth set in a hard line. "Where have you been? I looked all over the place for you."

Mike told him they went to a little party, but judiciously omitted the part about drinking and the police showing up. Monty narrowed his eyes. "You all look pretty beat up. What happened?"

Cynthia gazed at Mike adoringly. "He saved us all from the cops." She latched onto his arm. "He's my hero."

Mike shook loose from her. "Be quiet, Cynthia. You talk too much."

Monty sucked in his breath. "The cops? I've heard about parties like that, how could you be so stupid? Don't ever do that again. When I leave you someplace, stay put until I pick you up."

"Okay, okay don't make such a big deal out of it. Nothing happened." Mike shifted his feet.

"If you ever pull a stupid stunt like this again, I'll tell Dad."

Mike looked like he was about to argue, but in the end held his tongue.

They climbed into the car, and Meadow wondered what happened to the rest of the party goers. She hoped Scott was all right, but Jack deserved whatever he got. She glanced over at Lisa, scrunched into her corner.

What's wrong with her? Cigarettes and now this?

Chapter 9

Wendell

Wendell Halstead settled into a lounge chair, surveyed the back yard, and took a sip of his Pabst beer. The pool sparkled an invitation, but he really wasn't a swimmer—not much of an athlete at all, given his short, round physique. Lucy liked to splash around in it, though. She'd been sullen about the move back to Arizona after the excitement of Las Vegas, so he'd made the concession to rent a place with a pool.

Pleased with himself, Wendell took a breath of the cool night air. Ahh . . . alone at last. And quiet for a change. He'd sent Lucy to the 7-11 to get a six-pack, even though he still had a couple brews in the fridge. She'd been irritating the crap out of him with her interminable chatter. He needed time alone to think. It was only nine p.m., but the neighborhood was still as a crypt. Most of the old geezers that lived there were either glued to the tube watching Lawrence Welk or already in bed. Wendell chuckled. His parents used to watch that program every week, driving him wild with the sprightly polka music. He'd gotten his revenge when he stole their life savings.

He took another sip, savoring the quiet. What could be a better location than Mesa, Arizona? Gravel yards painted a lovely grass green and old blue-haired retirees who minded their own business. They could barely even dodder off to church, let alone suspect a wanted criminal lived among them, right on their street.

Lucy wasn't thrilled with the neighborhood, but who cared what she thought? All she wanted to do was dye her hair and paint her nasty cat-claws. Las Vegas suited her better, but the casino had started to catch on to his card-counting scheme, so it was time to move on. He'd always managed to fly under the radar—until last summer.

He gritted his teeth and clenched his fists into tight balls. That little brat ruined his plot to steal the Indian artifacts, and she was certainly going to pay for it. He took another swig of beer. A sneer curled his upper lip as he thought about his new plan. It had taken a while, but he finally found the right accomplice. Someone as evil as Rick had been, with no scruples. He was perfect—didn't even have a record. Wendell found it distasteful to perpetrate violence himself, but wasn't against using brute force if it served his purpose. He picked up the phone, dialed and spoke for a few minutes.

When Lucy slid open the patio door, he quickly ended the conversation. Her hair was now the same color as the ripe oranges that decorated the backyard trees. She sashayed over next to him, scooting her wide butt onto a lounger. "Who was that, hon? It's kinda late to be making social calls."

Wendell slitted his eyes. "Never mind. It's none of your business."

"You've got that snake-look. I hope you're not tormenting that girl again. What was her name . . . Meadow?" The effort of actually completing a thought seemed to exhaust her and she sank back in the chair.

"No, I was talking to a business associate, if you must know."

"Well, I'm glad you've given up trying to get revenge. I draw the line at hurting kids. Even teenagers, as revolting as they are." She lit a cigarette and inhaled deeply.

Wendell put his fingertips together and smirked. "Don't worry. *I* won't be hurting anyone."

Chapter 10

A Deadly Recipe

Meadow ignored the goosebumps on her bare arms as she diligently soaped and cleaned Foxfire's tack. The mid-December coolness felt good after a long, warm fall. She admired the sheen on her saddle, then scrubbed the bridle. The next day was the start of the final two-day show of the Pony Club fall series, and her equipment must be perfect. Kelsey perched atop a hay bale, ready at a moment's notice if Meadow should decide to go for a ride, and Foxfire had her head stuck over the stall door, watching the whole procedure.

Mike ambled into the barn. "Big show tomorrow, huh? Cynthia was moaning that you might beat her out of the high point medal, since you won open jumping in November."

Meadow put down her cleaning rag. "Good. I'm glad she's worried. She did win the hunter trophy, but we're ahead overall." She turned and stroked Foxfire. "This will be Foxy's last show. Her foal is due in April and I don't want to risk anything happening to her or the baby."

"Is Lisa bringing Major to the spring series?" Mike plopped down and patted Kelsey.

"She's planning on it. He's training well and I think she'll be competition for Cynthia in the hunter classes." Meadow picked up a straw and chewed on it. "I'm worried about Lisa, though. She's been pretty evasive with me. Is she still seeing Jack?"

"Uh . . . maybe."

"Mike, tell me. I know you're friends with Jack, but I'm not sure why."

"Jack's not such a bad guy. You know Lisa isn't totally innocent in all this."

"You mean she *is* still seeing him?"

"Why don't you ask *her*? And while you're at it, ask her why she's not in class one or two days a week."

"You mean she's been cutting school with Jack? I knew she'd been out a lot lately, but she always had some excuse, a headache, stomachache . . . but ditching . . . ."

"You didn't hear it from me." Mike got up. "Mom wants you to come in and set the table for dinner."

Meadow carried her saddle to the tack room, gnawing on her lip. How could Lisa be such a *liar*? She took a deep breath. It was time for a 'heart to heart' talk with her friend.

It was still dark when Meadow loaded Foxfire and Major into the truck the next morning. Wally heaved up a bale of hay and stood by while her father threw in a bag of sweet feed.

Dad dusted his hands on his jeans. "That should do it, plenty for one night. Wally, did you get the water buckets?"

Wally nodded, shuffling his feet. Pretty soon he blurted out, "You think I could come with you? I've never been to a horse show before."

Her father chuckled. "Sure, a break will do you good. You can help Meadow when she has to change tack."

"Oh, boy. I could even stay down there tonight, to make sure no one bothers the horses."

"That won't be necessary, they close the gates at night. But I appreciate the offer."

Meadow climbed in next to her father, and Wally sat by the window. Monty was at work, but when he finished galloping race horses, would bring Mom and Mike to watch the show.

After driving to the south side of Phoenix, they pulled into the fairgrounds, and Meadow saw the usual bustle of activity.

Butterflies flitted around in her stomach. Before long, she and Foxfire would be the champions. She could think of no reason why they wouldn't win high point.

In the middle of the fairway, food vendors and various booths were set up to sell all types of horse equipment, including show apparel.

At least she didn't need clothes anymore. Thanks to Linda Bowman, she was one of the best dressed exhibitors. It was too bad Linda wouldn't be there for her triumph, but Mrs. Bowman had taken her on a shopping spree. The butterflies started doing somersaults when she remembered Brett would be in town for Christmas vacation. He may have forgotten all about last summer, but she'd remind him when they were at the ranch. Her whole family had been invited to Brighten for the holiday.

Meadow helped her father unload the horses and put them into their assigned stalls.

He was antsy to get going. "I'm taking Wally with me to check out the booths. You never know, we might be able to make a trade with one of those used tack fellas. Right Wally?"

Wally's head bobbed up and down. "That's right, Mr. Shepherd." He gazed adoringly at his idol.

"Can you get ready by yourself, Meadow?"

"Sure, Dad, go make a trade." Meadow stared after them, feeling mixed emotions. She was glad her father had taken Wally under his wing. The big guy wasn't as dim-witted as everyone thought. His older brother, Rick, had kept him under his thumb his whole life, making fun of him and telling him he was stupid. No wonder he acted dumb. Who wouldn't, having to put up with that murderer? But on the other hand, she was a little jealous. Even though her father wasn't openly uncaring, they weren't close like they'd been in the past. He always acted like he couldn't wait to get away from her. It hurt.

Meadow swallowed a lump and began meticulously grooming Foxfire. When her mare was gleaming, she saddled up and headed to the arena. She saw familiar faces—Cynthia looking tense with her father shouting instructions from the sidelines, and Scott with his normal easy-going style, cantering Blondie around ring. It wasn't long before the first class was announced, and the show began in earnest.

By noon, Meadow was flying high, having widened the gap between herself and Cynthia Markowitz, the only real competition for the high point medal. A two hour lunch break was announced and she rode Foxfire to her stall, pouring her a scoop of sweet feed for lunch. Dad had brought the oat, corn and molasses mixture especially for her mare, knowing that she needed extra calories with her pregnancy. Foxfire lit into it, taking large mouthfuls.

Lisa appeared by herself and joined Meadow at the stall door.

"Where's your mom?"

"She saw your mother and they're walking around looking at saddle exhibits." Lisa smiled. "She wants to buy me one, so I don't have to use yours all the time."

"I don't mind."

"Yeah, but it'll be nice to have my own." Major stuck his head out of the stall and Lisa stroked him. "I heard you're really trouncing Cynthia. I'm glad, she deserves it."

Meadow nodded. "Yep, by the end of the day, she'll never catch us. Come on, let's get some food, I'm starved."

They walked along the line of vendors, decided on corndogs, then climbed into the grandstand. With plenty of room on the bleachers, they spread their lunches out. Meadow ate part of her dog, sneaking glances at Lisa. She sucked in her breath. It was time. "I know you're still seeing Jack."

Lisa chewed slowly, looking straight ahead. "Where'd you hear that?"

"It doesn't matter, but I think you're heading for trouble."

"And I think you should mind your own beeswax." Lisa picked up her bottle of root beer and took a sip.

Meadow plowed ahead. "You're my best friend. I don't want anything bad to happen. Remember the party?"

Lisa turned to her with a soft smile. "Yeah, I remember. You saved me. Jack was drunk, though, and he hasn't done anything like that since. But he *is* pressuring me to go all the way."

"You need someone that shows you more respect."

Lisa snorted. "Like *who* for example? There aren't any guys like that. They're all the same."

"That's not true. I met a guy at Brighten last summer that showed me respect. His name was Colt."

Lisa raised her eyebrows. "Who's Colt? I thought your boyfriend last summer was Rhett or Jet or something."

"Yeah, that's right, Brett. Um . . . that's who I meant." Meadow fanned herself with the program, then pursed her lips. "The important thing is that there *are* nice guys around. You don't have to see someone that only wants one thing."

"But he's the first boy that ever really liked me. It's nice feeling wanted. What if no one else wants me?"

"Lisa, you don't have to worry about that. You're smart, fun and pretty. Don't settle for someone like Jack. My mom says those kind of boys just use you and once they get what they want, they dump you for a new conquest."

"You talk to your mother about things like that? I could never tell my mom anything. She wouldn't understand."

"I'll bet she would. She's a doctor, you know." Meadow stood. "C'mon, let's go look at the exhibits before the next class."

"Okay." Lisa gathered the trash and followed her off the risers.

They walked around through the booths, admiring the expensive saddles and headstalls with silver Conchos. There was every imaginable type of horsey stuff, even tee-shirts, jewelry and coffee mugs.

"Good thing I don't have any money, 'cuz I'd spend it all right here." Meadow fingered a fancy breast collar.

"How about this?" Lisa tried on a flashy, turquoise-blue western hat with a tiara instead of a normal hatband.

"Cute. It'd be perfect for Princess Cynthia." Meadow took the hat, placing it back on the rack. "C'mon, we'd better get back to the barn."

They had just started for the stalls when Wally came rushing up, out of breath. "Meadow, come quick!"

"Wally, slow down. What's wrong?"

"Foxy." He gulped in some air. "She's acting . . . funny."

Meadow felt the blood drain from her face. "What do you mean? Funny how?"

Wally blinked rapidly. "I don't know, but you'd better come."

Stomach suddenly in knots, Meadow was already running toward the stable area with Lisa and Wally in close pursuit. As she got closer, she saw Major sticking his head over the stall door. The gelding neighed loudly when he saw them approaching. She couldn't see Foxfire.

Racing straight to the stall, Meadow peered over to see Foxfire down, sweat pouring off her. Her breathing was labored and her eyes were half-closed.

"Foxy!" Meadow yanked open the door and rushed to her side.

Lisa's hand flew to her mouth. "Oh my god! What happened to her?"

"Wally, find Dad," Meadow barked. "Lisa, get the vet, now!"

Wally and Lisa scattered in different directions. Meadow took off her show cravat, dipped it into the water bucket, and bathed Foxfire's face and muzzle. Her mare opened her eyes and Meadow could see she was suffering.

"Foxy, can you get up? Please, try to get up." If it was colic, her mare needed to walk.

Foxfire tried to rise, then fell back on her side, breathing heavily. Meadow clipped a lead into her mare's halter and pulled her head up, clucking. With great effort, Foxfire heaved up onto quivering legs, but almost immediately sank down again.

When the vet arrived, Meadow was nearly as sweaty as Foxfire from her frantic efforts to get her mare up.

"I'm Dr. Stevens. Let her alone for a minute." He went to the mare's head, and pulled her lip up, checking the color of her gums.

Meadow stood by, swiping at tears. "Is it colic?"

"Seems to be, although she is in more distress than usual. When did the pain begin?"

"She was fine when we left for lunch, about an hour and a half ago."

"Did you give her any food? Anything she's not used to?"

"She had a scoop of Omolene, but she's been eating that for a couple of months. She's in foal." Meadow kneeled beside the doctor as he listened to Foxfire's heart.

"Check to see if she ate it all."

Meadow went to the feed bin and noticed only a few mouthfuls were gone. "Most of it's still here. That's strange, she was eating when we left."

"Has she ever colicked before?"

"No, she's never been sick. I've had her since she was a weanling."

The doctor placed a hand on Foxfires's windpipe, then rose and peered in the feed bin. He took a handful of the mixture, smelled it, then turned to Meadow, frowning. "Has anyone else had access to her feed?"

She shook her head numbly.

"It appears to be oleander poisoning, judging from her rapid heartbeat and pale mucus membranes. This feed will have to be tested. Meanwhile, we need to try and empty her stomach as much as possible. I'll get the equipment." He left for his truck.

While the vet was outside, her father and Wally showed up. Dad lost all color in his face when he saw Foxfire.

Dr. Stevens returned with a long hose and a sling. He nodded to her father. "I'm glad you're here. This little gal and I would've had a hellava time getting this mare to her feet by ourselves."

Meadow and the men surrounded Foxfire and heaved her up, supporting her with the sling under her girth. The vet began carefully inserting the hose down one nostril. "I'm putting in the nasogastric tube to prevent the backward flow of intestinal contents into her stomach. As you know, horses are unable to vomit to rid themselves of poison."

After starting the procedure, they allowed Foxfire to sink to the ground again and Dr. Stevens filled a syringe and injected it into her neck. "This will make her feel more comfortable. Now we just have to wait." He shook his head. "It's good we caught it relatively early and she only ingested a couple of bites. It doesn't take much oleander to kill a horse."

Dad's face grew dark, like a gathering storm. "Someone must have put it in her oats. Who would do such a thing?"

"Cynthia really wants to win high point." Lisa put her arm around Meadow.

Meadow sniffed. "Even Cynthia wouldn't stoop this low."

Lisa pursed her lips. "I'm not so sure about that."

Dr. Stevens gathered a sample of the feed. "I'll have this analyzed to be certain it's oleander. I'll check back with you folks this evening. If she's going to survive, we'll know by tomorrow morning."

Meadow ran to her father, sobbing.

Dad held her tightly. "Take it easy. Foxy's healthy and strong. She'll make it through this, you'll see." He released her when the rest of the family and Lisa's mother appeared.

"Looks like Meadow and I will be spending the night here, Monty," Dad said. "Go home, bring back sleeping bags, a lantern, and a change of clothes."

"I'll help him," Mom said. "Mike, Wally, you come too. There's nothing you can do here."

As Meadow watched her family head for Monty's car, she gripped her father's hand. He pulled away and said, "Fill the water bucket and bathe her face some more."

She stumbled to the spigot on legs that wouldn't cooperate.

Lisa and her mother stayed for a while, then disappeared. They came back carrying drinks and snacks, but Meadow couldn't choke anything down. Lisa hugged Meadow before Dr. Wilson had to leave for hospital rounds. "Foxy will be all right."

By five p.m., Mom was back with the supplies, parking next to the truck. When she opened the car door, a black shape bounded out and sped through the open stall to Meadow.

"Kelsey! Mom, I'm so glad you brought her."

"I couldn't avoid it. She seemed to know something was wrong and wouldn't take no for an answer."

Mom insisted that Meadow take a break from Foxfire's side and brought out roast beef sandwiches and fruit. She stashed a thermos full of hot soup in the truck for later. Meadow managed a couple of bites of an apple, but when she heard her mare moan, she dropped it and bolted back into the stall.

As promised, the vet returned that evening about seven, but there was not much change in Foxfire. She still lay on her side, groaning occasionally. Dr. Stevens shook his head, and gave her another shot for pain. Then he took her dad and mom aside. Meadow couldn't hear what they were saying and was too upset to ask, fearing the worst. She sat by Foxfire's side hour after hour, bathing her muzzle, and stroking her.

It was late when her father told Mom to go home and get some rest. Her mother hugged Meadow tightly before leaving, but had nothing to say that would make it easier. The night dragged on and on, relentless. Her mind went blank, her tears dried. There was nothing left.

Finally, Dad pried the wet cloth out of her numb fingers. "Lie down and try to sleep. I'll wake you if anything changes."

She spread out the sleeping bag, but instead of snuggling with her, Kelsey stayed right by Foxfire, keeping a close watch.

Meadow lay awake for hours, cringing every time she heard a groan from her horse. In the wee hours, she fell into a troubled slumber. Her lids flew open early in the morning when Foxfire struggled to her feet.

Her father stood in the doorway, backlit by the morning sun. "She's going to be all right."

"Foxy, Foxy." Meadow jumped up and buried her face into her warm neck.

Foxfire nuzzled her, and then bent down to Kelsey, who licked her nose. Her father unhooked the water bucket, and then went outside to refill it.

Meadow was still stroking her mare when Dad returned with the pail and hung it up. Foxfire drank deeply, dehydrated from her ordeal. Her father slumped against the wall, eyes shadowed, and face drawn. She glanced around and her stomach lurched. The straw was stained dark red where Foxfire had been lying. Her hind legs were streaked with blood. "Daddy, what happened?"

His whole frame sagged. "Foxy lost her foal last night."

"Oh, no, poor Foxy." Her streaming eyes found her father's. "But she will totally recover from this, right? She can have another baby someday."

"Foxy should be fine, but the vet warned me she would lose the baby." He paused. "Dr. Stevens also said she wouldn't be able to have another foal."

It felt as though she'd been slammed in the middle with a sledge hammer, and Meadow collapsed in a heap, sobbing.

Chapter 11

Christmas at the Ranch

The shadows of dusk lengthened as Meadow watched her friend negotiate the jumps one last time. "He's doing great," she called, when Major sailed over the final fence.

Lisa reined her horse in. "I'm so proud of him."

"Major will miss seeing you while you're gone."

"He'll have a good time in the pasture eating grass all day." She patted her gelding.

"Are you excited about seeing your grandparents?"

"I guess so." Lisa made a face. "But not looking forward to the endless plane ride to Ohio." She gazed toward the barn, where Foxfire listlessly hung her head over the stall door. "When will you be able to ride Foxy again?"

"Dad says she'll recover more quickly if she doesn't have any stress, so we're taking her to the pasture with Major." She walked to the stall and with trembling lips, stroked Foxfire. Her mare's gaunt appearance and dull eyes always made Meadow want to cry. And hurt the person that made her mare suffer.

"I think whoever tried to murder Foxy should be shot." Lisa spat out the words as she led Major into the barn. "I'm still not convinced that Cynthia didn't have *something* to do with it."

"I know, but you can't accuse someone unless you have proof. When that reporter, Joel Adams, broke the story about the poisoning, even Cynthia seemed upset."

"She's a good actress or maybe it was her sleazy father who used that poisonous oleander. All I know is, she wouldn't have won the medal if you and Foxy had competed."

Meadow still got a knot in her gut remembering that terrible night. "We may never know who did it, but I hope whoever it was has a bad life."

"Me too. I think he should get run over by a garbage truck, and hauled to the dump." Lisa pulled out a straw of hay and chewed on it. "The barn will be empty with all the horses in pasture. Wally'll be sad without his friends to take care of."

"He's coming with us to Brighten for Christmas. We didn't want to leave him alone while we're gone. You know he hasn't got any family. When Dad told Bill Bowman his situation, he said to bring him along."

"That's nice." Lisa kissed Major on the nose to say goodbye.

"Yeah, they have plenty of room. My parents will sleep in the guest wing and the boys in the bunk house." Meadow grinned. "I get my old bedroom, as they call it."

"I'm glad to see you smile again. You've been either mad or sad ever since . . . well, you know."

Meadow nodded. "I know. I can't help but think about it."

That afternoon, Meadow and her father loaded Foxfire and Major to take them to the pasture on a farm a few miles south, where they purchased their hay. Dad had become friends with the family when he sold them a couple of riding horses.

They drove down the lane approaching the pasture, and Meadow smelled the sweet aroma of Alfalfa and Bermuda bales stacked high in an open shed. She spotted Rowdy, Elmer, Spot, and the rest of the stable horses ankle-deep in grass, grazing peacefully in a large open field lined with cottonwood trees. When Rowdy saw the truck, he whinnied and came galloping across the expanse. Foxfire answered him, bobbing her head to see her old friend again.

"Seems like Foxy's happy to be here." Meadow laughed as Rowdy followed them down the fence with her mare talking to him the whole way.

"She must be telling him all the news." Dad parked near the hay shed.

They unloaded the horses, and her father led Major through the pasture gate. Meadow stood for a couple of minutes petting Foxfire before releasing her. "Foxy, I'll be down to see you the minute we get back from Brighten. You don't have to worry about not seeing me every day, okay?"

Foxfire nuzzled Meadow as if she understood every word. She led her mare through the gate, and watched the renewed friendship with Rowdy, with them sniffing noses and nipping at each other. Rowdy squealed, stamped his foot, and then the young buckskin turned and galloped off playfully kicking and bucking. He skidded to a halt and turned back toward Foxfire, as if surprised she hadn't joined him. Meadow's shoulders sagged watching her trot after him stiffly.

Her father draped his arm around her. "This will do Foxy a world of good. She'll probably buck you off after a month of rest here."

Meadow managed a thin smile, but didn't answer. It hurt her to the core to see Foxfire without her usual energy and spirit.

"And going to Brighten will do *us* a world of good." Dad firmly escorted her back to the truck.

The drive north past Sedona was uneventful with all of them squeezed tightly into the Ford Ranch Wagon. There was barely room for six passengers, but Dad drove, whistling his tuneless song, and her mother sat by the window taking in the scenery along the mountain road. Piled between them were covered dishes Mom had insisted on bringing, even though her father said there would be enough food at the ranch to feed the Mongol hordes.

Her brothers and Wally were crowded into the backseat, with Monty and Mike elbowing each other for more space. Wally seemed to like the close quarters and jostling. It must've made him feel he was part of a real family at last. Meadow, being the smallest, was relegated to the way back area, with Kelsey. Dad diamond-hitched their suitcases crammed with winter garments on the luggage rack like he was packing a mule. Enough clothes for a full week at the ranch, until New Year's Day.

Meadow didn't mind sitting backwards, and dreamily contemplated seeing Brighten and the ranch in its snowy winter coat. It had stormed the day before in the high country, and the forecast called for unsettled weather the whole time they'd be there. She hadn't seen snow since they left Oregon. A fabulous white Christmas!

She secretly hoped to see Arrow, but figured it was unlikely. Nueme told her he hadn't seen the wild herd the last few times he'd gone to Hidden Valley. Her brows inched together. It would be disappointing not to see the stallion. What if something bad had happened to him?

Kelsey stirred and drew closer. Meadow's negative thoughts instantly melted away and she snuggled down with her dog to enjoy the ride through the glorious red rocks, now sprinkled with patches of white.

They drove past Brighten Resort with its little western village, giving the impression of a ghost town, forlorn and lonely. She might have expected a tumbleweed to blow across the road, if it hadn't been banked by snowdrifts. It was a good thing someone had plowed all the way out to the ranch. The Ford passed through the Lazy B gate, and the hacienda came into view, gaily decorated and lit up, along with the bunk house and barn, all glittering like jewels in the waning evening light.

The Bowman family came out to greet them, and stood on the porch together as if they were posing for a Christmas postcard, perfectly turned out in festive holiday sweaters. Brett was now taller than his father, and had filled out in the intervening months since Meadow had last seen him. He was even better looking than she remembered. Linda was as pretty as ever with a new pageboy haircut.

"Welcome everyone!" Bill Bowman greeted them, clasping Dad's hand, and hugging her mom.

"Please come in. Lupe has eggnog and hot cider ready." Mary Bowman offered them a frozen smile, always the perfect hostess. "Make yourselves at home. Juan will take care of your luggage."

Meadow followed the rest of the family into the great room. An enormous Christmas tree dominated one corner with dozens of beautifully wrapped presents underneath. She swallowed. They hadn't brought any gifts.

Mary Bowman seemed to have read her mind because she turned to Mom. "Rose, I told you not to worry about bringing anything for anyone and I meant it. I love to shop and have taken care of everything."

"That's good, because I took you at your word." Mom looked kind of pale. "But I did bring some extra food."

"Wonderful, I'll have Lupe put it in the kitchen." In spite of the words, Mrs. Bowman's tone reflected irritation.

Dad took Mom's arm, and she gave him a tentative smile. They all found seats and were served refreshments, with Bill pouring a little brandy into the adults' eggnog, before proposing a toast.

"Here's to good friends and may our continued acquaintance bring even more prosperity to us all." He clicked glasses with her parents and Mrs. Bowman before drinking.

Meadow thought he must be talking about the stable at Brighten Resort.

"I had Juan gather the ranch horses up. They're a little shaggy with winter hair, but we can all ride tomorrow," Bill announced. "If anyone would rather slide through the snow, we polished up the old sleigh."

Meadow clapped her hands. "Oh good, I love riding in the snow!"

Brett gave her a look. "You mean, you love riding. Period."

She smiled. "So true. I cannot tell a lie."

He arched one eyebrow. "After we ride, I'll take you for a spin in the sleigh."

Her pulse went up a notch. "Can't wait."

The next morning, Christmas Eve, the whole group gathered at the barn, with the exception of Mrs. Bowman, who stayed in to supervise Lupe's preparations for dinner that day. Juan, the ranch foreman, brought out the horses whose breaths turned to steam in the crisp morning air, and held them while everyone mounted.

Meadow climbed aboard a pretty sorrel mare with four white stockings.

"What's her name?" she asked Linda, who was already sitting on her bay.

"We call her Sugarfoot, since she looks like she just stepped in the sugar bowl. You'll like her, although probably not as much as Foxy."

"She's nice." Meadow patted the mare.

"I'm so sorry about Foxy's foal. That must have been terrible." Linda shook her head. "Are there any clues as to who might have done it?"

"Not really."

Linda reached over and squeezed her hand.

When everyone was mounted, Brett, Monty and Mike formed a line.

"Ready, set, go!" Brett hollered, leaning low over Calypso's neck.

His gelding leapt into action, galloping across the white powder with Monty and Mike in hot pursuit. Meadow grinned at Linda and they urged their mares after the boys.

After the wild ride across the open field, Meadow and the other teens pulled up their puffing mounts and waited for the adults to join them. Wally, the only inexperienced rider, was on a gentle giant of a horse and stayed close to her father. He wore a look of rapture as Dad gave him pointers on the correct way to sit and position his feet in the stirrups.

They all rode in a leisurely fashion up a steep trail onto a butte with an incredible view of the ranch and surrounding landscape.

"What a beautiful sight." Her mother sampled the mountain air. "I can see why you love this place so much."

Bill nodded. "Yes, it's a very special place. I'm grateful to have good friends to share it with."

"We're happy you invited us all. It's quite an undertaking to feed and house this mob." Her father shifted in his saddle, watching Meadow and the others jostle for position.

Bill laughed. "I love having a houseful of rambunctious teenagers. Keeps me young. Speaking of food, though, we'd better get back. I'm sure Lupe has something whipped up for lunch."

They made their way down the mountain trail, back to flat ground. Brett rode up alongside Meadow.

She asked him about his school, Eaton Military Academy.

"It's pretty intense, but I'm getting used to it. Sometimes it's even fun."

She tightened her lips and looked straight ahead. "Yeah, it must be, judging from all the letters I've gotten from you."

"Gimme a break! I've been pretty busy. And you've only written a couple of times."

Meadow raised her chin. "I've been busy, too."

He graced her with his irresistible grin. "Come on, let's not argue. How 'bout that sleigh ride after lunch?"

The ice in her veins thawed. "Okay, sounds fun."

The enormous Spanish dining table was formally set with linen napkins and real silverware, along with crystal water and wine glasses. Several fancy-looking hors d'oeuvres adorned the side board. Everyone took little platefuls.

Meadow sat where Mrs. Bowman indicated, then stared as Lupe began bringing more food. She was already full from the appetizers. This was more like dinner than lunch.

The meal dragged on, with Meadow sneaking glances at Brett, wondering when it would be over. Lupe kept bringing courses—did they really need soup and salad, plus huge hunks of tri-tip beef with all the fixings? Meadow had to admit, everything was tasty, but the adults were sure taking their sweet time eating it. She could've been done an hour ago.

She squirmed in her chair and Mom frowned at her to sit still. Meadow finally looked pointedly at Brett, and he rolled his eyes. At long last, he spoke up.

"Mother, can we please be excused? I promised Meadow a sleigh ride. It'll be dark soon."

"Oh, of course, Brett." Mrs. Bowman glanced around the table. "In fact, all of you children may go if you like. We can have dessert and coffee later."

The teens stampeded from the table, with Wally following. Even though he was in his late twenties, he acted more like one of the teenagers. Monty and Mike weren't too interested in a sleigh ride, so Linda offered to play them a game of pool. Wally trailed after Meadow and Brett to the stable.

Brett scowled at Wally after he got the driving horse, Dancer, hitched up.

"There's really only room for two in the sleigh, Wally," he said. "And I promised Meadow."

"Okay." Wally looked down and shuffled his feet.

Meadow couldn't stand it. "Can't he come, Brett? We can scrunch up a little."

Brett huffed. "Well, all right. Get in then."

Wally's face cracked open in a toothy grin and he practically leapt into the sleigh. Meadow climbed in next to him and then Brett eased into the driver's seat. He spread a quilt over the three of them, clucked to Dancer, and the sleigh glided silently across the frozen white. It was a little tight, but Meadow liked being so close to Brett, especially when he put his arm around her to make more room.

By this time, it was nearly dark, but a full moon was coming up on the horizon, shining its magic across the snowy wonderland. Just like a Currier and Ives print. Brett drove them around the grounds and through the field where earlier they'd raced their horses. Dancer enjoyed his job, putting his whole heart into pulling the sleigh at a fast trot, and the frigid air bit at Meadow's unprotected face. She loved it—her whole being engaged and acutely alive.

She saw Brett watching her with a smile. "It's nice to see a girl enjoy herself so much."

Warmth crept up her face, and she didn't trust herself to look at him.

Wally had a dazed expression, apparently mesmerized by the ride and unable to speak. She turned to Brett. "Thanks for letting him come along."

"Of course, anything for the little lady."

She giggled, remembering the carnival bear he won for her last summer. The bear still had a place of honor in her bedroom.

All too soon, Brett turned back toward the barn, saying he didn't want to heat Dancer up too much with a chilly night coming on.

They left the gelding with Juan rubbing him down, and joined the others in the game room. Linda's boyfriend, Sheriff Dave Redland, had arrived. They were curled up together on a fur rug in front of the fireplace. Her brothers were playing a game of darts, and Brett challenged Meadow to play pool. He was thoroughly trouncing her, so she was relieved when Lupe appeared at the doorway.

"*Senora* Bowman wants you all in the living room to sing carols."

Meadow quickly abandoned her cue stick. "That's sounds fun."

The boys all groaned a little, but obediently followed the rest of them to where everyone else had already gathered. Linda sat down at the antique grand piano, and it wasn't a surprise she played beautifully. Everything she did was perfect. They all joined in the singing except for Wally. He tried, but kept getting the words messed up and then grew quiet. Poor guy. He'd probably never had a real Christmas. Meadow took his arm and he turned to her, smiling.

After they sang Silent Night, Lupe brought in a large tray of hot cocoa, complete with whipped cream on top. They sipped and talked a while longer, until it was past midnight. Meadow was a bit drowsy by now and pretty soon everyone drifted off toward their sleeping quarters.

By the time she got to her room, Meadow was awake again. She opened the French doors to the courtyard and stood spellbound as white flakes floated down in the moonlight—like the snow globe she had back home. Her heart grew full with thankfulness for her family and friends. This was what Christmas was all about. She climbed into the four-poster and sank deep into the heavenly feather mattress. After pulling the down comforter up to her chin, she giggled. She'd probably dream of wild horses eating sugarplums.

Chapter 12

New Year

Meadow's eyes flew open with first light and she bounded up, racing to the window. The storm that had dogged them for a better part of a week was finally over, and snow sparkled in the glorious sunshine. She puckered her brow, trying to think up a plan to steal away to find Arrow. This was New Year's Eve and would be her last chance.

They'd been snowbound at the ranch while the puffy white stuff floated down endlessly, until it was over a foot deep on the flats and drifted much higher in some places. Not that it mattered to any of them, since they could have left in the four-wheel-drive vehicles if they really wanted to. There was plenty of food, the power never went out, and so far, no one got on anyone's nerves. It was a nice reprieve from their regular lives, with no phone or other outside communication to interrupt the tranquility of the ranch.

At first, the adults had voiced concern that the teens might get bored. But that didn't happen. In fact, the holiday week had flown by with a whirlwind of activity. Meadow went sledding, snow shoeing, and horseback riding with the rest of them. They even built a snow fort and had snowball fights, and everyone laughed when Kelsey kept retrieving the icy balls for Meadow and proudly dropping them at her feet.

And Brett was very charming and attentive. It made Meadow feel like she was living in a lovely dream—a dream she never wanted to end. If only Foxfire were there to share it all, everything would've been ideal. She hoped her mare was enjoying the pasture time with the other horses.

Her father and Bill were sequestered in the study every day until long after dark. Meadow wondered what they were cooking up, and couldn't wait to hear about it. Her mother seemed more relaxed since she was helping Lupe with the food preparation for the large crowd of ravenous eaters. Mary Bowman spent most of the time in her office, working on next year's business plan for her art galleries.

In spite of the fun she was having, Meadow still felt an urgent need to go to Hidden Valley to make sure the wild herd was all right, especially the stallion. She would have to go alone if there was any chance of seeing Arrow, so she waited, hoping for an opportunity to slip away from the others. They were leaving for home tomorrow—it would *have* to be today.

No one had come up with any firm plans for the morning, so she quietly dressed and opened the French doors onto the patio. Kelsey, snoozing outside of the door in a cozy alcove, rose and stretched when she saw Meadow.

"Hi Kelsey," she whispered, ruffling her dog's ears.

She tiptoed through the courtyard and toward the stable, with Kelsey following along. Juan had just finished throwing the horses some hay and swiveled to face her when she entered the barn.

"*Buenos Dias, Senorita* Meadow. You're up early."

"Hi Juan. Just wanted to say hello to the horses." She casually went to Sugarfoot's stall and leaned on it. Dang, it would be hard to sneak away with Juan around.

Juan went on with his morning chores, while Meadow stroked Sugarfoot. She stayed for a while, then returned to the house, still pondering how to get away without the others knowing.

The delicious aroma of frying bacon wafted to her nose when she opened the kitchen door and saw her mother whipping up pancake batter. Lupe was nearby cutting fresh fruit into a bowl.

Her stomach growled. Brett, her brothers, and Wally were already at the breakfast table looking hungry. She slid in next to Wally.

"Hi, honey, breakfast will be ready soon," Mom said. "Your father and I are going to Brighten with the Bowmans to use the phone this morning. What are you kids planning?"

"We're driving the jeep up to the range to get in some target practice," Brett answered. "Meadow, do you want to go shooting with us?"

"Don't invite her, she'll make us all look bad." Mike was only half joking, since Meadow outshot both her brothers last time they practiced.

"Thanks Brett. You guys go ahead." She chuckled. "I wouldn't want to ruin your fun by showing you all up."

Her father and Bill entered the kitchen together, heads close, talking. Dad looked up. "Good morning, everyone." He sat near Bill at the table. "Smells good."

Lupe served breakfast as Linda swept into the room. She was dressed warmly and her mouth rosy with lipstick. "Dad, do you think I could ride along with you to Brighten? I'll call Dave from there to pick me up. Mother wants us to go into Sedona and get some supplies for the big bash."

"Sure thing. There's room in the Range Rover. But probably no one will be able to get back here for the party tonight with all this snow on the ground."

Mrs. Bowman, who never ate breakfast, appeared in the doorway just as Bill finished speaking. "I know we won't have a problem getting out, but let's have Juan plow the road again for our guests this evening."

"Good idea. I'll tell him before we leave." Bill took one last sip of coffee before rising to get his coat.

Linda turned to her. "Meadow, would you like to come with us?"

"No thanks, I think I'll just read and relax today."

Meadow smiled to herself. This was working out perfectly. She waited until they'd all gone their separate ways, and watched Juan drive the truck with an attached snow plow past the main gate. It would take him hours to make it all the way to Brighten and back.

She raced to the stable, retrieved Sugarfoot's bridle, and jumped onto her bare back. The mare was fresh, and walked eagerly through the knee-high snow. They got past the main gate, and she tried to keep the mare on a path indented from years of use. The drifted snow made it hard to see. Kelsey playfully scampered through the white powder, once in a while burying her nose and taking bites of it.

Meadow breathed in the crisp air and her heart quickened to think that before long she might see Arrow after so many months. The amulet under her sweater felt warm.

They arrived at Oak Creek and crunched through patches of ice on the edges. Kelsey galloped through, sending water in every direction, seeming to know they were on a mission. Meadow rode up the steep canyon trail toward Hidden Valley, urging Sugarfoot along, but the mare was tiring from her long trek through deep snow. Finally, they rounded a corner and the wide valley greeted them, looking pristine in a veil of white.

She reined Sugarfoot in to give the mare a breather, and stared around, searching for any sign of the mustangs or the stallion. Even if he were there, would Arrow come to her without Foxfire? It was eerily quiet. So still that not even a bird chirped or a squirrel scolded them. Suddenly, a loud whinny rang out, and Sugarfoot threw her head up, startled by the break in the silence.

Meadow's pulse went into high gear as she scanned the valley to see where the sound came from.

Kelsey gave a low woof and sped across the expanse toward the tree line to the west. Meadow could just make out a silver silhouette against the backdrop of pines. The horse turned and fled into the forest with Kelsey trailing.

"Kelsey, come back!" She pushed Sugarfoot into a gallop.

When she reached the other side of the valley and got into the trees, Meadow found that the going was more difficult. The lee side of the mountain had heavy snowdrifts. They galloped on through an area thick with ponderosa pines, when the terrain took a steep downward pitch. The mare hesitated, then plunged down, slithering along the icy slope. Her hooves lost their purchase and she stumbled to her knees, throwing Meadow headlong toward a giant ponderosa. She fell next to the tree, the snow gave way, and a massive hole swallowed her.

Meadow frantically tried to grab onto something, anything that could stop the downward momentum. Dad had warned her about going near trees in drifted snow because of the danger of tree wells. He said the upper branches slowed the snowfall, not allowing it to pack in at the base. With nothing to grab onto, she kept falling and the snow caved in around her. She was buried alive.

Don't panic. Think.

She heard Kelsey's muffled yaps above her, and then some mournful howls. So far, she hadn't run out of air, but knew it would happen quickly. Methodically, Meadow tried to maneuver closer to the tree trunk. Her only chance was to try and pull herself up. She kicked her legs and moved her arms as if she were in a pool. Only snow was a lot heavier than water, like she imagined quick sand would feel. And just as deadly. Her throat began to close.

Inch by inch, she scooted toward the trunk. At last, Meadow could feel the rough bark, and gritting her teeth, she pulled. It felt like she weighed a million pounds. Sweat trickled down her forehead, stinging her eyes, but she was making some headway.

Whump! Another load of snow slipped off a branch and landed solidly on top, burying her deeper. Struggling was hopeless. This was it. Too tired to fight.

Unable to catch a breath, her hands uncurled off the trunk, and found the amulet. Her mind wandered. A vision, misty at first, then clear as the mountain air appeared—she was flying on Arrow through the red canyons and then up toward the sky. The last thing she remembered was the Indian medicine woman, Meda, beckoning to her.

It seemed like hours, but must have been only minutes before Meadow became aware of someone breathing into her mouth, his lips warm on hers.

"Meadow, Meadow, wake up."

She could hear Kelsey in the background whining. Her lids ratcheted up to see Colt's deep green eyes. He smiled as she gazed at him. She breathed in. "Is it really you or am I dreaming?"

"It's really me. I heard Kelsey bark and howl, so I came to investigate. When I saw her furiously digging and a riderless horse, I knew what happened."

Meadow shook her head to chase away the fog. "What are you doing up here?"

"I often come when I'm on school break. You know I like my solitude."

"Yes, I remember. It's lucky you happened to be around. You saved me." Meadow sat up and realized Colt had wrapped a heavy blanket around her.

Her teeth began chattering and suddenly she was shivering. Kelsey came over as close as possible and earnestly licked the snow off her face.

"I'm okay, Kelsey." Her voice quavered.

"We need to get you warmed up." Colt stood to gather wood.

Before long, he had a fire going and he laid his heavy jacket in front of it for Meadow to sit on. Then sitting next to her, he took her hands in his and rubbed them. Gradually, she stopped shaking and her brain cleared.

Meadow saw her mare and Colt's stallion, Smoke, standing nearby. Thank goodness Sugarfoot had waited for her. There would have been hell to pay if she needed to explain to her folks what happened. As it was, there was no need to clue them in. She stole a look at Colt, handsome in profile, contemplating the flickering flames. He wouldn't tell on her.

"Are you coming to the Bowmans' party tonight?" she asked.

"No, I have to get back to Flagstaff this afternoon, but my father will be there."

"I'm glad your father is coming, but I wish you were, too."

"New Year's parties are not really my thing." His chiseled face was solemn.

Meadow nodded. It made perfect sense to her, but she wasn't sure why.

"Have you seen the wild herd lately? I thought I saw the stallion. That's why I was galloping through here. I wouldn't normally be so careless."

"You don't have to explain anything to me, Meadow. But no, I haven't seen them for a few months now."

"I must have been wrong then . . . but I thought I heard him, too."

"Just because I haven't seen him, doesn't mean *you* didn't."

That simple statement made her feel light as air and she smiled. Colt always had that effect on her. Her eyes followed him as he rose and pulled her to her feet. "You need to go back now, before anyone looks for you." He led her to Sugarfoot and gave her a leg up. Colt smoothed his blanket across Smoke's bare back, and then jumped on with one fluid motion.

They rode for a while in silence, but as they passed the fork leading to the cliff dwelling, she asked, "Is the Medicine Chest okay?"

Colt smiled. "Yes, our secret is safe."

After they crossed Oak Creek, he reined Smoke in.

"I will leave you now. Take care, Meadow. There's someone who means you harm. You must always be vigilant."

Before Meadow could ask him what he meant, he turned his stallion and melted into the trees.

She still felt a little woozy—not sure if it was from the fall or from being in Colt's heady presence as she rode down from the high mesa. He was real, but always seemed a little other worldly to her. Wasn't it strange she had never seen him with other people around? But he always showed up when she needed him most. Then she smiled to herself. His lips were *definitely* real.

Meadow turned in front of the mirror, checking out her new cashmere sweater and wool skirt—a Christmas present from Brett and Linda. Brett told her he had picked out the teal green sweater for her, because he thought it would match her eyes. His sister helped to get the size right, and then Linda decided Meadow needed a skirt to go with the new top.

They both fit just right and Meadow loved the luxurious feel of cashmere against her skin. The sweater had a lower neckline than she usually wore, and the medallion shone softly in the evening light. She ran a brush through her long mass of dark waves, and wondered how it would look in a short page boy like Linda was wearing. No, her father would have a conniption fit if she cut it. He was so old-fashioned.

She gave one more passing glance at the mirror and touched the amulet. It was time to go meet the guests that had started to arrive. Ugh. She wasn't really in a festive mood after her near-death experience and seeing Colt. The party wasn't even starting until the fashionable hour of 9 p.m., and she would rather snuggle up with a book and go to bed early.

It was fortunate she got back to the ranch before anyone knew she was gone. She'd already showered and was sitting innocently in the den by a crackling fire when the boys got back from shooting. Her parents and the rest of the group came trailing in about an hour later.

After dinner, they all prepared for the gala evening that Mary Bowman had planned. Meadow was glad that many people had begged off from coming, reluctant to negotiate the long drive from Sedona on icy roads. Mrs. Bowman forged ahead anyway, unwilling to cancel the event.

Meadow entered the great room and saw Sheriff Dave there, cozy with Linda. Colt's father, Chief White Horse, stood with his back to the roaring fireplace. She grinned and made her way over to him. The chief clasped both her hands in greeting.

She tried to make her voice casual. "I'm so glad you came tonight. Did Colt mention he saw me today?"

Chief White Horse looked at her sharply. "No . . . he left before I spoke with him. I see you're wearing Meda's necklace."

"Hope you don't mind. I always have it on. Don't feel right otherwise."

He nodded. "Yes, you must wear it. You are the one chosen by Meda."

She was about to ask the chief what he meant, when Nueme joined them.

"It seems only cowboys and Indians made it to this party."

Meadow and Chief White Horse laughed, agreeing that he was right. None of Mrs. Bowman's socialite friends were there. Her brothers and Wally were all decked out in cowboy garb, including their gifts from the Bowmans—fancy hand-tooled belts with large silver buckles.

Dad and Bill Bowman showed up, and Meadow excused herself to go sit on a sofa near the fire. She was tired to the bone. Mike walked over and plopped down next to her.

"Don't be surprised if Brett tries to get you under the mistletoe," he said, with a little smirk. "I've seen how he looks at you, but keep in mind he's quite the lady killer back east."

She frowned. "What are you talking about?" Mike just wanted to stir things up.

"He likes you a lot, but he has a girl in New York that looks like a cross between Liz Taylor and Natalie Wood."

"How do you know?"

"He showed me her picture. He's been taking her out and said even his mother approves. Her name is Tiffany." He laughed. "*That* should tell you something."

Meadow felt a slow burn. So he just paid attention to her when she was the only game in town. Jerk. She huffed. Enough of Brett. "What do you think the big announcement is?"

"Who knows? With Bill Bowman, the sky's the limit."

It was getting close to midnight when Brett gathered all the teens together with a conspiratorial look. "I got some fireworks. Let's go out to the patio."

"Okay." Mike grinned, following him out.

Meadow tagged along with Monty and Wally to watch. The fireworks turned out to be a few colorful streamers, pop bottle rockets and some cherry bombs, all of which quickly became history. The last sparkler fizzled out, and just as the clock struck midnight, Brett hauled her under the mistletoe, kissing her full on the mouth. Her brothers snickered.

"How's that for a first kiss?"

She pulled away from him. "Who says it's my first kiss?"

His brows came together. "*What*? You've been kissing other boys?"

"Just one." Meadow vividly recalled Colt's lips. Even though it wasn't technically a kiss, Brett didn't need to know that. "Besides, you have a girlfriend back east . . . remember?"

"You mean Tiffany?" He shrugged. "She's not my girlfriend. Just the daughter of one of Mother's friends. But who have *you* been kissing?"

"Uh—no one." Shoot, she shouldn't have mentioned it.

"Tell me!" Storm clouds gathered on his face.

"It's none of your business!"

"Fine." He turned and stomped away.

Darn, she really blew it.

Now that the New Year had officially started, Bill rounded everyone up to make his big announcement. He motioned her father and mother closer and began speaking.

"As you all know, I have recently been in negotiations to purchase the old Fort Apache movie set. Well, the deal is now complete, and Mary and I are the proud new owners."

Everyone cheered and clapped at the news, but Bill wasn't finished.

"To make this type of venture successful, I need smart managers to run the place." He paused dramatically. "And I'm happy to announce that Shep and Rose have agreed to take it on."

Meadow looked at her brothers in stunned silence.

Monty recovered first. "You mean we're going to live at Fort Apache?"

Dad nodded. "Yes, we will be moving the end of January."

Mike sucked in a breath, then blurted out. "What about school? All our friends?"

"You will have to change schools, but this is a wonderful opportunity. We'll all have to adjust, but it will be for the best in the long run."

Meadow had figured something exciting was going on behind the scenes with her parents, but this was beyond her imaginings. She glanced at her brothers—standing still with dour looks. Oh well, they'll get used to it. Her father and mother were huddled with Bill—all grinning like they'd won the Irish Sweepstakes.

A tingle coursed through her. Oh boy, a new adventure.

Chapter 13

A Fresh Start

The next morning, Meadow woke up conflicted about the impending move. It would be exciting, but what if Lisa's mother was unwilling to board Major in Apache Junction? It was hard to contemplate the loss of her best friend. They told each other everything—well *almost* everything. Lisa was secretive at times, but to be honest, Meadow had secrets, too. One thing was sure, her best friend was miles ahead of her in the romance department.

Meadow couldn't wait to tell Lisa all about Christmas week at the ranch. What a wonderful time it had been with Brett . . . and Colt. She sighed and hugged her arms around her. It was sad they had to leave today. If it were up to her, they'd live full time at Brighten.

She pulled on her jeans and headed for the barn to pet Sugarfoot one last time.

Juan was nowhere to be seen and the mare put her head over the stall door briefly, then buried her face in the sweet Timothy hay again. Meadow smiled and watched for a moment before sensing a presence behind her. Turning, she saw Brett, his mouth set in a straight line. Her heart quickened at his nearness, but she was no longer tongue-tied in his presence, like last summer.

"Morning, Brett, you're out here early."

"Yeah, I wanted to talk to you alone before you left. I figured you'd be with the horses."

"I had to say goodbye to Sugarfoot. It's been a lot of fun riding her." She petted the mare over the gate. "The whole week has been wonderful. I think it was my best Christmas, ever."

"Me too. It's been special because of you . . . and your family being here." Brett paused. "Sorry I was so rude to you last night. About the kiss, I mean."

"It's okay. I was pretty rude, too."

He frowned. "I was just . . . surprised, that you had already kissed someone else."

"I shouldn't have said that. I haven't really been kissing anyone. You just made me mad, so sure you were the first. I know *I* wasn't the first for you."

"Well . . . no."

"Who've you been practicing with? Tiffany?"

"It doesn't matter." He stepped closer and took her hand. She caught her breath and waited while Brett leaned toward her.

"*Buenos Días, Senorita* Meadow, *Senor* Brett."

They both jumped a little at Juan's voice and turned to see him grinning, like he'd caught them in the hay loft.

Brett dropped her hand. "Mornin', Juan," he mumbled. "C'mon, Meadow, let's go get breakfast."

She giggled at him. *Now* he wasn't so cocky. "Yeah, let's."

Meadow and her family arrived back home in Scottsdale just as the sun was setting over the western mountains. The place seemed lonely with no horses in the barn and the house quiet after the non-stop fun and laughter of the holiday week. Now it was back to reality and time to pack once more.

Before they left, Brett had promised to write, but Meadow wondered if he would keep his word this time. It seemed like he forgot all about her when she wasn't in close proximity. In spite of that, Meadow did haunt the mailbox every day.

January flew by with a flurry of packing and preparation for the move to Apache Junction. Monty was down in the mouth about changing schools and leaving Susan. Finally, he proposed a solution to Dad, offering to give up his after school job so he could drive Meadow and Mike to and from Scottsdale for the rest of the term. Dad agreed to pay his gas expense plus give him pocket money. And Meadow heaved a sigh of relief when Dr. Wilson said she would bring Lisa out to Fort Apache every week to ride.

She went with her father to bring Major and the Navajo horses back from pasture. Meadow hugged Foxfire after she came trotting to say hello, almost back to normal. "Only a couple more weeks, Foxy, and we'll be together." Foxfire whinnied after them as they drove away.

Her father patted her shoulder. "She's coming along nicely. Be good as new before long. Meanwhile, I have some Navajo ponies that could use some training. How would you like to help?"

"What about Mike?"

"He'll make sure they're topped off, then you can teach them some finesse. How's that sound? From what I've seen, you're becoming a hellava horse trainer."

Meadow glowed. "Sure Dad, I'd love to." Finally, he was paying some attention to her.

She had her hands full riding the young horses plus working with Major when Lisa wasn't able to come over. Major was talented and his jumping improved daily. Lisa took him to the Pony Club show in mid-January, and did very well, winning a third place his first time out. Since Lisa's return from visiting the grandparents, Meadow noticed a big change. She wasn't seeing "Runnin' Jack" anymore or skipping school.

One Saturday after riding, Meadow and Lisa went to the kitchen in search of refreshments. As soon as she'd scrounged around and found some oatmeal cookies, Meadow sank down across from Lisa at the table. "I'm so glad you broke it off with Jack. What happened?"

"I had an epiphany."

"A what?"

Lisa grinned. "An epiphany. Nice word, huh?"

"Yeah, but what's it mean?"

"It means all of a sudden it came clear to me that you were right about Jack. While I was away, I kept thinking about what you said. You know, respect and all that."

"Uh huh, then what happened?"

"Mom talked to me and said she was really worried. She's had it rough, being alone. I'm all she has . . . and I was being a brat."

"Did you tell her about Jack?"

"Sort of. Well . . . not everything. Geez."

Meadow giggled. "I understand. I don't tell my parents *everything* either."

"Yeah, like almost smothering under the snow and then some mysterious dreamboat saves you in the nick of time?"

They laughed together, then Lisa became serious. "I'm going to miss having you live so close. When are you moving?"

"Next weekend. We'll see each other in school, and I hope you can come out and ride all the time."

"Mom promised at least once a week. If I bug her, maybe more often."

"You've got to come to the big grand opening at Fort Apache."

"That sounds fun. Will there be food and everything?"

"Tons of food. Mr. Bowman is having it catered. He's even invited a couple of movie stars that used the set before."

"Wow, I won't miss that!" Lisa got up and strutted around the room. "Maybe I'll be discovered."

"Don't get too excited. It's actors we've never heard of. John Wayne couldn't make it." Lisa snorted and they broke into fresh giggles.

After Lisa's mother picked her up, Meadow wandered to the mailbox, all set to be disappointed.

She pulled out a pile of mail and began leafing through it. Yay! At last, a letter addressed to her, in a bold, masculine hand. She sprinted from the mailbox, dashed into her room and flopped on the bed before ripping it open.

Dear Meadow,

Here I am, back in prison—but seriously, it's not so bad now that I'm used to all the discipline. Of course, that was Mother's plan, wasn't it? I have to look at the bright side, which is that I'm getting a well-rounded education and will be better prepared for college. Man, I can't believe I just wrote that! I sound just like my parents, for cripes sake. But it is hard to believe I only have one more year after this before I go off to University. Mother wants me to go to an Ivy Leaguer, but I would be happy with ASU, so I would be nearer to everyone.

I have some exciting news. I get to start flying lessons this term. By the time I see you again, I will be well on my way to being a pilot. Dad is happy about it, saying I will be able to fly him to out of state business meetings, and stuff. He's even planning to put in a runway at the ranch. I'll be able to take you flying next summer. Pretty cool, huh?

It was great seeing you, we always have such a good time together. Write soon and tell me about all the changes at Fort Apache. I can't wait to see it. I'll try to come out during Spring Break.

Always,
Brett

P.S. I'm taking Tiffany to the Winter Wonderland Dance. Mother insisted. Maybe I'll practice some more kissing . . . ha ha

Meadow smiled while reading the letter, until she got to the postscript. She could picture Brett's teasing look as he wrote it, but wasn't so sure he would be able to resist the rich, beautiful Tiffany. Meadow pulled out her stationery, intending to pen a response. But then, after she started to write, she frowned and crumpled the paper. Serve him right to wonder if she would reply.

Lying back on the bed, her thoughts turned from Brett to Colt, and how different they were from each other. She shook her head. Colt didn't think of her that way. More like a little sister, probably. Whenever she was with him, though, it was as if their destinies were intertwined. What was it Chief White Horse had said? Something about being Meda's chosen one—chosen for what? Gradually, the amulet warmed next to her skin, just as it had the day Colt rescued her.

That evening they all sat around the dinner table discussing the move.

"We've already taken most of the household items. The rest will fit in the truck and the Ford next Friday." Dad pushed away his plate and sat back.

"It worked out perfectly with the day off from school," Mom said.

"I can't wait to have Foxy back and be able to explore the Superstition Mountains." Meadow hoped her mare would be ready to ride by the end of the week.

"The whole area is pretty interesting," Monty said. "I'm reading a book about the Lost Dutchman Mine that's supposed to be up there somewhere."

"I've heard something about that." Mom began gathering the dirty dishes. "Wasn't it a German prospector who found a large gold deposit in the mountain?"

"If he was German, why do they call it the Lost *Dutchman* Mine?" Mike asked.

"Germany is also known as Deutschland, so people used to call them Dutchmen when they came here," Dad said.

Monty nodded. "Yeah, that's what the book says. The Apache Indians were the first to know about the gold and when Coronado and the Spanish Conquistadors came searching for the Seven Golden Cities of Cibola, the Indians told them about the mountain.

"Then what happened?" Meadow perked up at the mention of Indians.

"When the Spaniards wanted to explore, the Apaches refused to help, believing the mountain was protected by the Thunder God, so the Spanish went on their own."

Mike leaned forward. "Did they find the gold?"

"No, the men started vanishing mysteriously, and if they were found, the bodies were mutilated with their heads cut off. Of course, the survivors were terrified and refused to return to the area, and it became known as Superstition Mountain."

"Wow, cool." Mike shook his head. "But how did the German get into the act?"

Monty gave Mike a big brother look. "I'm not that far into it yet. Maybe *you* should read the book yourself."

"I want to read it," Meadow said.

"You can borrow it tonight, I have homework anyway. It's next to my bed."

Mike tapped his fingers on the table. "Maybe we'll find the mine and be rich."

"It's just a legend, Mike, don't get too excited," Dad said. "Although, I think maybe Clay has been looking for it. He's got a couple of mules and goes up the trails regularly."

Meadow turned to him. "You mean the caretaker at Fort Apache?"

"He's pretty creepy with those weirdo, colorless eyes," Mike said.

Mom pursed her lips and looked at Mike. "You can't judge someone by their looks."

"Well, he *is* a little odd, but Bill wants to keep him on as a wrangler, so I guess we're stuck with him." Dad was actually agreeing with Mike for a change.

Meadow left to find Monty's book and was sprawled on her bed, deeply engrossed, when the sharp jangle of the telephone brought her back to the present. The rest of her family was still in the dining room. She jumped up, and raced down the hall to pick up the receiver.

"Hello?" she said, a little out of breath.

"I know where you're going, you can't escape me," the raspy voice threatened.

Meadow slammed down the phone, her pleasant interlude ruined. She went back to her room and peered around the blinds into the outer darkness.

Colt's chilling words came back to her. "Someone means you harm."

Chapter 14

Fort Apache

Meadow sat on the top rail of Foxfire's new corral, the early morning sun warming her back. She smiled, watching her mare explore, snorting and skittering away from imagined boogeymen. Thank goodness Foxfire was back to normal.

It was the end of January, and the previous day's move had gone smoothly. Meadow already felt at home, although it was a little strange living at a place with so many empty buildings. Kind of like living in a ghost town. If those walls could talk, they'd have some great stories about past movie shoots. She loved the enormous barn—large enough to house every one of the dude horses, plus trading stock.

Foxfire galloped by, tossing her head, then came blasting back and skidded to a stop right in front of Meadow. She thrust her nose over the fence, demanding attention. Meadow laughed, patting her. Kelsey put her front legs up on the bottom rail and Foxfire leaned down, blowing softly.

Meadow heard crunching steps behind and turned as her father joined them at the corral. "I see the old Foxy's back with her usual feisty attitude," he said. "Looks like she's made a total recovery."

"Yeah, I plan to take her for a long ride today."

"That's good, you can scout out trails for the dude rides. How do you like it here so far?"

"I love it. Especially since we won't have to change schools, after all."

"I'm glad it worked out. C'mon, time for breakfast." Her father turned and headed toward their new quarters.

She hurried to catch up. "How will we guide the dude rides while we're in school?"

"You kids are off the hook, for now. We're hiring wranglers after we get busy."

"Oh, cool."

They walked up onto the wrap-around porch of the log house that had been under renovations for the past month. The structure was huge, with tall ceilings and six bedrooms. It had originally been built for the director and movie stars to stay in while filming on location. All those bedrooms were a real luxury and allowed Meadow and her brothers to each have their own. Even Wally got to choose one.

The caretaker, Clay, lived in a cabin near the back of the complex. He was a skilled horseman and could help with the dude rides. It turned out he'd been an animal trainer in a circus at one point.

Meadow followed her father into the main room of the house, with several sitting areas and a large stone fireplace dominating one wall. Mary Bowman had insisted on helping to decorate, so the house was embellished with expensive antiques and beautiful artwork. Colorful Navajo rugs covered the polished pine floors.

They entered the kitchen, where her mother was frying a pan of potatoes, with eggs going in another skillet. A pot of oatmeal bubbled cheerfully. The kitchen had been equipped to feed an entire movie crew, having a massive gas range, double ovens and more counter space than seemed necessary. It even had an automatic dishwasher. Washing dishes was a chore Meadow was pleased to relinquish to a machine.

Anxious to get back on Foxfire, Meadow grabbed a bowl of oatmeal, and scooted in next to Wally in the dining hall. She picked up a spoon and began shoveling in the cereal. Her father sat at one end of the mahogany table that looked small in comparison to the size of the room.

Her mother came in with a stack of toast. "Don't gulp your food, Meadow."

"Uh, okay." She made an effort to slow down. "Where's Monty?"

"He's keeping his job at the track on weekends, so he left early." Her father buttered a slice of toast.

Mike came in the room and guzzled some orange juice. "Okay if I go to Jack's house today?"

Mom brought in a platter of eggs and sat down at the table. "How are you getting there?"

"His father said he'd come get me."

Dad looked at him over the paper. "All right. Your mother and I are going to pick up the rest of the horses from pasture."

Meadow finished her breakfast and stood. "I'm taking Foxy out this morning."

"Is Lisa riding with you, honey?" Mom asked.

"No, she's going to the mall. She wanted me to come along, but shopping didn't sound fun when I could be riding."

A furrow appeared between her mother's brows. "I hope she's not losing interest in Major already."

"No, she's coming out tomorrow to practice jumping." Meadow started for the door. "She's showing again in a couple of weeks."

"I'm glad she's continuing with that. She did very well in the first show. Came close to beating Cynthia."

Meadow turned and nodded. "She'll probably win high point next time. See ya later."

It was pure bliss being back on Foxfire and exploring new trails with Kelsey following along. In the last month, busy with school and packing for the move, Meadow had almost forgotten this feeling of independence and freedom. Foxfire was frisky, and before long, the trot turned to a canter, and then they were galloping with sheer abandon up the old jeep track. All too soon, the road narrowed, and petered down to a faint path leading deep into the Superstition range.

Her head swiveled from side to side gawking at fascinating rock formations, some with cave openings high on the mountainside. She couldn't help but think of Monty's book detailing the Lost Dutchman Mine said to be located here. How cool to actually find it. It must be real with so many people looking for it. Even creepy Clay.

According to the book, the first man to find the gold of the Indians was Don Miguel Peralta, a member of a prominent family who owned a ranch near Sonora, Mexico. He gathered men to work the mine and was soon shipping millions of pesos of pure gold back to Sonora. This angered the Apaches and they raised a large force to drive out the Mexican intruders. Peralta got wind of the impending fight and prepared to withdraw his men from the region, packing up all the mules and burros with gold. He planned to return some day, and took elaborate precautions to conceal the entrance to the mine and wipe out any trace that they had ever worked there.

A shiver went down Meadow's spine. Right here, somewhere, the Indians attacked and massacred the entire company. The pack mules and burros were scattered in all directions, spilling gold as the Apaches drove them over cliffs and into ravines. For years afterwards, prospectors and soldiers found animal remains and rotted leather packs brimming with gold. Meadow watched for any signs of bones or packs, but hoped she wouldn't see any. It was just too creepy.

The legend went on to say that a German, Jacob Waltz, reportedly saved the life of a descendant of Don Miguel Peralta, who as a reward, let him see the map. Waltz found the lode, then mined furtively, only coming out of the mountains when his saddlebags were full of ore. The German died without telling anyone the whereabouts of his find and since then it has been called the Lost Dutchman Mine.

Meadow rode on, her brain working overtime, wondering where the mysterious gold deposit might be. She rounded a corner, and looked across an intervening canyon. She caught her breath. A magnificent spire rose straight out of the surrounding rocks, towering above them.

"That must be Weavers Needle!" She reined Foxfire in, and sat staring at the formation.

The column of rock rose one thousand feet from the canyon floor, and figured prominently in the legend of the Lost Dutchman Mine. It was claimed that when the sun hit just right on the needle, the shadow would point to the entrance of the mineshaft. It was close to noon now, so there wasn't any shadow. She would have to come later in the day to see it.

She patted Foxfire. "I guess we won't be finding the Lost Dutchman today. We better turn back now anyway. I think you've had enough exercise."

On her way back through the winding canyon trails, Meadow wondered if Colt or Nueme had any knowledge of the mine's whereabouts. Their tribe had traveled the whole of Arizona before being put on reservations, and they seemed to know all the tribal legends, passing the lore down to younger generations.

The old truck was parked, and her father and Wally were unloading the horses by the time Meadow rode through the stockade gate. They turned the dude string loose in a large corral and then Dad turned to her. "You and Mike can tune these critters up before the Grand Opening next weekend. We don't want any mishaps that day."

"Don't worry, Dad. They'll be ready."

"Good. And I have another important job for you. Come over here."

Meadow followed him to a low corral with interior poles in odd angles that Clay was constructing. "What's this, Dad?"

"It's a pony maze. You get the honor of running it on Saturday."

"Oh, great. You mean I have to babysit little brats all day."

Her father laughed. "Exactly. And I know you'll do a great job."

"Can I have Lisa help me? At least then it'll be a little more fun."

"Sure, it takes two, anyhow. One person at each end."

"So the kid gets to ride through like he's in control. That's ingenious, Dad. Much better than a pony ring that just goes in circles."

Dad chuckled. "I thought so. And Mike and Monty will be busy giving rides in the arena." He glanced at Wally. "And you will be helping folks to mount."

Wally beamed. "Yes sir, Shep."

Meadow headed for the house. "I'll go call Lisa right now and tell her she's been drafted."

After Lisa agreed to the plan, Meadow hung up the phone, and lay back on the couch, smiling. In spite of grousing to her father, she was excited about the events for the coming weekend. Her father was acting pretty normal and the movie people were coming!

Chapter 15

The Grand Opening

Fort Apache was ablaze with red, white and blue pennants decorating the top of the stockade for Grand Opening Day. Food vendors arrived early to set up inside the grounds, and Meadow could already smell the tantalizing aromas of popcorn and cotton candy. For the special invited guests, Bill Bowman had hired a caterer to use the kitchen in the main lodge. Her mother was keeping a close watch to make sure everything went off without a hitch.

Mike, Wally, and Clay had the stable horses curried and saddled, ready for the onslaught of eager wanna-be cowboys. The admission price included everything, but the dudes would not be going out on trail rides. The arena had been carefully groomed, and a few steers milled around in the corrals for the team penning contest.

Lisa arrived early to help Meadow run the pony maze—a labyrinth built so the ponies went in one way, and wound through to the opposite end. Then they would be turned around and sent back with the next group of kids, Meadow at one end and Lisa in control of the other.

They were busily braiding the pony's manes and tails, entwining ribbons to match the flags, when Meadow noticed a long, black limo pull in through the stockade gate. Her heart beat double time. "Look! It must be the movie people!"

"Those B rated stars?" Lisa giggled.

The liveried driver got out and went to the passenger door, holding it open for an oldish man, small and thin. Bill Bowman, followed by Meadow's parents, came out of the house to greet him. They shook hands and began talking on the porch.

Lisa boldly flounced right over, with Meadow lagging behind.

"Girls, come up here and meet Donald Lord, the foremost director of Westerns in Hollywood." Mr. Bowman waved them up the steps.

Donald Lord, wearing a tweed sport jacket with a cravat, eyeballed them. "Well, here are a couple of young ladies that would make outstanding additions to my stable of starlets in a couple of years." He wiggled his thin mustache and extended a manicured hand to Meadow.

"Pleased to meet you." She wondered how he got his golden blond hair to wave perfectly across his forehead. "I'm Meadow and this is my friend, Lisa."

The director's gaze settled on Lisa. "What a great, exotic look you have. Would you like to be a movie star?"

"Yes, I would." She lifted her chin and met his stare.

His wicked smile broadened. "Come and see me when you turn eighteen." He turned back to Meadow. "Both of you."

Her father stepped between them. "Meadow, I think you'd better get back to the ponies."

"Okay, Dad." She grabbed her friend by the arm. "Nice meeting you, Mr. Lord."

Donald Lord chuckled. "Believe me, the pleasure was all mine."

She practically dragged Lisa back toward the maze, where some kids were petting the ponies. "He probably says that to all the girls, you know."

"Probably, but I wanted to call his bluff." Lisa sighed. "But wouldn't it be neato if he was serious? Just think, me in the movies . . . and you too, of course."

Meadow rolled her eyes. "Forget it. Haven't you ever heard of the director's couch? I think he's a dirty old man, and besides, he dyes his hair."

"Oh, yuck." Lisa made a face. "Hey, we have customers."

Two little boys, the bigger one wearing a Junior Ranger cowboy hat, were waiting to ride. They kept shoving each other to be first.

"Simmer down, you two." Their tired-looking mother sounded exasperated. "Tommy, you're the oldest, you can go first."

Tommy gave a triumphant last shove to his brother, who lost his balance and fell on his bottom. The smaller boy wailed loudly, and his mother tried to console him, without much success. Meadow approached to offer assistance. She took the sobbing boy's hand. "It's okay. You can both go at the same time. And look, you get to ride the black pony. He's the biggest one."

The mother smiled as Meadow took the boy over to Blackjack. She lifted him up and his little face broke into a grin once she placed him on the pony's broad back.

"What's your name?" she asked.

"Bobby."

"Okay, Bobby. You're in charge of Blackjack."

Bobby sat proudly holding the reins, his short legs sticking almost straight out from the saddle.

Meadow hoped the ponies would behave themselves. She didn't worry about Blackjack, he was steady as a rock. But the other three were a different story. They were Shetlands, and had a totally different way of viewing work. The two pintos, Nip and Tuck, were sweet, but Tinker, a chocolate brown with a flaxen mane and tail was a challenge. He had a tendency to turn around and go the wrong way through the maze, causing all the ponies to get jammed up.

Her strategy was to let Blackjack lead the pack, Tinker second, and the pintos bringing up the rear. With Bobby taken care of, Meadow picked up the older boy, Tommy, seating him on Tinker.

"I was supposed to be first." Tommy stuck out his bottom lip. "I want the big black one. I'm bigger than Bobby."

Meadow looked at him seriously. "This one needs a real cowboy to ride him. Blackjack is for really little kids, not big boys, like you. I'm counting on you to keep Tinker in line. Deal?"

Tommy's chest swelled. "Deal."

Two little girls showed up and Meadow put them on Nip and Tuck. Lisa got in position at the opposite end to take the children off the ponies as they arrived.

"Everyone ready?" Meadow lifted the whip that was next to the maze.

All the kids nodded and she tapped on the wooden rail behind Blackjack. He obediently started forward with the rest of the ponies following his lead. Meadow let out a sigh of relief when all of them, including Tinker, made their way through the maze, coming to a stop at Lisa's end.

"Mommy, can we go again? Pleeease?" Tommy pleaded, as Lisa was about to take him off.

"I guess so," his mother said.

The two girls got off, but both boys wanted to ride again. Lisa turned the ponies and started them back through the maze. This time, midway through, Tinker decided he really liked going the other way better. He suddenly turned around, causing Nip and Tuck to stop, confused.

Blackjack kept going forward and the two pintos squeezed past Tinker, who was still intent on going the wrong way. Tommy giggled and gave Tinker a kick to reinforce his decision. Tinker broke into a trot, while Tommy squealed and kicked harder.

Seeing the problem, Lisa moved into the maze to try and get the pony turned back the right direction. Tinker was sneaky, though. He waited until Lisa was close, then dodged around her to continue with his escape plan. Before long, he had trotted out the end of the maze and into the stable yard. They were near the back gate of the stockade which opened into the desert. Tinker was determined to go explore those wide open spaces.

"Woohoo!" Tommy yelled, as they went out the gate. "I'm a real cowboy!"

"Tommy, come back here this instant!" His mother shouted after him.

Meadow knew she had to act fast. Blackjack arrived with Bobby, and she quickly handed him to his mother.

"What'll we do now? Tommy may get thrown and be killed!" She patted the wailing Bobby. "That boy will be the death of me yet."

"Don't worry, I'll go round them up." Meadow dashed for Foxfire's corral.

Tommy's mother held tightly onto Bobby. "Please hurry!"

Foxfire met Meadow at the gate. She swung unto her back, without a bridle, using just her legs for control. They flew through the stockade after the rapidly disappearing pony.

Tinker's little hooves were churning the dust when they caught up.

Meadow took hold of the pony's bridle. "I thought you were a cowboy, not a horse thief." She shook her head. "You know what they do to horse thieves, don't you?"

"No, what?" Tommy had a silly grin. No doubt this was the greatest adventure of his young life.

She narrowed her eyes, trying to look mean. "They hang 'em."

Tommy's jaw went slack and tears welled up. "I didn't mean to steal him. Tinker just wanted to come out here. It's not my fault!"

"Maybe they'll let you off this time. First offense, an' all— you haven't done this before, have you?"

"No, ma'am, never."

"Okay, pardner. Let's head back to the fort and I'll try to get you cleared."

Meadow kept hold of Tinker's reins, afraid that the wayward pony might take off again. By the time they got back, a crowd had gathered and was watching their return.

"There she is! She saved my little boy!" the mother gushed, snatching Tommy off of Tinker. "And with no bridle or saddle!"

"How do you control your horse?" asked an onlooker, as everyone crowded around Meadow and Foxfire.

She shrugged. "I never thought about it. Foxy always knows what to do. But I usually have a bridle. I didn't have time to put one on."

Meadow answered some more questions and was trying to extricate herself from the crowd when she saw a familiar rumpled figure making his way over.

"Nice job." Joel Adams snapped a picture of her on Foxfire.

"Thanks, I didn't know you were coming today."

"Another human interest story for the Gazette. Linda Bowman called to make sure I would cover the Grand Opening. Of course, whenever *you're* involved, something dramatic happens."

"Is Linda here yet? I haven't seen her."

"Don't know. Just got here myself. Glad I made it in time for the impressive rescue. Can I quote you in the article?"

"Sure, I guess." She glanced over at the pony area. "I'd better get back. More customers are lined up."

The children wanting to ride had multiplied tenfold when Meadow returned. As she led Tinker over to the maze, most of them clamored to ride him.

"Sorry, Tinker is retired from the ring, but you can sit on him, if you like." She tied him securely to the outside rail. Parents sat their kids on the Tinker the Stinker and took photos. Many of them wanted Meadow to pose with the children and she reluctantly complied.

She and Lisa were busy the rest of the day, not even having time for a lunch break. Meadow was about to expire from lack of food, when Linda showed up with sandwiches.

"Thanks, Linda, am I glad to see you!"

"Seems like our Grand Opening is a big success."

"A lot more people showed up than I expected. And they all have kids that want to ride."

"Glad this isn't my regular job." Lisa snatched a sandwich. "I'm really sick of the little brats."

Linda laughed. "You'll be happy to know that your father said you could close down now. Tell everyone to go watch what's happening in the arena."

Meadow thankfully put the ponies away. It was more work than she'd imagined looking after a passel of kids. When they got to the arena, a crowd had already gathered. Monty and Mike were giving a team penning demonstration. After they finished, Mike asked who wanted to try it. Earlier, a group had practiced riding in the arena and now these people came forward to learn team penning. Before long, they found out it wasn't as easy as her brothers made it look.

It was pretty funny to watch the novice riders trying to maneuver their mounts to round up uncooperative cattle. The audience loved it, though, calling out helpful advice when the bawling steers escaped, dashing back to the safety of their friends, while frustrated riders glared. Total chaos reigned and not one of the herd went into the pen. Finally, Monty and Mike rode back into the arena and in short order, the rebellious steers were all in their proper place.

By now, it was nearing dusk and people started to leave, looking tired but smiling. A sure sign they would be back to spend money on trail rides next time.

Bill Bowman announced it was cocktail hour and ushered his invited guests into the lodge. Meadow and Lisa snuck away to shower before coming to the party. When they crept back in, Donald Lord and the rest of the adults were swilling drinks at the bar. They seemed to be deep in a serious discussion.

Meadow followed Lisa to the davenport and they both sprawled out, then started giggling about Tinker's antics. Linda joined them, drinks in hand.

"Big news." She offered them each a Shirley Temple. "Donald Lord wants to make another movie here at Fort Apache. He said Shep can supply all the horses and be head wrangler. I think that was Dad's secret plan all along."

"Really? How soon?" Meadow asked.

"It will be a while. He's right in the middle of a picture now, just took a short break to come here for the opening. Still needs to get funding and all that. And Meadow, he saw you rescue the boy, without using a bridle or saddle. He was quite impressed. Said you and Foxy would be tremendous for some stunts."

"Wow, that's so cool!" Lisa said.

Meadow stared at Linda. "Really?"

Linda nodded. "I agree with him." She glanced over at the adults and stood. "Better get back and see what else my father's cooking up."

After Linda left, Lisa leaned toward Meadow. "Just think of all the cute boys you'll meet in Hollywood! You're so lucky."

Meadow giggled. "It'll probably never happen. But if it does, you can come be my assistant."

"Cool!"

The rest of the evening was spent conjuring up all sorts of impossible scenarios where they were both discovered and became big stars.

Chapter 16

The Plot Thickens

Wendell sipped iced tea by the pool, carefully reading through the Phoenix Gazette, page by page. You never knew when the opportunity for a fresh scam might present itself. The slider squeaked open, footsteps slapped on the deck, then a big splash sprayed drops onto his paper. He shook the water off and scowled. "Can't you jump in at the other end?"

Lucy poked her head up, rivulets running down the side of the white swim cap. "What'd you say, hon?"

"Nothing. Forget it."

His eyes followed her as she climbed out of the pool, bursting out of her bikini top. She shook out her orange tresses, put on oversized white-framed sunglasses, then lay back on the lounge next to his. A tall, frosty Pina Colada sat in a puddle of condensation on the small table separating the two chairs. Wendell limited himself to a few beers, never drinking hard liquor. He didn't like the feeling of being less than clearly focused at all times, but Lucy obviously didn't share his fear of losing mental acuity. This was her third drink since noon. In a few minutes, she was snoring like a cat lying in the sun.

Wendell turned to the *Variety* section of the paper, then sat up straighter and studied the photo featured on the front page. It was of a girl sitting bareback astride a bridleless horse. After reading the article, he swore under his breath, and threw the paper onto Lucy's bare midriff. She nearly jumped off the chair, then pushed up her dark glasses.

"What's the big idea?"

"That little bitch is in the news again!" he said, unable to control the anger in his voice.

"Huh, what? Who are you talking about?"

Wendell groaned and looked at her in disgust. How had he ended up with this dimwit? She was a real millstone, lazy, and only interested in what small luxuries he could provide. Why did he put up with her? Then his eyes traveled down from her pouty face and rested on her scarcely contained, ample bosom. That's why, but he wasn't sure it was worth it.

"Meadow Shepherd," he spat out. "It says she heroically saved some little boy whose pony ran away with him."

"Oh, is that all?" Lucy lay back on her deck chair. "Why do you continue to fixate on her? Some silly teenager."

"You just don't get it, do you? Because of that stinking brat, the cops are after us. We might even have to move outa this *lovely* neighborhood. Besides, she knows where the Indian Medicine Chest is. You know it's worth a fortune."

At the mention of a fortune, Lucy sat up. "How can you be so sure she knows where it's hidden?"

"I can feel it and I'm never wrong about these things."

"How will we get her to tell?" Lucy screwed up her face. "You can't just kidnap the girl and torture it out of her."

"Hmmm . . . not such a bad idea. But no. I'll be much more subtle than that. I'm working on a plan that will make her *want* to confess everything. Go back to sleep."

He waited until snores purred from her tanned body, then reached for the phone, and dialed. "Hi, it's me. Keep an eye on her, whatever she does. And up the pressure."

"My pleasure. You leavin' the method up to me?"

Wendell curled his lip. "Yeah, whatever it takes. She'll sing like a canary when we're through."

He clicked the receiver with his mouth set in a thin line.

Chapter 17

Trouble Brewing

Meadow rode along the trail with her head in the clouds, still thinking about the fun and excitement of the Grand Opening. She figured it was silly to dwell too much about actually being in a movie—that was a long shot at best, but it was fun to dream about.

Her attention returned to reality when she saw Kelsey sniffing some hoof prints. Meadow stopped to get a better view, and saw they were unshod. Her pulse went up a notch. A whole herd of unshod hooves. Nueme said there was an old Indian path along the rim that wound its way into the Superstitions. Arrow must have moved his herd down from the high country. Their winter grazing area must be somewhere close.

Heart thumping, she put Foxfire into a trot to follow the tracks. The amulet grew warm against her chest as they twisted and turned through the rocky terrain. She reined in when her mare started acting spooky, swiveling her ears back and forth. Prickles popped up on Meadow's arms.

"What is it, girl?" She scanned the surrounding area. Nothing.

She clicked to Foxfire and they rode on, but her mare continued to act funny and Meadow had an eerie feeling of being watched. When the tracks faded out completely, it was almost a relief to head for home, except for the sharp disappointment of not finding Arrow. The elusive quarry had disappeared without a trace.

It wasn't until they were safely back at the fort that her nerves quieted. As she passed the pony maze, it occurred to her how abandoned the place seemed after the whirlwind of activity from the day before. Better enjoy it. The dudes would start coming soon, then there'd be plenty to keep them all busy.

But no one was around today. Donald Lord wasn't leaving until Monday, so her parents were taking a break from work. Monty called early that morning with a hot tip from his boss, the race horse trainer, then everyone got excited about trying their luck at the races. They'd taken Wally with them—a brand new experience for him. He practically danced a jig when Monty said he could help groom one of the thoroughbreds.

Even Mike was gone. He spent the night at Jack Dawson's house. Mom and Dad hadn't been too happy about the arrangement, but finally gave in. Mike argued that he wouldn't see much of his friends with the move to the outback, as he called it.

Meadow couldn't see why her brother wanted to stay friends with Jack, and the rough crowd that included Frankie and his gang. They were not a good influence, and he'd been cutting class with them. His grades were starting to suffer, and she'd overheard him and Dad having angry words about it.

Her attention was focused on refilling the water trough, when Meadow heard the loud rumble of an engine. She swung around and saw Mike pull up on a Harley motorcycle, idling to a halt next to her. He had a huge grin on his face, obviously enamored with the monstrous machine.

"Where'd you get that?" Meadow covered her ears as he shut it down.

"It belongs to a friend of Jack's. Remember Frankie?"

She scowled. "Yeah, I remember him, but why are you riding it? You don't even have a license."

"They told me the cops won't care, as long as I stay on the back roads."

Meadow raised her brows. "Really? I don't think Dad would like it."

"Don't be such a spoilsport. C'mon, I'll take you for a ride. It's a blast."

"I don't know . . ."

"Oh come on, Meadow." Her brother held up two fingers, like a Boy Scout pledge. "I promise I'll take it right back afterwards. No harm done. It's so much fun, you'll love it. C'mon."

"Well . . . all right." She couldn't resist. It *did* look fun, plus she'd never ridden on a motorcycle before.

Mike started the Harley and the engine roared to life, the sound reminding Meadow of the party that went south. She swallowed, hoping this didn't turn out as badly. She climbed on board, and felt the unrelenting vibration as he revved up the motor and let out the clutch. The back wheel dug in, dirt spewed out behind and they were propelled forward at a high rate of speed. She clung to Mike as he turned out of the stockade and onto the main road towards Apache Junction.

"This isn't a back road!" She called to him, but her words were torn from her lips by the wind.

Mike hunkered down and gave the bike more gas, and she saw the speedometer climb until it indicated more than 80 miles per hour. Meadow had never gone that fast before. It was exhilarating, with the wind whipping her hair and the landscape flying by. She could see why Mike liked this. They were moving so fast her eyes started watering, and she buried her face against his back.

He had already slowed, and was turning around toward the fort, when Meadow's heart dropped. Crap! There was a patrol car parked behind a large billboard.

Wheeling out from the shadow of the sign, the policeman pulled up next to the Harley, and waved them over to the shoulder of the road. Mike wasn't grinning any longer, as he and Meadow dismounted and watched the blue uniformed man get out and walk toward them.

The cop was young, with short, sandy hair barely visible under his cap. The badge on his chest read "Dan Billings."

"Do you know why I pulled you over?"

Mike shrugged. "Guess we were going a little fast. I just got this bike and it has a lot of power. Sorry sir, it won't happen again."

Officer Billings offered a friendly smile. "Well, I can understand that. I have a bike myself. Driver's license and registration, please."

Mike put on a show of searching his jean pockets, then looked up, eyes wide. "Shoot, I must have left my billfold back at the house."

"Heck, I've had that happen before. I'll just follow you home, and you can get your wallet. What's your name and address?"

"Mike Shepherd, Fort Apache . . . in Apache Junction, but I must have left it in my jacket at a friend's house . . . in Scottsdale."

The policeman narrowed his eyes. "That's out of my jurisdiction." He made a note on his pad and turned to Meadow.

"Your name and address, Miss?"

"Meadow Shepherd, same address. Mike's my brother."

"Wait here," Officer Billings said curtly. Before returning to his car, he wrote down the motorcycle license plate number.

They could see the cop talking on his car radio.

"We'd better get out of here." Mike started to climb on the motorcycle.

She grabbed his arm. "No, that'll make it worse!"

"I guess you're right." He slowly brought his leg to the ground.

Mike shifted uneasily as he watched the officer. Before long, the policeman strode back toward them, his earlier friendliness replaced with a stony face.

"Young man, you're under arrest for the possession of stolen property. Sorry, regulations say I have to put these on for a felony theft."

Meadow gasped and watched, speechless, as Officer Billings took out handcuffs and clicked them onto Mike's wrists. The cop looked over at her.

"You'll have to come along, too." He nodded to the car.

"But my sister didn't have anything to do with this. Uh. . . I mean, she didn't steal anything, but neither did I!" Mike blurted out.

"How do I know she isn't an accomplice?" the officer asked. "Now both of you, get in my cruiser."

He ushered them over to his patrol car, pushed on their heads as they clambered into the back seat and firmly closed the door. After he got into the front, he grabbed the radio receiver, saying he was on his way in with two suspects. He replaced the handset, but the radio crackled static and disembodied voices all the way to the Mesa police station.

This can't be happening, Meadow thought in desperation, peering through the screen that separated them from the officer. We're not criminals!

She leaned toward her brother, asking in a hushed voice, "What's he talking about? Didn't you borrow the motorcycle?"

Mike just nodded his head, looking a little green.

"Tell him then!" Meadow hissed.

"Frankie must have taken it, but I don't want to get him or Jack into trouble. The bike was at Jack's house," he finally whispered back.

"You have to tell, even if they get into trouble."

"But I was riding it. They'll never believe me."

At the police station, they were escorted into a waiting area, and then Meadow watched as Mike was taken through a heavy door. A large female officer, with dingy hair pulled back into a severe bun, took Meadow's arm and guided her into a small room. There was a table with chairs on either side. There were no other furnishings, and the room's drab putty walls were devoid of adornment except for a poster declaring, "CRIME DOES NOT PAY."

"Sit down." The policewoman checked her paperwork. "I'm Detective Cook, and I'm going to ask you a few questions. All right?"

Meadow nodded.

"Do your folks have any idea of your whereabouts today? Tell me what happened." The woman appeared to be very no-nonsense.

After swallowing, Meadow took a deep breath. "They left me at home, then I went for a ride on a motorcycle with my brother. Mike didn't do anything wrong. He borrowed it. He didn't know it was stolen."

"Uh huh. Were you with him when he *borrowed* it?"

"No, he rode it out to our place and picked me up. Mike spent the night with a friend. The motorcycle belongs to him . . . or another friend."

Officer Cook pursed her lips. "That all sounds a little murky. What are their names, and which one supposedly owns the vehicle?"

"I'm not sure. Jack Dawson is Mike's friend, but the other guy's name is Frankie. I don't know his last name. I think the bike belongs to Frankie."

"According to my records, the owner is a Homer Munson. He's the one that reported the vehicle stolen." Officer Cook paused. "Someone is lying."

Meadow's guts, already in knots, twinged painfully.

The detective rose and started toward the door. At the last minute, almost as an afterthought, she turned back to Meadow.

"What's your phone number? We need to contact your parents."

She gave her the number, and then the woman left her alone in the austere room. Her stomach churned and Meadow thought she might be sick. The thought of her parents finding out about this made her want to retch.

More than an hour passed while she fidgeted, and finally Detective Cook came and told her that they'd been able to get her folks on the telephone. She brought Meadow out to the waiting area, and offered her a stale-looking donut.

"No, thanks. But could I have a glass of water?" Her mouth felt as though she'd just crossed the Sahara without a canteen. Detective Cook took her time, but eventually brought some tepid water in a paper cup.

The waiting room was like a tomb. This must be a slow crime day, Meadow thought as she awaited her parents' arrival. The minutes crawled by as she squirmed and paced, nervously watching the clock, wondering where her brother had been taken.

The only relief in her complete boredom was when a scruffy looking man came staggering in and went straight up to the admission counter, as if he was familiar with the routine.

The officer in charge said, "Disturbing the peace again, Floyd?"

"Thought I'd save everyone some trouble and arrest myself." The slurred words were hardly discernable and the guy weaved, clutching the counter.

The man was escorted past Meadow on the way to the drunk tank. He grinned and gave her a sly wink, and she wrinkled her nose at his foul smell, which lingered long after he disappeared through the doorway.

At last, when she was close to screaming in frustration, Meadow saw her parents enter the police station. Bounding up, she ran to her father and flung herself into his arms.

"I haven't seen Mike in hours. I don't know what they did with him." She tried to stifle tears. "I know he's innocent."

"Everything will be all right, sweetheart." Her father held her for a moment. "We'll get this straightened out. I'm sure it's a misunderstanding."

Meadow followed her parents to the sergeant's desk, and stood by while they signed papers.

"Your son has been charged with grand larceny," the sergeant said brusquely. "He's being released to your custody, with a hearing scheduled in ten days. Meanwhile, you'll be able to meet with the County Defender, unless you want to retain your own attorney."

"Grand larceny!" Mom echoed, grabbing Dad's arm.

Her father clenched his jaw. "What evidence do you have that he actually committed the crime?"

"He was caught red-handed with the stolen property. That's all the evidence we need. See you in court." The sergeant abruptly ended the discussion and bent over a stack of paperwork.

Mike was finally led out of another area. Instead of her normally tough brother, he seemed frail, stumbling over to them and looking at the floor.

"C'mon son, let's get out of here." Dad put his arm around Mike, and helped him out of the station.

On the way home, her brother was unusually quiet, offering no excuses to Mom and Dad. She wondered if he'd told the police about Jack's involvement.

Stupid Jack! First Lisa, and now this. How would Mike ever get out of this mess?

That evening, the family turned in early. Meadow sighed as she slipped into bed. What a terrible day. Anticipation of the fun new venture was ruined. Now worry about Mike overshadowed everything else.

Chapter 18

A Major Win

Meadow winced as Mike banged his way out of the house the next morning. He'd been in conference with their parents for the better part of an hour. She followed him into the barn and found him pacing like a cooped-up racehorse.

"Just as I figured, nobody believes I didn't steal that stupid motorcycle." His words were belligerent, but his eyes betrayed the hurt.

"I believe you."

"Dad doesn't, and now I'm grounded forever. He's never liked me as much as his firstborn son, and you've always been his darling little girl."

"That's not true. He loves you just the same. Did you tell him what really happened?"

"Not about Jack or Frankie. I can't squeal on my friends. I said I borrowed it but didn't tell him any names."

"Did you tell the police what happened?"

Mike glared at her. "No, I *told* you—I can't rat on my friends." He kicked at the dirt, then swallowed, "I . . . I told the cops I did it."

"What! Why'd you do that?"

"They kept pressuring me and telling me to come clean . . . it was horrible. I was in this little room for hours, and two of them just kept badgering me. They said I would get off with probation, if I confessed. Jack's already on probation. I couldn't tell on him."

Meadow took hold of both his shoulders. "You *have* to tell the cops and Dad about his involvement. Do you want to be on probation . . . or go to jail?"

"I won't go to jail. This is my first offense." He shrugged. "Probation's no big deal. I'm not a criminal."

"You shouldn't even get probation. If Jack was a real friend, he would come forward and tell what happened."

Mike gripped her arm, his fingers biting into her flesh. "Promise me you won't say anything to Mom or Dad about this."

"I can't promise that. They need to know the truth."

"No, I'm handling this my way. Promise me."

Meadow pried his hand off, shaking her head. "All right, but I think you're wrong."

The next Sunday, Meadow sat alone at the Pony Club Show, watching Lisa and Major have a perfect round, qualifying for a jump off against Cynthia. She stood up, cheering as her friend reined the gelding in. Lisa waved and flashed the audience a brilliant smile. She was doing so well it was a shame that none of her usual supporters were in attendance.

Earlier, Dad had dropped them off at the show, then left to deliver one of the Navajo ponies to a buyer. Dr. Wilson was performing an emergency surgery, and Meadow's mother had stayed at Fort Apache to supervise Mike. He was still grounded and was helping Wally and Clay clear the riding paths of debris. They'd be open for dude rides in a couple of weeks.

After Lisa exited the ring, Meadow stepped down from the grandstand to join her while the jumps were being raised. Just as she got to the lowest step, she saw Jack Dawson talking to her friend. When Lisa was in an event, he always seemed to show up. They appeared to be arguing. Meadow gritted her teeth, tore over to them, and got right into Jack's face. "Why don't you tell the cops that Mike is innocent?"

Jack gulped and took a step back. "I don't know anything about it."

"Liar! It was you and Frankie that stole that bike!"

"No, it wasn't me." His eyes darted around, as if he were being watched. "Leave me alone." He turned and fled.

"Jack, wait! Who was it then?" She was about to go after him, but Lisa grabbed her arm.

"Let him go. He wouldn't tell me anything either. He's scared of Frankie's gang."

"If he told the truth, Mike wouldn't be in trouble."

"He thinks if he talks, Frankie will beat him up . . . or worse."

"He could at least tell them that Mike wasn't involved."

"I know." Lisa put her arm around Meadow.

Scott rode up to them and pulled Blondie to a stop.

"Congratulations, Lisa. If you keep this up, you'll win high point today." He chuckled. "Cynthia is over there pouting right now."

They both looked where Scott indicated and Cynthia stared back at them, face strained. The blonde's father was standing next to her, spewing advice. Ben Markowitz finally dried up, apparently running out of useless instructions, and strutted off. Cynthia slunk over to speak to Meadow, managing to ignore Lisa.

"I hope Mike isn't in too much trouble. But even if he has to go to jail or juvenile detention or whatever, I won't ever forget him." Cynthia's flair for drama came on full force. "I will *always* love him no matter what. Of course, my father is being just *horrid* about the whole thing. He says your whole family are a bunch of hooligans."

"I don't want to talk about it." Meadow turned from her. "Just go away."

"Well, you don't have to be so *rude*. I was just trying to help." She dabbed at her eyes with a lace handkerchief. "Tell Mike I'll *always* be true."

As Cynthia departed, Meadow saw Joel Adams, the reporter, sauntering toward them in his usual rumpled shirt and baggy pants.

"Hi, girls." He nodded to them. "It looks like I'll have a new star to write about. What a relief not to interview that Markowitz girl and her overbearing father again."

Lisa laughed. "I haven't won yet. But thanks to Meadow, Major is doing great."

Joel's brows came together. "Thanks to Meadow? I thought you were riding him."

"She schools him when I can't come out to ride and he has really improved."

"Thanks Lisa, but Major is doing so well because he works his heart out for *you*."

"He's my best friend, except for you, of course." Lisa gave Meadow a peck on the cheek.

"Uh-oh, they're saying get ready for the jump off. You better get back on." Joel offered to give her a leg up. "Soon you'll be the champion." He winked at her.

While Lisa prepared to go to the arena, Joel accompanied Meadow back to the grandstand to watch the event. They climbed to the top for a better view.

Joel cleared his throat. "I'm sorry about your brother."

"How do you know about that?"

"I saw the police report. I have a friend at the Mesa station and follow what's going on. You never know what you might dig up."

She firmed her lips. "He's innocent."

"Don't worry, Meadow. He doesn't have a record. No judge in his right mind will give him more than probation, even if he did it."

"He didn't steal anything!"

"Okay, okay. I'm sure you're right. There *is* something else I want to talk to you about, though."

"What?"

"I told you I read the police reports. Well, the cops have a lead on Wendell Halstead. They tracked him back to the Phoenix area."

"Oh, no." Suddenly the air felt like an artic chill had set in. It made sense, the phone calls and maybe even the ghost . . . .

"Yeah, so be careful."

He was the second person to warn her to watch out. But careful of what? What could Wendell do besides make threatening phone calls and scare her?

Joel touched her shoulder. "Look, it's Lisa's turn."

Lisa rode in confidently and started the round, taking each obstacle with precision. Cynthia already had a fence down, so if Major jumped clean, they would win. Going into a big loop, Lisa headed toward the last row of jumps, when suddenly there was a muffled pop.

Meadow gripped the side of her seat as she saw her friend's stirrup fall to the ground and Lisa slip sideways on the saddle. Major scooted over slightly to get under her again, and Lisa pulled herself upright. She continued on, riding with just one stirrup. Meadow let out her breath, clapping and whooping with everyone else as they finished the course without a fault.

The loudspeaker blared out, "What a fantastic ride that was, ladies and gentlemen! Please welcome our high point winner back into the ring, Lisa Wilson!"

Lisa's face was wreathed in smiles as she rode her victory lap with just one stirrup amid more cheers. Meadow's heart swelled with pride for her friend and she hurried down to welcome her out of the arena, trophy in hand. Joel followed at a more leisurely pace.

She raced to Lisa's side. "I'm so proud of you! You could have been hurt if that happened over a jump."

"I'm glad my mom wasn't here. She would've had a stroke." Lisa handed the trophy to Meadow and slid to the ground.

The ring steward retrieved the stirrup leather and brought it over. "You're a lucky girl this came off where it did. The leather's intact. The metal keeper must have broken."

Frowning, Lisa pulled up the saddle flap. The stirrup retainer was fractured. "Wow, this is a new saddle."

The steward tsked and shook his head. "We've had it happen before on this model. You'll have to send it back to the dealer. I suggest a different brand." He walked away from them muttering.

Lisa looked stricken. "Mom will be furious. What'll I do now? The new one will never arrive in time for the next show."

"You can borrow mine. I'm not showing anymore." Meadow felt a little twinge saying it, but had no stomach for the show ring since Foxfire's poisoning.

Joel shuffled over to them, grinning. "Well Lisa, thanks to you, I have a great story to write. You and Meadow always provide much more interesting copy than certain others that shall remain nameless."

They both laughed, then walked arm in arm back to the stable area where Dad was just pulling in with the old truck. After they loaded Major, Lisa chattered about the show until being dropped off at her house. Meadow smiled, it was pretty special winning the trophy.

Dad didn't say a word on the rest of the drive to Fort Apache. Finally, she couldn't stand it anymore.

"Everyone says that Mike will probably get probation. But he's innocent."

Her father whipped his head around, giving her a sharp look. "Do you know anything about what happened?"

"I just know he's not guilty."

He sighed and stared at the road.

Meadow shifted uncomfortably, at a loss. She desperately wanted to tell him what she knew. Why had she promised Mike? She certainly felt no loyalty to Jack Dawson or Frankie.

The steady grind of the old engine was the only sound as they continued down the road.

Chapter 19

The Hearing

Meadow's stomach lurched and threatened to erupt the morning of Mike's hearing. She lay still for a minute, allowing it to settle, then rolled out of bed and dutifully trooped into the dining room. When her mother brought out bacon, eggs and toast, she sipped orange juice and pushed the food around, making a mess out of the yolks. She finally shoved the whole plate away.

Her father took only black coffee and after his third cup, he pushed back from the table. "We'd better get going. The hearing is in an hour."

The tension was thick as Mike stood, his face strained. Meadow followed him to the Ranch Wagon and climbed into the backseat. Monty hadn't been able to take off work, and Meadow got the feeling he was relieved to miss the hearing. They passed Wally and Clay shoveling manure as they drove toward the gate. Wally grinned and waved, but the white-haired man with the dead eyes just watched them go, expressionless as always.

The courtroom was cold and sterile, much like Meadow had imagined it would be. Mike was taken up front to wait for the judge to come in. He sat down, but his leg jiggled as though it had a mind of its own.

Meadow slid into a pew-like seat, next to her parents. She glanced around and spotted Joel Adams across the aisle. He must have found out about the hearing from the police department. His unsmiling face was far from reassuring. He mouthed something to her. It looked like, "Bad judge."

She frowned, feeling her neck tense even more.

Then the bailiff announced, "All rise for the honorable Judge Polk."

They stood while a large, grim man marched in, his robe flowing out behind. He sat with purpose and banged the gavel. "You may be seated."

The judge shuffled his papers and nodded to the bailiff, who announced, "First on the agenda is the State of Arizona versus Michael Shepherd. The charge is grand larceny. Please stand, young man."

Mike stood, his eyes flitting around, as if he were trying to find the nearest exit where he could flee.

 The judge's stare was cold as he peered down at Mike from his bench. "I see that a plea has been entered of 'guilty as charged.' Do you want to let that plea stand?"

Mike nodded like a wooden figure being controlled by an unseen puppeteer.

Even though Meadow knew Mike had confessed, to hear it from the judge's lips felt like a blow to her middle. It somehow hadn't been real until this moment.

Her mother sucked in her breath and Dad scrambled to his feet. "What's going on here? He's not guilty!"

The judge rapped his gavel. "Order. Order in the court. I won't tolerate any such outbursts. If it happens again, I'll clear the courtroom." He glared directly at her father. "Understand?"

Dad collapsed onto the seat as if his legs were suddenly made of soft rubber. Mom grabbed his arm, her hand shaking. Meadow waited, holding her breath for what the judge would say next. It didn't take long.

"I understand this is your first offense, young man, and generally we are more lenient given those circumstances. But due to the seriousness of the crime, and the fact that recently, this court has seen an uptick of juvenile delinquency throughout our community, I have decided to make an example of you to deter the criminal behavior of other youths. Therefore, I hereby sentence you to three months detention at Fort Grant State Industrial School for Wayward Boys."

The bang of his gavel reverberated throughout the courtroom, echoing his words.

Fort Grant! The kids at school whispered about that place. A place where really rough boys were sent, not her brother, not Mike.

Meadow and her parents sat in stunned silence as Mike was led away without a backward glance.

Chapter 20

The Mine

Meadow left the fort early and rode up the steep, winding trail to the overlook where she could see Weaver's Needle. The sun rose with fiery brilliance and she grinned when the shadow it cast lengthened across the expanse to some rocky crags. It pointed the way to an opening in those rocks only a mile or so from where she sat aboard Foxfire.

"C'mon, girls. Let's go find it." Kelsey wagged her tail and her mare eagerly started forward, as if they both knew an important quest lay ahead.

It had been more than three weeks since Mike left for detention at Fort Grant, and none of her family had heard a word from him. That was part of the sentence—no contact for the first month. Meadow's whole family was devastated by the punishment and separation. Her father had ceased whistling his favorite tuneless song and her mother had a permanent worry line on her forehead. Monty threw himself into his job at the track and they seldom saw him except for the evening meal.

Meadow took to riding long hours in the Superstitions on Foxfire, with Kelsey as her only other companion. Lisa didn't trail ride much since she'd started dating Scott. She only rode to practice Major over jumps, but was doing quite well in pony club shows, beating Cynthia at least half the time. They were neck and neck for the high point medal competition coming up in May.

The stable continued to draw customers, making a profit right off the bat. Her father hired another wrangler, Hank, to help Clay and Wally with the rides. Sometimes, Clay mysteriously disappeared for hours at a time, riding off on his mammoth mule, but Dad hadn't seemed to notice. When Meadow tried to talk to him about it, he brushed her off. Her father hardly spoke to her at all anymore.

The search for the mine kept her thoughts off family troubles, and Meadow forged ahead, even though a path was nonexistent. Foxfire nimbly crossed the boulders, sure-footed as a mountain goat, but it still took more than an hour to reach the crevice in the rocks. The opening was big enough to enter, and they wound through a slot canyon, the sandy bottom still wet from a rainstorm that tore through the night before. In places, water dripped from the top, making tiny waterfalls down the sides of the sheer rock faces.

The canyon widened and finally gaped open, and they entered into a protected basin surrounded by cliffs. Grass grew in thick clumps and a few mesquite trees dotted the landscape. At the far side, a group of cottonwoods stood in a stately assembly, their early spring leaves already in full foliage. Foxfire looked toward the trees, flared her nostrils, and nickered softly.

Meadow's heart pounded when she saw a silver form emerge from the green backdrop and rear unto his hind legs.

Arrow! She had discovered his winter retreat. Behind him, his herd drifted into view, the mares stopped short at seeing encroachers in their sanctuary, and the new foals peeked from behind.

The Sky Horse thundered across the expanse, and circled, silver mane and tail flying. As he danced around them, the amulet glowed warm under Meadow's shirt. She bubbled with laughter as he and Foxfire sniffed noses, stamping and squealing at each other. The stallion led them over to the copse of trees, where a small stream meandered, lazily making its way to the wall of rocks and then disappearing from sight. Meadow was certain it must only run until the blazing summer sun dried it up, but by then Arrow and his herd would be back in the high country.

She dismounted and slipped the bridle off Foxfire. "Go play. You two have some catching up to do."

The stallion galloped away, and Foxfire followed, bucking and kicking, exuberant to see her old friend again. Meadow sank down onto a carpet of grass next to the stream. Kelsey lapped the water, then waded in and flopped down in a shallow pool.

"This is a great place, right, Kelsey?" Her dog wagged vigorously, bounded out and shook all over Meadow, then clambered into her lap. She lost her balance with the dog's weight and fell over, laughing. She hadn't felt this good since Mike's ordeal had begun.

Meadow lay back in the shade, and closed her eyes. It wasn't long before she felt a soft blowing on her face. When she looked up, one of the foals was checking her out, tentatively poking his little nose toward her. He sprang back when he realized she was looking at him. He was only a few days old, and soon his mother was calling for him to come to her. Meadow watched him scamper away with a prick of sadness that Foxfire would never know the joys of motherhood.

Out in the field, the stallion and Foxfire settled down and became involved in the serious business of cropping grass. Meadow let them graze for a while before calling her mare over. "C'mon Foxy, we'd better get going."

Both horses came at her call, and the stallion put his head down to her level. She pulled his forelock and fondled his ears. "You don't know how I've missed you. I've been worried, you know." He rubbed his head against her, as though he understood and missed her, too.

"I'll bet you know where the mine is, don't you, boy?" He looked at her with his dark, liquid eyes, and then backed up and tossed his head. "I swear you understand everything I say. You *do* know where it is."

Meadow retrieved the bridle, slipped it on Foxfire, and then swung onto her back. With a quickened pulse, she let Arrow lead them out of the valley on a different route, deeper into the mountain. The band of mares with their babies were content to let them go, seeming to know the stallion would be back. Where was he taking them? Would it really be to the famous Lost Dutchman Mine?

A series of switchbacks led them on a circuitous route, past outcroppings and cliffs. After a couple of miles, Arrow hopped up a seemingly impossible boulder and then dropped from sight. Meadow grabbed tightly to Foxfire's mane and her mare lunged forward. They leapt and scrambled up the huge rock, then slid down a steep grade.

Meadow sucked in her breath when they landed in a clearing that looked like an old camp site. Off to one side was a fire ring, remnants of a shack, and other debris. Situated in the middle was a circular pit paved with flat rocks. Drag stones were connected to a center post by a long arm. Around the edge, horse or mule hooves had dug a shallow trench from long use of dragging the stones in a circle. She knew from reading about mines that this must be an arrastra, a primitive mill used for grinding and pulverizing gold ore.

Her eyes searched their surroundings for an obvious mine shaft, like in the movies. Darn, is this it? No doubt someone had mined here in the past, but it didn't fit her romantic notion of what it should look like.

Kelsey began sniffing and digging at a pile of rocks nearby. Meadow was just about to go investigate when a crack of thunder startled her. She hadn't even noticed the gathering clouds with all her attention focused on the campsite. "C'mon, Kelsey, we'd better get going, before it pours."

She looked around for Arrow, but he had disappeared, like he'd done so many times before. She sighed. Oh, well, at least she knew he was safe.

Meadow turned Foxfire in the direction where she thought they came into the clearing, but couldn't find any hoof prints. That was odd. What happened to the tracks? They had just gotten there a few minutes ago. She shook her head in confusion, and thunder cracked again. Large drops wet her face. She rode around the clearing, but found no way out. Meadow reined Foxfire in and sat still, feeling disoriented. Now what?

Foxfire stamped and pulled at the bit. "Okay, girl. You find the way out."

Meadow gave Foxfire her head and she started walking in a totally different direction from where they'd come in. Soon they ended up at the sheer wall surrounding the clearing, facing a large, brushy mesquite. Foxfire skirted around the tree and Meadow saw it concealed an entrance to a short tunnel. They passed through and discovered thick brush at the opposite end of the opening. It was highly unlikely that a casual passerby would spot the tunnel to the campsite clearing.

After making their way through the brush, Foxfire found a faint trail heading in the general direction of the fort. The rain spit and spat for a while, but never developed into a real downpour. It turned out her mare had found the most direct route home and in a couple of hours they were riding through the fortress gate.

Clay had just returned from guiding a dude ride, and his bad-tempered mule was hitched to a rail. Once Meadow had attempted to pet the beast, but he laid his giant ears flat and bared his teeth. Definitely takes after his owner, she decided. Behind the mule's saddle were the largest set of saddlebags she'd ever seen. What did he carry in those?

After he dismissed the guests, Clay turned and eyed her without smiling. She hurriedly took care of Foxfire, then ran to the house, creeped out by the strange man who never said a word to her, just stared.

She was eager to tell someone about her interesting find and went in search of her parents. Everyone was gone somewhere, and she rattled around the large house until her mother showed up to start dinner.

"Mom, guess what I found today?"

"I have no idea." Frying chicken hissed and popped in a skillet while her mother busily chopped vegetables for a salad.

"I think I found the Lost Dutchman Mine!"

"That's nice, dear. Can you set the table?"

"Mom, did you even hear what I said?"

Her mother frowned. "Just set the table, please. We can talk at dinner."

Meadow scowled and got the plates out. It had been this way for weeks now. No one listened to a word she said. She went about setting five places. Mike wasn't there, but Wally was part of the family and always ate with them. Thank goodness the hired men didn't come for meals. She didn't mind the new guy, Hank. He was an amiable older fellow, grizzled and bandy-legged, who like to tell stories of a hell-raising youth working for a cattle outfit. He had a wife tucked away somewhere and went home to her in the evenings. Creepy Clay preferred to eat in his own cabin. Probably dined on rats with a side of scorpions. It would have been awkward having him at their dinner table, just staring at everyone.

She was glad to have a neutral topic of conversation. The silence had been awful since Mike left. He had always livened things up, one way or another. When they were all seated, she tried again. "I found the Lost Dutchman Mine today."

Monty snorted and nearly choked on his food. "You found the mine? Yeah, right. How did you manage that?"

"Well, I saw Arrow and he led me to it . . ." Her voice trailed off when she saw everyone had stopped chewing and were gawking at her.

Monty recovered first, laughing out loud. "Some horse led you to the mine? Wow, your imagination has really run amok this time."

Dad wrinkled his brow. "Bill's stallion is in the Superstitions? He won't be happy about that. Rough country, to say the least. He's always worried something will happen to his prize horse."

This conversation was not going the way she planned. "He's fine, Dad. But what about the mine? There was an old campsite and even an arrastra."

Her father patted her hand. "I'm sure there's plenty of old campsites all over the mountain. After all, people have been searching for gold there for hundreds of years."

Meadow sank lower in her seat and clamped her mouth into a pout.

Wally put down the chicken leg he was working on and turned to her with worried puppy-dog eyes. "I believe you, Meadow. I'll bet it really is the Lost Dutchman Mine."

"Thanks, Wally. I'm glad *someone* believes me."

Dad put down his fork. "It's not that we don't believe you. But we have other things to worry about right now. Like what to tell Bill about Diablo."

"Don't tell him anything. Arrow will move his herd back to the ranch before long and he'll never know the difference."

"If anything ever happened to that horse, there'd be hell to pay. Remember the deal you made with him."

Meadow's belly twinged. Yes, she remembered the deal. She promised Bill Bowman that Arrow would be safe running free, but she hadn't considered he might end up in the Superstitions. Anything could happen in that dangerous place.

Chapter 21

Spring Break

The next morning, Wally followed Meadow out of the house, yapping a mile a minute. All he talked about was the mine, ever since she made the announcement about finding it. He had great plans for them all making their fortune.

She let him rattle on, barely listening. After being doused by her parent's lack of interest, it was nice that somebody was enthusiastic. She was chomping at the bit to get back up there. What if there *was* a shaft nearby with gold just waiting for her to discover it? It would have to wait, though. Today they were going to the annual Easter Fling and gymkhana at the Apache Junction fairgrounds. It would be a fun play day, and they were taking Foxfire and Major for the horse events.

A tingle of excitement coursed through her. Brett would be there. Linda called the night before to let her know he was back from the academy for spring break. She said the whole Bowman family would be at the Fling and were coming to the Fort afterwards for a barbeque. Meadow frowned. Geez, her parents hadn't even told her about it. Like it wasn't really important.

Deep in her own head, Meadow stopped short in the tack room doorway when she saw Clay already in there. Wally, following closely, almost bumped into her, then pushed past.

Wally's fervor was written all over his face. "So, whataya think, Meadow? When can you take me up to the mine?" He turned to Clay. "Meadow found the Lost Dutchman Mine, you know."

"That so?" Clay's normally expressionless eyes sparked before he quickly averted them. He grabbed a saddle and hauled it out the door. Kelsey growled as he passed her.

"Wally, please don't broadcast to everyone I found the mine. It's our secret, okay?"

He nodded eagerly. "Sure, Meadow. I won't tell anyone, cross my heart."

She smiled. He was so darn cute, she couldn't be irritated with him. "When I'm sure I can find it again, I'll take you up there. Okay?"

His eyes shined. "Okay!"

She grabbed a box of grooming supplies and called back over her shoulder, "You can get Major ready for Lisa."

Their old truck chugged into the fairgrounds, then sputtered and hiccupped to a stop. A big tent-like pavilion was set up with refreshments, and dozens of children were already scrambling around the grassy baseball field hunting for Easter eggs. Bleachers framed one side of a large roping arena, where the gymkhana would take place.

Meadow and her father unloaded the horses, and before long, Lisa arrived with Scott and his parents. They'd brought Scott's mare, Blondie. Dr. Wilson was on duty at the hospital and wasn't able to attend.

Lisa ran over and hugged Meadow, then kissed Major on the nose. "I've missed you both so much!"

"Yeah, you haven't been out to see us in a while."

Lisa looked at her feet. "I'm sorry, Meadow. I've been really busy."

Meadow watched Scott unload his mare. "Busy with him, you mean."

"It's okay to like boys, you know." Lisa's tone was defiant, then she softened and hugged her again. "I'll always love you the best, though."

Meadow couldn't help but laugh, and they went arm in arm to get the horses ready. They were participating in several events, and all required western tack. Meadow was intent on fastening Foxfire's breast collar, when she heard a familiar voice.

"Hello, Little Lady."

She looked up, straight into dreamy blue eyes. "Brett, you're here!"

Meadow was just about to hug him, when she noticed a gorgeous girl standing close by. She wore a pink cowboy hat, and had a cute kerchief tied around her neck that screamed dude. Her tight jeans were tucked into pink cowboy boots that glittered with rhinestones. As Mike had put it, a cross between Natalie Wood and Liz Taylor.

Brett turned to the girl with a flourish. "Meadow, I'd like you to meet Tiffany. Tiffany, Meadow."

Tiffany narrowed her eyes and held out a limp hand. "Hello. So you're Meadow. Brett said something about you. The *outdoorsy* one." She made it sound like it was a terrible fault.

Meadow lifted her chin. "And you're the *debutante*."

Brett chuckled at their exchange. "C'mon, girls. We're all friends here."

Meadow turned back to arranging Foxfire's tack. She didn't want Brett to see her face burning like a hot poker. Why did he have to bring that hoity-toity witch along?

"We'll see you later, Meadow. Tiffany's never been to an Easter Fling, so I'm going to show her around." The horrid girl latched onto Brett's arm as they wandered away.

Linda rushed up, just as Meadow mounted for the Egg and Spoon contest. "I should've warned you that Tiffany was staying with us this week. It really wasn't Brett's idea. Tiffany told

Mother that she'd always wanted to come see the Wild West, and of course Mother invited her to stay with us. Her parents are family friends, not to mention Mother's best clients for expensive artwork."

"She's beautiful. I'm sure Brett's happy she's here."

Linda shrugged. "Tiffany *is* pretty, and knows it. Thinks she can wrap everyone around her manicured little finger. Mother adores her for some unknown reason."

"Riders enter the ring," the loudspeaker blared. "You will each be given a spoon with a raw egg on it. The idea is to get to the finish line first, without dropping or breaking the egg. Good luck to all our contestants. This could get messy."

Meadow rode into ring and then she noticed Brett was participating, too. He sat aboard his roan, Calypso. He tipped his hat to her and she stiffly nodded back. She hoped he got egg all over him. Lisa and Scott were already in the arena, armed with loaded spoons. A couple of other riders were lined up, ready to go.

When the starter gun fired, one horse reared and nearly lost its rider, and another one bolted to the side, eggs flying. Two down. Meadow hunkered on the saddle, concentrating hard to keep her spoon steady. This should be easy, Foxfire had smooth gaits. She didn't care about anyone else, but wanted to beat Brett.

Lisa got going too fast, the egg bounced off her saddle horn and a yellow streak appeared on Major's bay coat. Scott was looking at Lisa when Blondie tripped and the yolk marred the mare's lovely flaxen mane. It was just Meadow and Brett now. Calypso's fast jog-trot kept him right next to her. They were closing in on the finish line. She glanced over at Brett and he stuck out his tongue at her. Meadow giggled, and the spoon started jiggling the egg, making a clicking noise. Foxfire's ears flicked back at the unusual sound and she did a bunny-hop. The egg flew up, then came down smack on top of Meadow's head. Eggshell matted her hair and sticky slime streamed down her face. Brett crossed the finish line and turned to look at her. He let out a hoot of laughter. She wiped egg out of her eyes, and saw Tiffany watching, beautiful, cool, and composed. Oh, great.

Meadow galloped out of the arena and skidded to a halt at the water trough. She jumped down and put her head under the faucet, washing the goo out of her hair.

Brett rode up, still chuckling. "I've heard that egg is a good conditioner."

She made a face at him and continued drenching her hair, until it squeaked clean.

Lisa and Scott showed up at the trough and hosed the horses down. Meadow grabbed the hose and pointed it at Brett, getting him full in the face.

"Hey, cut it out," he sputtered, leaping off Calypso.

It turned into a full-fledged water fight, and pretty soon they were shoving each other into the muck. By then, they were laughing uncontrollably, covered with mud.

"Brett! What in the world are you doing?" Mary Bowman walked up with Tiffany beside her.

Brett peered at them through the streaked grime. "We were just having a little fun. Want to join us, Tiffany?" He threatened to squirt her.

The debutant recoiled in horror. "Heavens, no!"

Brett laughed. "Don't worry, Mother. It will wash off." To prove his point, he began rinsing the mud off himself and Meadow. She turned for him to get her back, then took the hose and sprayed him down. Scott and Lisa hosed each other off, and they all led their horses to the trailers and removed the saddles to let them dry.

"This afternoon is the Rescue Race. Do you want to be my partner, Meadow?" Brett was at his most charming now.

Meadow looked away. "I dunno. Mike and I always rode in it. Anyway, what about Tiffany?"

"Never mind her. She's not a cowgirl. I think she was only on a horse once—in Central Park."

She was still miffed at him. "Mike was always a really good partner. I don't know if you can measure up."

His face lost the grin. "Listen, I'm sorry Mike's not here with us. He's my best friend and I miss him, too. But he'd want you to have fun." He touched her arm. "C'mon, I promise not to drop you."

"Okay, I guess so."

Brett smiled broadly. "Great!" He started to walk away. "I have to go make amends to Mother and Tiffany. See you later."

Meadow basked in the sun during lunch and it didn't take long to dry out. Afterwards, the announcer came on, "Everyone get ready for the Rescue Race. Rescuers at the entrance gate, and Ladies in Distress at the other end of the arena. Riders will gallop down, swing their lady up behind them, turn and race for the finish line. Good luck!"

Meadow waited at the far end of the ring, near the calf roping chutes, her heart thumping in anticipation as she saw the horses line up. Lisa stood nearby, face tense, waiting for her rescuer, Scott. Two other girls stood farther down.

The gun sounded, and Calypso leapt forward, well in front. In no time, Brett was circling her, his hand outstretched. Meadow grasped it firmly, and he pulled her up. She wrapped her arms around his middle, and they were off in a cloud of dust, crossing the finish line without any challengers.

Meadow looked back to see how the others were faring. One girl still hadn't got off the ground and another was on her bottom, sitting in the dirt. Lisa finally made it up behind Scott, but Blondie didn't like the arrangement and crow-hopped in a circle. Lisa dropped down, and landed on her feet. She threw her arms up, like a bronco buster, grinning.

Brett turned to Meadow. "Too bad this isn't an Olympic sport. We're a great team!"

She laughed. "True, we did blow away the competition." Her amusement dried up when she saw Tiffany, standing on the sidelines, shooting daggers at her. Meadow slipped to the ground and dusted off her pants. "We're heading for home now, to get everything ready for the barbecue."

"Okay, we'll be over after we drop off Calypso. Probably Tiffany will want to freshen up, too. Thanks for riding with me."

"Sure, anytime."

Meadow paid more than usual attention to her clothes that evening. She tried on several outfits, finally deciding on a red and white striped top and white Capri pants. She slipped her feet into sandals, and stared at her toes. Some polish was desperately needed. She went to find her mother.

"Mom, do you have any nail polish?"

Her mother raised her eyebrows. "Have you ever known me to paint my nails? Why do you want it anyway? You've never been interested in those sort of things."

Meadow lifted one foot. "My little piggies are naked."

Her mother studied the wiggling toes and decided to be helpful. "Why don't you call Lisa? Oh, that's right, she's not coming." She wrinkled her forehead, then brightened. "I know, Linda—wait, on second thought, she doesn't color her nails . . . hmmm, what about Tiffany?"

"Mom, no! You just don't get it." She ran back to her room, and began brushing her hair. Man, parents were so thick sometimes. As if she'd ask the debutant for *anything*. After a few fumbled attempts at a French braid, Meadow huffed, then marched back in the kitchen and asked her mother to help.

The Bowmans arrived, and Brett opened the car door for Tiffany, who stepped out, looking like the Ice Queen. She was wearing a silver cocktail dress and matching heels, for cripes sake. The slinky outfit emphasized her tiny waist and curves in all the right places. Her shining cap of stylishly short, black hair only needed a tiara to complete the effect. Of course, she latched right on to Brett's arm like he was her Prince Charming.

When the Ice Queen saw Meadow, she said, "Well, don't you look *sweet*? All that mud did *wonders* for your complexion."

There were hugs and back-slaps all around and everyone moseyed out to the patio. Mom had set out hors d'oeuvres and made Sangria full of raspberries and citrus fruits. The teens were offered sodas. Meadow watched Wally take a glass of Sangria and gulp it down. She wondered if he had ever had liquor before. They usually didn't have that option at their house. Her parents rarely drank, only on social occasions.

Meadow soon tired of listening to Brett and Tiffany discuss the wonders of "Back East," and went to join the adults. She got there just in time to hear Wally, seeming to be a little tipsy, spill the beans. "Meadow followed Arrow and found the Lost Dutchman Mine." He grinned crookedly until he saw Meadow glare at him. He clapped his hand to his mouth. "Oops, I told our secret."

Wally headed to refill his glass, but Dad stopped him. "You've had enough, Wally. Here's a cola."

Bill Bowman was staring at Meadow. "Diablo is in the Superstitions?"

She swallowed and nodded. "He is perfectly fine, though. Not even a scratch."

He glowered at her. "He'd better stay that way."

Meadow was relieved when her father, standing by the barbeque, told everyone to come get their steaks. She heaped a load of potato salad next to her ribeye and dug right in, but noticed the Ice Queen just nibbled, like a rabbit. Probably afraid she'd rip one of those tight seams.

By the time dinner was over, Meadow was thoroughly sick of Tiffany fawning over Brett, so she left the party and went out to say goodnight to Kelsey and Foxfire. She was startled when someone came up behind her. "Hey, Meadow. What ya doing out here?"

"Hi, Brett." He definitely looked better sans Tiffany. "I just needed some air. It was getting a bit sticky on the patio."

"I know what you mean. Tiffany can be a little clingy. Don't worry about her—she's really not my type."

"What is your type?"

He grinned. "I like independent girls that go find cliff dwellings and old mines."

"Could a fooled me."

"Do you really think it's the Lost Dutchman Mine?"

She shrugged. "I dunno, maybe. I didn't find an actual mineshaft."

"Let's ride up there tomorrow. I'll help you search."

Meadow warmed, as if the sun just came out from behind a cloud. "All right. Be here early, we can take a lunch and make a day of it."

"Sounds good."

They went back to the party and the rest of the evening, Tiffany tried to freeze Meadow with icy stares, but nothing could dampen her inward glow.

Chapter 22

The Skull

Meadow surveyed her handiwork with satisfaction. The assembled lunch items on the kitchen counter represented all the food groups—steak sandwiches, cheese and crackers, carrots, apples, potato chips, and oatmeal cookies. That should do it.

It was five a.m. and no one else was up yet, but pretty soon Monty ambled in. He was starting work later, ever since his race track boss hired a new guy that took the earlier shift. He eyed the pile of food. "Man, you taking the whole crew with you today?"

"Just me and Brett."

"You're crazy. You'll need a pack mule just to carry this lunch." He shook his head, slurped some orange juice and headed out the door

Meadow hesitated, looking over her goods, but in the end stuffed everything in her saddlebags. She hummed a little as she filled two canteens with water. Brett would be here any minute.

She sprinted for the phone when it jangled insistently. It was him.

"Sorry, Meadow. Mother put the kibosh on our ride today. She insists I pay attention to Tiffany. She's our guest, after all. Hope you didn't go to any trouble. We'll go another time, all right?"

Meadow felt the fair wind leave her sails and her mood hit the deck. "Sure, another time." She slouched back to the kitchen, methodically unpacked the lunch, leaving just an apple, carrots for Foxfire, and the cookies. She'd show him. She'd find the mineshaft all by herself.

It wasn't as hard finding the entrance to the campsite as Meadow feared it might be. Foxfire remembered the way and found the tunnel opening with no trouble. Once there, Meadow let her mare graze while she searched the area.

Kelsey went straight to the mound of rocks and began sniffing and pawing again.

"What did you find, girl?" Meadow moved a few of the stones, but tired of the manual labor rather quickly. She abandoned the pile and passed behind the old shack to see what was there. A little path wound back through the brush and ended up next to the canyon wall. When she got closer, it looked like a landslide had slumped off the side. She clambered to the top and her breath caught. The debris wasn't flush against the cliff. It had been dug out. Down the other side there was an opening into the mountain.

She skidded down the slope and peeked in. A mineshaft! It dropped down at about a forty-five degree angle into darkness and had the remains of support timbers, but was partially caved in. The hair stood up on the back of her neck. Someone had been working here recently. There was evidence of digging and picking, and a shovel, rake and pickaxe were leaning against one wall. Her eyes darted around and she backed up. Better get out of here before the miner showed up. He might not be friendly.

Meadow hurried back to the clearing, intending to high tail it out of there. She looked around for Foxfire, but her mare wasn't in sight. She hiked to the far edge of the clearing, around a large boulder and finally discovered Foxfire near a spring trickling from the rocks and pooling below. Of course—this is where whoever had lived in that cabin got their water. She smiled, Foxfire was not alone. Arrow stood next to her and they were scratching each other's backs. Meadow's frayed nerves calmed as she watched them. There was no one else here, or the stallion wouldn't have come.

She heard barking, and went to see what was bothering her dog. Close by the cabin, Kelsey was still working on the pile of rubble. Meadow ran over to see what she had uncovered. As she neared the mound, she stopped short and then crept up to get a closer look. A chill ran through her body as she inspected Kelsey's prize. Grinning grotesquely from the sand lay a hideous looking human skull.

Meadow gulped and shuddered, a sick feeling growing in the pit of her stomach. Inching closer, she saw a gold tooth glinting from inside the gaping mouth. Who was it? How had he died? Someone had buried him here, in this shallow grave, next to the cabin. Now her uneasiness returned full force. This was too creepy. Maybe this guy had been murdered. Maybe the killer would return any minute. It was definitely time to go.

She turned back toward the horses, but the stallion had disappeared, and only Foxfire came trotting over, blowing and snorting. Her mare kept gazing up above, to the top of the cliff. Meadow squinted in the same direction. Was something up there? A few pebbles came bouncing down, and quick flash caught her eye, then it was gone.

"Let's get out of here." She hopped on Foxfire and galloped to the tunnel. They made good time getting home, trotting and cantering when the rocky trail allowed. She turned her mare loose to drink, then dashed for the house.

Her parents were eating lunch. "I found a skeleton up at the mine!" She dropped into a chair, panting.

They both stared at her, then her father spoke. "Human remains?"

"Yes. A man, I think. He had a gold tooth."

"I'll ride back up there with you and take a look. But first, eat something."

She got up and started pacing. "We should go right now, Dad."

"A skeleton won't be going anywhere."

Her mother nodded. "That's right, honey. Calm down while I fix you a sandwich."

Meadow fidgeted until the food was ready, then ate, taking huge bites. "Okay, let's go."

Shadow's long strides kept pace with Foxfire, and they made short work of the trail up to the tunnel. Her father had to dismount to go through, given the combined height of a large horse and tall man. When they made it into the clearing, he gave a low whistle. "By golly, you did find an interesting place. Not that I doubted your word, but this is really something. You say you found the mineshaft, too?"

She pointed to the shack. "It's over behind there."

"Where's the skeleton?"

"C'mon, I'll show you." She led the way, but when they got there, the stones were back in their original place. "That's strange. Kelsey and I had this all dug up." She slid off Foxfire.

"Are you positive this is the right spot?"

She started moving rocks and rubble. "This is it, but someone's been here. The skeleton is gone." Meadow's eyes scanned the clearing, then up to the canyon wall. "Dad, I forgot to tell you. When we were about to leave, I saw something up there, on the cliff. It flashed in the sun, like binoculars."

"The bones are gone now. Whoever took them covered up their footprints." He faced her, taking hold of her shoulders. "I want you to listen to me, Meadow. This place is off limits, understand? Who knows what type of crazy person is lurking around, working an old mine and moving skeletons. Promise?"

"But what about the mine? What if it *is* the Lost Dutchman? Don't you want to know?"

"The chances are pretty slim. Prospectors have been poking around here for hundreds of years. This is more likely one of dozens where someone tried their luck. Trust me, a big mining corporation would be on to it by now if the mother lode were really here." He turned and led Shadow toward the tunnel opening. "Let's go. It'll be close to dark by the time we get home."

Her father's logic was hard to ignore, and Meadow wasn't as upset as she might have been about being forbidden to go back to the mine. It *was* an eerie place, especially since someone had been there and moved the remains. That person must have been watching her. She shivered. Whoever it was, might be a murderer. She certainly didn't want to run into a crazed, murderous prospector.

"Dad, shouldn't we report this to the sheriff?"

"I'll mention it to Dave, but there's really nothing to tell. He can't do anything without the remains. No body, no crime."

As they passed by the Weaver's Needle lookout, Meadow glanced toward the slot canyon entrance. She hadn't mentioned the refuge of Arrow and his herd to anyone.

That secret belonged to the Sky Horse and was not hers to tell.

Chapter 23

The Letter

The next couple of weeks, Meadow tried to focus on school and help with the stable, but it was torture staying away from Arrow. When she couldn't stand it anymore, she managed to steal off to see him. After all, her father hadn't forbidden that. She studiously avoided the old mine site, but even so, it felt like someone was watching her.

Meadow haunted the mailbox every day—not only hoping to hear from Brett, but from Mike. Brett hadn't bothered to write, and she refused to make the initial effort. He was the one that had broken their date, and needed to write first. He was probably way too busy escorting Tiffany to all the dances and whatever other affairs those Back East people attended.

She slumped in the seat next to Monty on the drive home from school. It was a crappy day. Lisa was paying more attention to Scott and less to her. She never came to ride anymore. Major wouldn't have gotten any exercise if Meadow hadn't continued his training.

The squatty mail truck arrived at the same time they got to Fort Apache. A hand came snaking out to deposit a pile of envelopes into their box. It had been over a month since Mike was sent to Juvie and even though they'd been warned there would be no contact, it didn't make it any easier. Monty braked in front of the post box.

When she didn't budge, he said, "Hurry up and get the mail, dopey."

"What's the use? It'll just be junk mail and bills."

He patted her hand. "Maybe there'll be one today. You need to get the rest of it, anyway."

"Yeah, I guess so." She scooted out and her brother drove on to the house. Her mood lifted when she opened the box. Monty was right. Placed on top of the stack, like the postal carrier knew it was important, rested a legal-sized envelope addressed to the Shepherd Family in Mike's scrawling hand.

Meadow raced to the house, waving the letter as she ran. She burst into the kitchen. "It's from Mike!"

Her mother turned from the counter and snatched it away, then hugged it to her breast, appearing to be afraid to open it. Monty hovered in the doorway.

Meadow began dancing around. "C'mon Mom. Let's see what he says."

With agonizing slowness, her mother took a knife and slit the top. She began reading out loud.

Dear Family,

I just got all your letters. They wouldn't let me have them until last week, but I know you wrote right away from the postmarks.

I miss all of you. Please write often, I can only write back once a month, but it helps knowing someone is out there that cares. Tell Cynthia that I can't receive anything from her or send her letters. I think she wrote—the mail guy told me I got a pink, smelly envelope, but can't have it since it wasn't from my family.

You're probably wondering what it's like here. I'll give some free advice to any of you considering a life of crime—think twice before breaking the law, or aiding and abetting a criminal. And definitely don't take the rap for any so-called friends. I've learned my lesson.

The first month was agony, being locked in a tiny cell. I would've given my right arm to get some fresh air and exercise. It was the worst time of my life, with time crawling by. The food stinks. Mom, I always knew you were a good cook, but NOW I really appreciate just HOW good. I think I've lost at least 20 pounds already.

Lately, things have looked up. I've been a model prisoner, so was allowed to volunteer for a brush clearing crew in the forest. It's very hard work—for suppressing wild fire danger, but a million times better than being locked up.

We live out in the woods, in tents. Pretty basic. The food still stinks.

Anyway, don't worry about me. I'm fine.

> *Love,*
>
> *Mike*

By the time the letter was finished, Meadow had a lump in her throat and her mother was wiping away tears.

Monty just looked mad. "I told him not to hang out with that crowd. Serves him right." He turned on his heel and stormed away.

Meadow touched her mother's arm, then went to Monty's car to retrieve her homework. In her bedroom, she put the books onto her desk and sank into the straight-backed chair. Poor Mike. In spite of his words, it was hard not to worry. At least he would be home before too long, then they could get back to being a family again.

She opened a textbook, but was having trouble concentrating. Wait, it was Friday. She had all weekend to finish. She closed the book with a snap and glanced at her calendar. Why was tomorrow circled? Oh yeah, it was the last show for Pony Club.

Lisa would triumph over Cynthia at last!

Chapter 24

The Final Show

Flags floated lazily in a soft breeze and colorful vendor tents peppered the fairway for the last Pony Club show of the season. A feel of festivity and promise were in the air—sort of like graduation ceremonies. The chance to compete for the high point medal was a validation of the clubbers' hard work for the whole season.

Meadow stood next to the fence at the warmup area watching Lisa practice. She breathed in the distinct horsey smell and gazed around at riders all decked out in their finery with a twinge of regret. She did love the competition and excitement of the shows. The decision to opt out of the events after Foxfire's brush with death had been an emotional knee-jerk reaction. Dad assured her they would watch Foxfire like a hawk if she wanted to bring her today, but the image of her mare lying helpless from oleander poisoning was too vivid. It still made her shudder. What kind of sicko would do that?

Lisa finished her round, rode over, and petted the gelding. "Did you see Major take that oxer? Isn't he wonderful? And you too, for training him so well!"

Meadow nodded. "He's easy to train. Always gives his best effort."

Lisa bubbled on. "I'm so lucky to have you as a friend. I don't know what I would have done for a saddle if you hadn't loaned me yours. It rides like a dream. Mother is fit to be tied it's taking so long to actually get my new saddle. She called the company and threatened to cancel the whole order. You're such a good pal to let me borrow yours."

"You can use any of my stuff whenever you want."

Lisa flashed her beautiful smile. "Like I said, you're the best!"

"You, too. I'm sure you'll win the medal. Is your mom going to make it?"

"She'll be here after seeing her patients. She wouldn't dare miss my big victory!"

"Where's Scott? I haven't seen him."

Lisa shrugged. "He said something about Blondie getting a stone bruise. Guess he's not coming today."

"He's not going to be here to watch you ride?"

"No." Lisa averted her gaze.

"What's wrong?" Meadow scaled the fence to be eye-level with her friend. "Did you guys break up or something?"

"Yeah, but it's okay. A mutual decision. To tell the truth, I think he still has a crush on you."

"You've got to be kidding. I made it perfectly clear we're only friends."

"That's not how it works when it comes to the heart." Lisa sighed. "I should know."

Meadow knew she was talking about Jack, and patted her leg in support.

Lisa leaned over and squeezed Meadow's shoulder. "Let's look at the bright side. Now I'll have lots more time to come and ride. I've missed you. My best friend in the whole wide world, forever and ever." She urged Major forward and cantered away.

Meadow swallowed back a lump. This was the first time she'd ever had such a close friend. It felt great having someone to share with. Especially since her family was such a train wreck lately.

Another person climbed up beside her and wiggled his bottom onto the rail, wobbling a little. She giggled. Joel Adams seemed totally out of his element on a fence. She was pretty sure he looked just right behind a desk, frowning in concentration as he typed away to make his deadline.

"I want the real scoop, Miss Shepherd. Is it true that Lisa Wilson will edge out Cynthia Markowitz for the high point today?" He pretended to put a mic up to her mouth.

She played along. "It's absolutely true, Joel. They've been going at it head to head for months, and now we're down to the wire. The story on the street is that Lisa has the will and determination to beat Cynthia's pants off."

Joel chortled. "I can't wait to see Ben Markowitz's face when his daughter ends up pant-less."

They were both still laughing when Cynthia entered the ring, spotted them, and rode over.

She raised her pert nose in the air. "What's so funny?"

Joel smothered his laugh and became the consummate professional. "Just getting some background info. Are you feeling confident about your chances today, Miss Markowitz?"

Cynthia puffed out her chest. "Very confident, thank you. There's no way *that* person is going to beat me." She nodded her head toward Lisa. "After all, my father paid an absolute *fortune* for my Majesty, and he's a pure Thoroughbred, not some grade horse like hers. Plus I have riding lessons every week and a *professional* trainer. We're the best and that's that." She stuck out her lower lip and yanked her poor horse around, riding off in a huff.

Meadow caught Joel's eye and they both snickered. Then he got serious again and took out his pencil from behind his ear. "I heard you found what might be the Lost Dutchman Mine, not to mention some human remains at the site."

She scowled at him. "Where'd you hear that?"

"I'm not at liberty to disclose my sources."

"It was Wally, wasn't it? I'm going to kill that big mouth!"

"Don't be too hard on him. I wangled it out. With you riding the Superstitions all the time, I figured something interesting might happen. So what's the story?"

"I didn't find anything. You can quote me on that."

"C'mon, Meadow. Give a guy a break."

She shook her head. "You'll have to stick to the show winners this time. Here's a headline for you, 'LISA WILSON CONQUERS ALL,' then underneath, 'She arose out of obscurity and fought her way to the top of Pony Club Elite.'"

He smiled. "Hey, that's pretty good. Have you ever thought of a career as a journalist?"

Meadow slid down from her perch. "Let's go, the show's about to start."

They headed to the grandstand for a good view of the morning classes. Meadow whooped and cheered whenever Lisa prevailed and won another event. Joel had to be tactful and clapped equally for all contestants. Her friend continued to battle it out with Cynthia, and by the noon break, Lisa led by a narrow margin. She rode out of the ring, grinning, and holding up her latest blue ribbon.

Lisa tied Major to the truck, while Meadow brought a bucket of water and gave him a flake of hay. They both petted and praised the gelding until Lisa pulled at her arm. "Let's get a hamburger. I'm starved."

They finished eating, and were whispering about the finer points of a cute boy at the next table, when Dr. Wilson rushed up, her eyes shining. "Lisa, you'll never believe what just happened!"

"What, Mom?"

Dr. Wilson grabbed both her hands. "Your father phoned me before I left the hospital." She took a deep breath. "He's here."

Lisa jumped to her feet and swiveled her head back and forth. "Here?"

"No, not yet. But he will be soon. He called from the airport. I told him about your show. He said he's so proud of you and can't wait to see his beautiful daughter again." A tear slipped down her cheek and she latched onto Lisa, hugging her tightly.

After a moment Lisa pulled back, a pucker between her brows. "Mom, I'm scared. I don't remember him at all."

"Don't worry, honey. You'll love him. Everyone does."

"What's he been doing all this time? Why hasn't he contacted us before?"

"He wanted to make a success of himself first, so joined the military to finish his medical schooling. He saw action in Korea and was wounded the last year of the war. Seems it messed him up mentally and took a long time to recover. After being promoted to Lieutenant Colonel, he decided it was time to get his family back."

Lisa sank into the seat, overwhelmed.

Dr. Wilson put an arm around her. "I know it's a lot to take in. The important thing is, he's back now. He still loves us."

When the announcer called the next event, Lisa took Meadow's hand and led her to the warm-up area. Her eyes were unfocused, totally unlike her usual razor-sharp gaze. "I want you down here with me. You'd be too far away up in the stands."

"Of course. I'll be your groom. Just like at the big shows."

Dr. Wilson, now sitting next to Meadow's parents, waved down to them from the grandstand. Lisa seemed oblivious, so Meadow waved back. She gave Lisa a leg up and hoped her friend would be all right to ride. Lisa entered the arena as if she were in a trance, and rode like a zombie. Major did his job, but his rider's lack of concentration showed. Cynthia ended up winning and closed the gap between them.

When Lisa came out of the ring, Meadow handed her an iced tea. "You better snap out of it. You have to pay attention.

Your dad will be here before long. Don't you want him to see you win the medal?"

She blinked and stared at Meadow. "Huh?"

"Your father will be here soon. Remember? Make him proud."

The fog slowly lifted from her eyes. "I guess I let that rich, spoiled brat catch me, didn't I?"

"Yes, you did."

The old Lisa came into view as she set her jaw. "It won't happen again. She *will not* have the satisfaction of beating me out of the medal."

"That's the spirit, as my mother would say. The most important class is coming up. Open Jumping. You'll have to be in top form to win this one."

Lisa squared her shoulders and rode into the ring with her chin up. The competition was stiff, but one by one the others fell by the wayside until Lisa and Cynthia were tied. Even though Cynthia's horse had more natural talent, Major was trying harder and it showed. The ring steward raised the bars for a jump-off between them.

Meadow stood next to Major and briefed Lisa about the new pattern. "This is a timed round and every second will count. Don't be reckless, but cut corners where you can. Cynthia isn't very good at tight turns, especially with Majesty's long stride. I know you can do it."

"Of course I can." Then she took Meadow's hand. "I'm so happy. Totally happy, I think, for the first time. I have you, and I'm going to have a real dad. A real family. Just like you!" She gathered her reins and guided Major into the ring.

Meadow's heart swelled with pride as she watched Lisa take the first fence. She rode with precision and Major responded gallantly. Out of the corner of her eye, Meadow noticed a tall, dark man join Dr. Wilson in the stands. He grabbed hold of her like a life preserver in a rough sea. When they parted, Dr. Wilson pointed toward the arena. The man smiled broadly. It was Lisa's smile, beautiful.

Lisa took two more fences, clearing them with room to spare. Then it happened. Instead of the usual sweeping turn, she wheeled Major abruptly on his haunches and kicked him toward the chicken coop, shaped like a three and a half foot tall A-frame house. The gelding surged forward and made a huge leap to clear the fence at an angle.

Suddenly, mid-jump, the girth popped, then flapped down, hanging loose. The saddle shifted to the side, and Lisa came off, crashing down onto the sharp edge of the solid coop. Meadow heard a sickening crack as Lisa hit. Her best friend lay still, the saddle nearby.

The crowd hushed, then there was screaming from somewhere. Meadow flung open the gate and raced across what seemed to be an endless expanse of dirt before she reached her friend. Major had circled back and was standing over her, head down, eyes big and sad.

Meadow kneeled beside Lisa, taking her hand. A trickle of blood seeped from the gash on her head. The ambulance drove in from the sidelines and a burly man emerged. "Move that horse back and stand out of the way, Miss." He worked on Lisa for a couple of minutes, but she still didn't move.

It was mass confusion as Dr. Wilson, the tall man, and Meadow's parents came onto the scene. Everyone was talking at once, but there weren't any answers. They loaded Lisa onto a stretcher and slid her into the vehicle. Dr. Wilson and the tall man both climbed in with her and they all left in a swirl of dust.

Meadow stood next to Major, watching as her world seemed to shrink. It got smaller and smaller, till there was nothing at all.

Chapter 25

The Broken Girth

Meadow felt a cool sensation on her forehead and her eyes slowly opened, coming into focus on her mother's anxious face. Had it all been a bad dream? Mom removed her hand from her brow and held some water to her lips. She sipped it.

"What happened?"

"You fainted, honey." Mom sniffed, while trying to blink away tears. "Do you remember anything?"

The image of her friend lying in a crumpled heap came washing over her. She struggled to a sitting position. "Lisa. Is she all right?"

"We haven't heard anything."

Fear gripped Meadow's heart like a vise. "She'll be okay, though, right?"

Her mother looked at the ground and mumbled, "I don't know. I've been praying for her."

Meadow gulped and fought for air.

Mom encircled her in comforting arms. "You've got to be strong. Take deep breaths. Worrying won't help anyone. Come on, we have to get out of here."

It was then Meadow realized they were both sitting in the dirt, still in the ring. Had it really only been moments since the accident? It seemed like days, weeks even. She gazed around and saw her father leading Major away, the saddle on him with the dangling girth. The judge, ring steward and some other people were off to one side, heads close together. A crew busily dismantled the jumps and loaded them onto a waiting truck.

Her mother rose, bringing Meadow up with her. She stood, unsteady on shaky legs. Pushing the dread to the back of her mind, she concentrated on walking next to Mom, slowly putting on foot in front of another, like a very old person.

On the sidelines, Ben Markowitz held up the high point medal that Cynthia had won by default. How could he possibly be smiling and laughing after what happened? Next she saw Joel. He waved for her to come over, but she ignored him and continued toward the gate.

Dad had already put Major in the truck and was examining the saddle when she and her mother arrived. He was frowning—that dangerous look he got sometimes.

"I checked the girth myself before we came this morning. It was fine." He pulled up the flap and sucked in his breath. "Son of a b—! It's been tampered with!" He showed them the edge of the elastic connector. "See here. Some of it was cut, the rest is frayed from tearing apart. It ripped slowly and finally let go with Major's big effort at that last jump. It must have been done here at the show."

"Who would do such a thing?" The look of horror on Mom's face reflected how Meadow felt. Her mind began a slow whirl and she swayed.

Her father reached out to steady her. "Easy, sweetheart. I don't want you hitting the deck again." He sat her down on the running board. "Did anyone know you were loaning Lisa the saddle?"

She shook her head, then looked up. "I guess Cynthia knew, but she would never do something like this."

"But Ben Markowitz wanted his daughter to win pretty badly. I've always had my suspicions about Foxy's poisoning, although I didn't think he would stoop to that. Now I wonder."

Meadow wasn't so sure. She remembered the weird phone calls and the feeling of always being watched.

Maybe Lisa wasn't the target. Maybe it was her.

Chapter 26

Farewell

The next few days were a living nightmare for Meadow. With Major still in the truck, they had driven directly to the hospital. The ride there seemed long, but Meadow dreaded arriving. She glanced at her parents' tense faces and her worries only deepened. The silence dragged on—even the old truck ran quietly, without the usual hiccups and burps.

Her father braked in the emergency parking lot and they filed through the door. The lady at the reception desk looked up as they entered the sterile room. "May I help you?"

"We're here to inquire about Lisa Wilson," her father said. "She was just brought in. A fall from a horse."

The woman frowned as she studied her list. "Are you family?"

"Yes . . . well, actually, no." Her father shifted his feet.

"Please have a seat in the waiting room. Someone will be with you soon."

They walked across the hall where several Naugahyde chairs and couches were assembled. A Coke machine stood in one corner occasionally making gurgling noises. Several people in white uniforms scurried in and out of the doors marked Emergency Room, and each time, a whoosh of antiseptic odors assaulted Meadow's nose.

Her mother had a tissue and dabbed at her eyes, while Dad stall-walked around the room. Every so often, he stopped and stared at the doors, as if willing someone to come out and speak to them. It finally worked, when a nurse, starched and unsmiling, pushed through and came over.

"Are you the Shepherds?" They all nodded and she continued, "I've been given permission by the Wilsons to tell you." She paused. "I'm so sorry, Lisa was unresponsive when she arrived, and we were unable to revive her. Massive head trauma."

The faint ray of hope Meadow had nurtured sputtered and died. She dropped like discarded rag onto a seat.

Mom fell beside her and held her close. Her father stood dumbfounded for a moment, then turned into a wild man. He slammed out of the room, striding so fast that Meadow and her mother had to run to catch up. His jaw was tight as he drove to the Mesa police station, carried in the saddle, then demanded to see the person in charge. The same gruff sergeant that booked Mike appeared. He listened to the story with skeptical eyebrows. "The evidence seems pretty flimsy, Mr. Shepherd."

"At least have a detective look at the saddle. I can show him where the girth's been cut."

The sergeant sighed, like it was a big bother. He disappeared for a moment, then waved them into another area, where several men in suits were sitting at desks either on the phone or writing reports. The sergeant led the way to a heavy-jowled man with crew cut hair standing on end. The smell of burnt coffee hung in the air. "Put the saddle here on my desk," he said.

Dad placed it there and showed the man where the girth came apart. The detective turned it over, checking both sides. "It looks like it snapped from stress. You say the girl was jumping a horse? No wonder it broke. Seems like an open and shut case to me. Accidental death."

Her father's mouth became a thin line. "Are you at all familiar with horse equipment? It's made for stress."

The man narrowed his eyes. "I'm familiar enough. It was an accident." He lowered his head and began typing.

Her father banged his fist on the desk, rattling the coffee mug with a spoon in it. "You mean to tell me you won't even look into this? What kind of a detective are you? A young girl is dead—it was no accident!"

"Mr. Shepherd, you need to leave now. I deal with real cases all day long. What I don't need is made-up problems to take up my time."

Her father looked like he was about to jump over the desk and pummel the guy, when two uniformed officers came up and grabbed his arms. The detective asked, "Will you go quietly, or do you want to cool off overnight in a cell?"

The next day, Meadow hadn't wrapped her brain around the fact that Lisa was gone. When her father suggested they go question everyone that had been at the show, she was glad for the distraction. Maybe it didn't really happen and they were playing a detective game. They got the roster of competitors and their addresses from the show secretary. She was very helpful when they explained about the girth.

It took a few days, but one by one, they crossed people off the list. It seems no one had seen any unusual activity or a suspicious person lurking around during the event. When her father confronted Ben Markowitz, he denied knowing anything, and had an alibi since he was with friends the whole time. It all turned out to be a dead end, and Dad's face turned to granite and his shoulders sagged.

Meadow had been somewhat successful in containing her misery during the legwork, falling exhausted into bed at the end of each day. During the night though, she'd wake, sobbing. On the eve of the funeral, the blackness became complete, and she awoke screaming, reliving the horrifying fall.

The weather was hot that day at the graveyard, especially wearing funereal black. Some people were hunkering under the shade of the few leafy trees while they listened to Lisa's eulogy. Meadow, her family, and Lisa's parents stood close to the open grave, with the bright sunlight glaring off the casket.

The pastor said all the right things, but his words brought no peace to Meadow. She glanced around at the faces. It was a big turnout. Most of the kids from Pony Club were there and even some classmates. Their sniffling and blowing of noses seemed so false that it turned Meadow's stomach and she had a bitter taste in her mouth. *Now* they all show support. Why couldn't they be nice when Lisa was alive?

Lisa's dad was one that had real tears streaming down his face. How sad they never got to know each other. Dr. Wilson stood by his side as if carved from marble, like the angel on a nearby headstone. Maybe she felt the same as Meadow herself, numb.

She turned her attention back to the eulogy to see if it would bring comfort, but the words seemed empty and meaningless. A senseless death of a beautiful girl, so young and full of life. And it was murder. Meadow gritted her teeth. She would discover who did it. She wouldn't rest until she found out.

At the reception after the funeral, Meadow was with her parents when Dr. Wilson approached them. She was pale and drawn, but in control. "I want to thank you all for your support and friendship." She took Meadow's hand. "Lisa loved you like a sister. You made her time here special." Then she turned to her parents. "Perry has been stationed at the Air Force base in Los Angeles. I will be joining him as soon as I can pack up the house and get it on the market. Shep, can you take care of selling Major?"

Meadow had been dry-eyed up until the mention of the gelding. Now the tears started rolling down her cheeks. Major was the last link to her best friend.

Her father squeezed Meadow's shoulder. "Rose and I would like to buy him back."

Mom managed a sad smile. "Yes, I want him for my personal riding horse. He'll have a good home with us."

Dr. Wilson grabbed her parents' hands. "That's wonderful. I'm so grateful to you both. Please come and visit us in California. I'll write when we get settled." She turned and went back to her husband and Lisa's grandparents.

Linda Bowman made her way over to them and reached out for Meadow, enveloping her. "Meadow, I would like you to come and visit sometime soon, and stay the weekend. We can swim and ride. You can bring Foxy and Kelsey, too. If it's okay with your parents."

Her mother nodded. "Of course, Linda. Anytime."

"I'll be in touch."

After a little while, everyone began drifting away and climbing into their cars. The ride home had a finality—the door closing on Lisa forever. Meadow felt a heavy weight, as if an anvil had settled on her chest. What would she do without her best friend?

When they got home, she couldn't stand the somberness in the house, and stole away on Foxfire. Meadow found herself on the trail to the wild horse sanctuary. With the weather warmer the last few days, and she wondered how long Arrow would keep his mares in the Superstitions. After they wound through the slot canyon and into the open field, the stallion spotted them. He pounded across, greeting them in his usual exuberant manner. At the stand of trees, near the stream, she unbridled Foxfire. Her mare cantered away with the stallion chasing after.

Drained from recent events, she sank onto the grass with Kelsey snuggled close, and cried herself to sleep. The next she knew, Kelsey gave a low woof. Meadow flinched and her eyes popped open. The most welcome figure she could have wished for came into focus.

Shirtless, Colt wore only buckskin trousers. Bronzed muscles flexed as he moved to ease down beside her. His presence was balm to her troubled soul.

She smiled for the first time in days. "What are you doing here?"

"I heard about Lisa. Are you all right?"

"I don't know. I'm so empty inside . . . and feel guilty."

"Why?"

"It was my saddle. Maybe it was meant for me."

Colt took her hand. "Even if it was, you have no reason to feel guilty. You're not responsible for what someone else did."

She wiped at a tear that escaped. "How can I find who *is* responsible? I feel so helpless, but somehow, I have to find Lisa's murderer."

He cupped her chin in his hand. "You will discover the truth. In the end, it will be made right. Lisa fulfilled her role in this life and has gone on to where a person's color has no meaning."

"But I miss her. It's just horrible—she was so full of happiness right before it happened."

"It's good to be content when you leave this world."

Meadow shook her head. "*I'll* never be happy again."

"You are stronger than you think. You will go on and fulfill your own destiny." He smiled. "And you will be happy. Lisa will always have a special place in your heart." He stood and held out his hand. "Come, the sun is getting low. Your parents will worry."

Colt pulled her up, then whistled for Smoke. The grulla stallion trotted over, with Foxfire at his heels.

Meadow bridled her mare. "Hey, girl, what happened to your buddy?" She looked around, but didn't see Arrow anywhere. "Where do you suppose he went?"

"The mares are gone, too. Probably took them to a different grazing spot." He vaulted onto Smoke. "I'll ride with you part-way. I'm camping up higher."

They rode together until they reached Weaver's Needle, then Colt turned north. He quickly disappeared from view, melting away into the rocky landscape.

She watched him go, wondering, not for the first time, how he always knew to show up just when she needed him most. Their talk had lightened her burden. The weight that had been sitting on her chest evaporated like a mist.

That night, for the first time since the accident, she slept straight through till morning.

Chapter 27

A Plot Gone Awry

Wendell zipped past the row of houses, barely noticing the little windmills and pink flamingos that adorned the painted gravel yards. He slowed the Renault sedan as a patrol car passed going the opposite direction. Damn! It wouldn't do to get a ticket. Why are the cops cruising this neighborhood? He usually drove carefully to avoid drawing attention to himself, but today he was preoccupied.

He had just taken Lucy to the mall and dropped her off. That stupid broad always drove too fast. Which is why he mostly chauffeured her around, only letting her use the car to go on short errands. She sulked, but he ignored her pouty looks and silent treatment. God, if she only knew what a blessed event her silence was, she would never use that tactic.

Wendell pulled under the carport, opened the door and swung out his short legs. He padded inside the house, and went straight to the telephone to dial a number he knew by heart.

"It's me. When were you going to tell me you screwed up the plan?" His voice was icy. "I had to read about it in the paper. Killing her friend was not part of the deal. You were supposed to scare her, that's all. What if Meadow had been using that saddle? She'd be dead and we'd be at a dead end. We need her alive. At least for the time being. After we get it out of her, you can do any damn thing you want." He chuckled. "I know you like torturing dumb animals. Does that include kids, too?"

"I rigged the girth to break sooner, on the flat. It was supposed to scare her, not bust her head open. Although that was entertaining."

Wendell clenched his fist. "You're a real weirdo. And there's no room for mistakes. It's lucky they ruled it an accident. No inquiry, but I did hear that Shep's been nosing around, asking questions. Keep an eye out. I wouldn't want to have to tangle with him."

"He won't be a problem. Anyway, I know how to lure the girl away."

"Whatever works. Just stay on point this time with no foul-ups. It'll be worth your while." He hung up the phone and narrowed his eyes. That guy was a born killer. He enjoyed it a little too much. But if he screwed up and got caught, there'd be no way to connect Wendell to the crime. Just the way he liked it.

He spent the afternoon looking at the "house for rent" ads. It was time to move. Cops in the neighborhood were never a good sign.

Chapter 28

Some Clues

The encounter with Colt had eased Meadow's pain, but it did nothing to alleviate the deep anger that filled her entire being. She rarely laughed now and looked upon others with suspicion. Who could have wanted to harm Lisa? Or if she wasn't the target, then her own life might be in danger. She didn't dare confide in her parents. They would worry so much it would restrict her from any possibility of finding the killer. Mike would have been her best ally, if he wasn't still in the slammer. She couldn't tell Monty. He was so straight-laced, he would go right to her parents. She was alone in this.

School was agony— sitting in class, seeing Lisa's empty desk, not to mention the lonely cafeteria. Monica and Beth tried to be nice and invite her to their table, but Meadow didn't accept their offer. It felt disloyal to Lisa to associate with that crowd. She sat by herself, gazing out the window and feeling powerless.

The three-thirty bell rang, and Meadow headed out to the curb to wait for Monty to pick her up. A dilapidated Volkswagen Beetle rolled to a stop in front of her and Joel Adams emerged. It was a fitting car for a guy that always looked like he left his clothes in the dryer too long.

"Hey, Meadow. I've been wanting to talk to you. Is there someplace we can sit?"

She nodded toward a bench in the shade of a Palo Verde tree. "Over there. Then I can see Monty when he comes."

They sat down and he faced her. "First of all, I'm so sorry about Lisa. Very sad. A great gal."

Meadow silently stared at him.

Joel pulled at his collar, as if it were suddenly too tight. "I'll get right to the point. I know you and your father think the girth was tampered with. Detective Kramer mentioned you came in the day it happened. Kramer said your father acted crazy and he almost booked him."

"Yeah, the stinking cops wouldn't even listen." Her lip quivered. "And Dad's not crazy, he's right. It was murder."

"Kramer's kind of a jerk. Anyway, after he talked about it, I remembered some fella was over near Major during lunch break that day. I walked by the truck and he left. At the time, I didn't think anything about it. You know there were throngs of people at the show for the finals."

Meadow straightened up and searched his face. "What did he look like?"

"Medium height and build. Had a hat pulled real low, so I couldn't see his hair. Sunglasses."

"Darn, I was hoping you'd describe Wendell. Then we'd have something to go on."

"What's Wendell look like? There aren't any mug shots of him on file."

"Short, round, and bald."

Joel shook his head. "No, definitely not him. It might have been some harmless bystander at the show, but I wanted to tell you."

"Thanks, Joel." She prepared to stand.

"Wait, there's one more thing. I know you denied finding any bones in the Superstitions, but I've been snooping around, and guess what? There *is* someone missing, from two years ago. He was a miner and worked with a partner. His son contacted the police after his father didn't show for a month." He shrugged. "Apparently they weren't real close."

Meadow swallowed. "Maybe the partner killed him. The skull had a hole in it." She grabbed Joel's hand. "Let's talk to the son. He must know who the partner was."

He smiled. "I'm way ahead of you. He said we could come over tomorrow and ask him whatever we want. He's eager to know what happened to his father. I can pick you up after school."

"Okay, I'll ask my parents. It should be all right, they know you."

Her parents hadn't been much problem. They seemed relieved to have her doing something, anything, other than moping around with a scowl. Joel had almost become a fixture in their lives, with his constant coverage of Meadow's exploits throughout the year. Even so, her father called his editor to make sure it was a real story he was working on. To Meadow's relief, it all checked out and she was given permission to go on the interview.

That evening, she pondered Joel's revelation about the missing person. In her gut, she was convinced it was the same man whose skeletal remains Kelsey had dug up. Maybe the Superstition killer had something to do with the cut girth. She knew it was a long shot, but it made a weird kind of sense to her. Someone at the mine camp had been watching her and moved the skeleton when she found it. Maybe Lisa's fall had been meant for her because she had stumbled upon the real Lost Dutchman mine.

The next day, school dragged by even more agonizingly slow than usual. Meadow counted the minutes until the bell sounded, then raced out the doors. Finally, she was able to do something positive.

Joel waited in his little car parked under the Palo Verde. He reached over and pushed the squeaky passenger door open when he saw her. "Are you ready to solve a cold case?"

She dove into the seat, pulling the door shut with a thud. "Yes, I am. Let's go."

They drove toward Mesa, wound through a modest residential area, and ended up at a small apartment complex. Joel led the way past a pool with a few kids splashing around and some adults sunning themselves. At apartment 24C, Joel knocked on the door. It swung open and a voice said, "You must be the reporter."

"Yes, Joel Adams, and this is my assistant, Meadow."

"How do you do. I'm Robert Edwards. My father was George. I'm assuming he's dead. It's been over two years since he disappeared. Come in."

They stepped into the dark room and Meadow wondered how anyone could live in such a depressing place. All the shades were drawn, the air was stale, and there were remnants of cigarette butts in overfilled ashtrays. Everything about Robert Edwards was dreary. The only thing that stood out were his bulging eyes behind thick lenses. He invited them to sit, but first had to clear away piles of *Playboy* magazine's off the couch. Meadow gingerly sat, trying not to touch anything.

"Do you think you could draw the drapes a little and maybe crack the patio door?" Joel asked. "I want to show you the police report on file."

"Oh . . . sure." The man hastily went to the slider and pulled the curtain back. After opening the door, he stepped back blinking, as if unused to light and fresh air.

Joel retrieved the report from his briefcase and went over it with the man. "Is everything correct, the way you remember it?"

Mr. Edwards nodded. "Except there's no mention of his partner. I told them about him at the time."

"The detective that worked the case said they never located him, and didn't pursue it because there was no reason to believe it might be foul play. People go missing all the time. But now, some remains have been found in the area."

Mr. Edwards's eyes bugged out a little more. "Remains, you say? Do the police have them?"

"No, not exactly. But we know where they were. Did your father give you any sort of map to the mine?"

"He wasn't very forthcoming about it. No map. All he said was the site had some ancient mining equipment. A long wooden arm that attached to some kind of animal that went in circles to crush the rock. To get the ore out or something like that."

Meadow sucked in her breath. He was describing the arrastra. It had to be the same mine camp she found.

Joel kept probing. "What was the partner's name? What did he look like?"

"I never met him, but Dad called him 'Whitey'. Maybe his last name is White?"

"I'll check it out on the wanted list. Is there anything else you remember?"

Mr. Edwards shook his head. "Sorry, guess I'm not much help. You will let me know what you find out, won't you?"

Joel stood. "Of course. Thanks for speaking with us."

After they exited and got around the corner from the apartment, Meadow gasped in clean air. "Whew, it was awful in there! How does he stand it?"

"I don't know. I was about to suffocate before he opened that door." He frowned. "Sorry, he wasn't much help, except the name, possibly."

Meadow took Joel's arm. "I didn't say anything, but he described the mining camp I found. It must be his father's skeleton."

"You're kidding, that's great! Now I feel like we made real progress."

"What's the next step?"

"I'll check for criminals at large with the name of White and see if I find any matches. It's a good thing you came along today, Meadow."

She told her family about their findings during dinner that evening.

"At least it's something to go on. I hope Joel finds the mysterious Mr. White," her mother said.

Dad drummed his fingers on the table. "Could be that 'Whitey' is a nickname, though, with no relation to his last name. It might be difficult to locate the guy. Especially after two years."

"Like finding a needle in a haystack." Monty shook his head.

The always supportive Wally put in his two cents worth. "I think you'll track the killer down, Meadow."

She firmed her jaw. It wouldn't be easy, but she had to try. The phone rang, and Meadow jumped up to answer it. Had Joel found something already? But no, it was Linda on the other end.

"Can you come over for the weekend? I'll bring the horse trailer for Foxy, and of course, Kelsey is invited. I've missed seeing my little sister."

"Sure, what time will you pick me up?"

"Not too early. Say ten o'clock?"

"Okay, I'll let my parents know."

Her mother beamed at the news. "It'll do you good to get away for a couple of days. Linda is the sweetest person I know. Make sure you pack some of your nicer things—not just jeans and boots."

"Okay, Mom." She actually felt a little thrill of anticipation. It *would* be good to visit Linda. She would tell her about the investigation and maybe her boyfriend, Sheriff Dave, could help.

Chapter 29

A Change of Plan

Meadow carefully packed her overnight bag the next morning, making sure to include a swimsuit. The Bowmans Scottsdale estate reminded her of a posh resort. She loved the huge pool with its waterfall and slide. And not only that, their place backed up to open desert with riding trails. What could be more fun? It would be great to see Linda for the whole weekend. She hadn't seen much of her since she started college.

Her mother peeked in Meadow's room. "Have fun with Linda, honey. Your father and I are going to the auction. Wally is coming with us. Clay can handle the stable. See you Sunday afternoon."

She gave her mother a quick hug. "Okay, Mom. See ya. Tell Dad 'bye."

Meadow finished packing and went to the barn to get Foxfire ready. After she brushed her copper coat to a shiny gloss, she tied her to the hitching rail, then went back inside and glanced at the clock. Geez, it was still only eight o'clock. What was she going to do for two hours? She wandered over to the bookcase and pulled out *Under the Light of the Western Stars*, one of her favorite Zane Grey novels. She was just getting into it when the phone jangled. Her pulse quickened, maybe Joel had found something out.

She raced to pick up the receiver. "Joel?"

"Yeah." His voice sounded a little weird.

"Do you have a cold or something?"

"Just a little hay fever." He coughed, then went on, "Listen, I got a call. The guy said you need to go up to the mine.

Something about the horse . . . the stallion. Hurt or something. I would go with you, but I'm covering another story. You'd better hurry, it sounded serious."

"Who was it? Why'd he call you? How did he know about the stallion? How's he hurt?"

"Don't know. That's all he said. I gotta go."

The phone clicked. Meadow's heart thumped double time. Arrow was hurt. She needed to get up there right now. She started for the door, then stopped. Oh crap! Linda. She ran back to the phone and dialed the Bowmans.

She made her voice scratchy. "Hi, Linda, I have to cancel. I woke up with a terrible headache and sore throat. Must be coming down with something."

"Okay, sweetie, we'll postpone. Take care of yourself."

Meadow felt terrible lying to her friend, but she couldn't risk Linda telling her father the stallion might be hurt. Bill Bowman worried enough about his prize horse as it was. She sprinted to the tack room and began gathering everything she could think of, including ointment, liniment, and bandages. At the last minute, she grabbed her father's Bowie knife, then stuffed everything into her saddlebag. She was well familiar with horse injuries, having assisted her father with doctoring since she was just a tot.

Without bothering to saddle Foxfire, she threw the bag over her mare's shoulders, leaped aboard, then galloped toward the mine. Meadow pushed Foxfire as fast as she dared over the treacherous terrain, and they were both panting by the time they made it to the tunnel. Kelsey's tongue was lolling out so far she threatened to trip on it.

Meadow dismounted and paused for a moment inside the passageway to catch her breath and think. She had to be careful. What if the person that hurt Arrow was still at the camp? But he couldn't be, if he made the call to Joel. Wait, there could be two of them. A chill skittered down her back, and she felt for the amulet. It was warm. She gulped in a big breath and started forward, cautiously stepping into the light.

The brush that dotted the valley provided some cover, and she led Foxfire, hiding behind trees until she saw the cabin with the arrastra close by. Her heart sank.

Tied to the long arm, head down, sides heaving from fighting the rope, stood Arrow. Blood dripped from his foreleg where the rock on the other end of the pulley had swung against it when he pulled back. Meadow forgot all caution and raced to his side. At first, he threw up his head, eyes wild.

"Easy boy, I'm going to help you." His face softened as she spoke.

The rope was pulled so tight it would be impossible to untie. She reached for the saddlebag, retrieved the knife, and began to saw. It took several minutes, but gradually the fibers separated, then snapped apart. With the rope loosened, she was able to untie the knot around his neck

"C'mon, Arrow, let's go." She could swear he understood, and when she slowly led Foxfire to the far end of the field, around the big boulder, the stallion hobbled behind them. Painfully slow, hopping on three legs, holding up the injured front foot.

Meadow took them to the spring, where a rivulet still splashed down from the cliff to the rocks below. Arrow came close, as though he knew she needed to tend his wound. First, she washed it, then patted on some dressing before wrapping a bandage and tying it securely.

Afterwards, she stroked his neck. "Good boy. I've had tame horses that didn't stand nearly as well as you. Just relax now."

Again, as if understanding her, he sank to the grass on his side and closed his eyes. Meadow crept away, leading Foxfire, so as not to disturb his much needed rest. She slipped off Foxfire's bridle so she could graze, then walked back to the arrastra. The cruel animal torturer seemed to be gone, but had he left any clues?

Intent upon her search, she was startled to hear a creaking noise from behind, then Kelsey growled. She whirled around to see a hooded figure, with slits where the eyes should be, coming out of the cabin. His clothing was all black and he wore heavy, tall boots. He carried a small rope with a loop in one hand and had a rifle slung over his shoulder. She began backing away, not sure which way to run.

"Stay put, and I won't hurt you. I just want to ask a few questions." His voice was gravelly, as though unused to speaking.

Meadow swallowed and kept backing up. "Who are you? What do you want?"

"Information, that's all, then you can go." He still approached, faster now. Suddenly, he rushed at her. Kelsey lunged forward, placing herself between the man and Meadow, hackles raised and snarling. The man deftly threw the loop around Kelsey's neck, pulling it tight. Her dog gasped and choked.

"Don't hurt her!" Meadow's eyes brimmed over.

"I won't, if you cooperate."

He dragged Kelsey to a tree and tied the rope.

Meadow had put some distance between herself and the hooded man, but now he rapidly started for her again. She whistled for Foxfire, grazing in the middle of the field. Her mare threw up her head and flared her nostrils, then galloped toward them. She passed Meadow, stopped short of the stranger and snorted, as if daring him to come closer.

"You've got a lot of animal protectors, kid. Better call her, if you want her alive." He raised the rifle, aiming straight at Foxfire.

Her mare reared up, bared her teeth, and charged the stranger.

"Foxy, no!"

Foxfire tilted her head at the sound of Meadow's voice just as the shot rang out. The gun cracked and in the same moment, her mare fell heavily to the earth and lay still. Meadow screamed and ran to her side, sobbing uncontrollably. "Foxy, Foxy!"

The man came up to them. "Too bad, kid. That was a nice horse."

Something snapped in Meadow and she jumped to her feet, hitting and kicking him. "Murderer!"

"Easy, kid." He tried to hold her off.

She wouldn't be stopped. Her pent up rage about Lisa's death and now her beloved Foxfire flowed out of her in a wild torrent. He retreated a step, then swung at her with the butt of his rifle, catching her temple. A sharp pain and colored lights, then blackness.

Chapter 30

Trapped

The first sensation was incessant throbbing in her head. Then total confusion. She couldn't move her arms or legs. Was she paralyzed? No, she could wiggle her fingers and toes, but her extremities were restrained somehow. She warily opened her eyes, but the darkness was complete. It must be nighttime. Where was she?

Meadow squirmed, trying for a more comfortable position, but the rope bit into the flesh of her arms tied behind her back. She touched the surface she was propped against. Cold, hard and rough. She listened—silence, except for the faint whoosh of wings. Bats? A sick feeling crept up from her toes and landed in her gut. The mineshaft. Where was the hooded monster?

Her parents must be worried sick and had probably sent out a search party by now. But wait, they thought she was at the Bowmans for the weekend. No one would be looking for her. She swallowed the bile that rose in her throat.

Time passed, but there was no way of knowing the hour or how long she'd been there. An all-consuming thirst took over. Parched throat and tongue like a cotton ball. Her mind drifted to the cool, sweet water of the gorge at Brighten. Then she mentally yelled at herself.

Stop it! Find a way out.

She struggled against the bindings, rubbing the rope along the rocks, hoping to wear it away. Her arms and legs chaffed and burned with the pain. She refused to let herself think about Foxfire, stubbornly pushing the horror away, but every once in a while a cold hand would grip her heart and squeeze. The agony of continual rubbing finally wore her down, and she sank back with her head drooped into her chest. No use. It wasn't working. She descended into a stupor of jumbled nightmares of a hooded man chasing her with death in his eyes.

A dim light filtered into the shaft when Meadow jerked awake, covered in cold sweat. The sun? It must be daybreak.

In a slow consciousness, she realized an animal lurked in the entrance, darkly backlit. Fear gripped her anew. A coyote or mountain lion?

The animal sampled the air and cautiously stalked into the mine. Meadow cringed against the wall. As it neared, relief seeped into her.

"Kelsey," she croaked, barely above a whisper. Her dog bounded over and began licking Meadow in earnest. Trailing around her neck were the remnants of the rope, chewed through.

Seeing her dog renewed Meadow's resolve and she tried to summon some moisture in her mouth. "Kelsey, fetch. Fetch saddlebag." She hoped and prayed Kelsey would remember the games of 'go find' they'd played for hours when she was still a pup. Meadow had taught her names of various items, then hid them for her dog to fetch and retrieve.

Kelsey cocked her head and whined, eager to please.

"Fetch saddlebag." It was as though a switch flipped in Kelsey's brain and she turned and sped away. Meadow fell back, drained from the effort.

It seemed like hours, but was probably only fifteen minutes or so, before Kelsey was back, dragging the bag like a lion with a kill. "Good girl," Meadow croaked. "Here."

Kelsey brought the saddlebag up next to Meadow, flat on the rock surface. The knife. But how could she get it out? If she could prop the bag up and then tip it over . . .

She worked her body around, then pushed the saddlebag with her feet, inch by inch, until she had it shoved against the wall, the middle part looped up. With a last bit of energy, she kicked up under it hard as she could. The bag flipped up, then came down, spilling the contents out of her reach. The knife glinted dully in the dim light of the shaft, at least five feet away from her.

"Kelsey, fetch knife." Her dog sniffed around the various contents, and retrieved the roll of bandages. "No, fetch knife." Her voice was fading fast. Kelsey went back and sniffed again. When she came to the knife, Meadow nodded vigorously. "Good," she whispered. Her dog picked it up, dropping it next to her side.

Now, to get it in her hand. She tipped herself over backwards onto the knife, where she could grab it. Then, using her feet and bottom she pushed and scooted until she was propped back against the rock wall. She maneuvered the blade edge so it was facing the rope, then tried to work it back and forth. Crap, her limited range of motion made it really awkward.

Dang, it fumbled out of her hand. Now she had to start over. It fell from her numb fingers two more times and doggedly she tried again.

Sweat streaked her face and her wrists ached from the constant sawing. But there was no choice, she had to keep going.

The hooded horse murderer might be back at any time.

After a couple more hours of work with little result, tears of frustration sprang out, and the knife slipped from her fingers and clunked down onto the rock, skittering away. She didn't attempt to get it, sinking back in defeat. Kelsey came, licked the tears away, and retrieved the knife.

Meadow inhaled deeply. "Ok, girl, you win." Don't think, keep sawing.

At long last, she could feel the fibers loosening. Heartened, she sawed faster, at the same time working the other wrist. When she could feel it was nearly sawn through, she dropped the knife and pulled with all her remaining strength.

Pop! Hooray, her wrists were free! But she wasn't loose, yet. She painfully brought her arms around from behind her back. Stiff and aching from being in the same position, she rubbed and flexed until some circulation returned, but it was still hard making her fingers work to untie her legs. She stubbornly kept at it until the restraints came undone. After stuffing the medical supplies back in the saddlebag, she heaved it over one shoulder. Her thirst raged. Darn, should have remembered the canteen. Got to get out of here, fast. Rising onto trembling legs, she staggered toward the mine opening. Water, need water.

Meadow labored across the open field, deliberately skirting the area where Foxfire fell. She couldn't face that. When she reached the spring with the pool, she sank down and buried her face in it, then gulped in great mouthfuls. Water had never tasted so good. She would never go anywhere without a canteen again.

Now that her thirst was quenched, the pain from the angry burns and welts on her wrists came on full force. She bathed them in the cool stream, then opened the saddlebag, pulling out the ointment and bandages. Her head cleared with hydration and the soothing effects of the medicine. It occurred to her that Arrow was not there. Good, that meant his leg was feeling better.

Then Kelsey growled, low and menacing. Meadow swung around and her blood ran colder than the stream. Near the boulder stood the hooded killer, rifle slung over his shoulder. Her eyes darted, as she desperately looked for a way out of the grotto. There were sheer walls on three sides, and the man was blocking the entrance. She refused to let him capture her again. He moved closer and she edged to the side, intending to make a run for it. But the man was too quick, latching onto her, and skillfully pinning her arms.

Kelsey viciously attacked his legs, and he kicked out at her, missing by inches. "Call her off or I'll shoot!"

"No, Kelsey, back!"

Instead of obeying, Kelsey renewed the attack, but the man's heavy boots protected him. Undeterred, the monster kept pulling her backwards, till they were next to the cliff. Meadow's head whirled. This can't be happening. What's he want? Was he going to kill her?

A sudden trumpeting whinny rang out, reverberating against the surrounding walls.

Arrow! He came thundering around the corner, fury in his eyes, but he wasn't alone.

Foxfire! She was alive, gloriously alive, running at his side. They charged across the terrain straight at them.

The hooded man violently shoved Meadow to the ground and aimed his rifle.

"No!" She sprang to her feet and shoved his arm up, just as the shot cracked. The slug went wild and a puff of dust appeared above their heads in the cliff wall. A rumbling sound began and grew, and almost instantaneously sand and rocks of all sizes came careening down.

The stallion charged the man and he stumbled backward. Foxfire raced to Meadow and she swung onto her back. They galloped away from the rockslide, as the man's leg was pinned under the debris. She heard him cursing and looked back to see him struggling to free himself, but didn't wait to find out. They galloped straight through the tunnel with the stallion close behind.

Arrow came with them as far as Weaver's Needle, then veered off to join his herd. His bandage was still in place, but he only limped slightly, and Foxfire had dried blood across the side of her head where the bullet had creased it. Meadow knew it was an old Mustanger's trick to crease a wild horse and knock it unconscious, so they could get a rope on. She was sure that wasn't the killer's intention, though. He meant to murder Foxfire, and he would have if she hadn't turned her head.

By the time they reached home, exhaustion blanketed Meadow like a shroud. She clung to Foxfire's back, barely hanging onto her mane, then slipped to ground next to the porch. Her legs gave way and she fell to the earth. It was impossible to summon the energy needed to rise, so she lay prone with Foxfire and Kelsey standing guard.

Chapter 31

The Amazing Ninja

Her parents found her crumpled near the porch, barely conscious. Dad carried her into the house, and Mom put a cool compress on her forehead.

"Maybe we should take her to the emergency room." Mom hovered over Meadow anxiously, holding a glass of water to her lips.

She drank greedily, and sat up, feeling somewhat revived. "No, I don't need a doctor, but I am kinda hungry."

"What happened to your wrists? You were supposed to be at the Bowmans this weekend." Her father touched the bandages, frowning.

She explained the urgent call from Joel, and related the subsequent events in jerky, halting sentences, her voice fading away at times. Mom's face lost all color and she gathered Meadow in her arms. "Oh my poor baby."

Her father tried to get more details, but Meadow was too weak to answer sensibly, mumbling responses or just shaking her head.

Mom finally intervened and fed her soup, then ran a hot bath. By the time Meadow stumbled out of the bathroom, groggy from the relaxing interlude, her father was on the phone with the police. After listening for a minute, he got deathly quiet and slammed down the receiver.

His face had that dangerous look and he began ranting. "Useless idiots!" He said many more choice words that could be heard echoing throughout the house, but Mom led Meadow away to her bed and told her to rest.

Sleep, without dreams, came at once and lasted until the first beams of sunshine brought her out of blessed oblivion. Her eyes squinted open against the bright light and her first panicky thoughts of being back in the mine were quickly soothed by the sight of her own room.

The kitchen was saturated with the sweet smell of warming maple syrup, with her mother flipping pancakes when Meadow dragged out of the bedroom. There was no sign of her father, Monty, or Wally.

"Where is everybody?"

"Monty's at school. Everyone else is searching for your abductor. Sheriff Dave and Nueme came yesterday, after you were already asleep. They went to the mine camp, but didn't find anybody. Dave and Nueme spent the night here and they all went searching again at first light."

"He escaped from the rockslide." She couldn't help the bitter sound of her voice.

Her mother cradled her in her arms. "Yes, but they'll find him. If anyone can figure out the tracks, it would be Nueme."

"But that guy's like a demon or something. The way he just appears out of nowhere."

"Eat some breakfast. You need to get your strength back."

A large stack of pancakes materialized in front of Meadow. She didn't have to be told twice. "Maybe I should ride up and help them look," she said in between bites.

"Absolutely not! You're going to stay right here where I can keep an eye on you."

"Since Monty already left, guess I'm not going to school."

"You're staying home a couple of days. Your teachers will send work home with Monty. I arranged it this morning."

"Good, then I won't have to answer any dumb questions about what I did to my wrists."

Her mother inspected the rope burns. "You did a pretty good job doctoring them. They'll heal in no time." She got up and began loading the dishwasher. "Joel called and wants to come over today. I told him what happened and said I didn't think you were up to it."

"Yes, I am. Maybe he found something out about the partner. I think it's all tied together. Please, Mom, I really want to talk to him."

"Well, all right. Make sure he doesn't tire you out."

Joel must have jumped in his beetle and drove over the minute she hung up the phone, since he rapped on their door less than an hour later.

"Couldn't ferret out anything about the name." He stared at her wrists. "But what about you? Tell me why you went up to the camp."

"After you called me about Arrow . . ."

His expression stopped her. "Whataya mean, after I called? I didn't call."

She sucked in her breath. "Someone did. He said he was you and the stallion was hurt."

"The stallion?"

"He belongs to Bill Bowman, but runs wild with a herd of mustangs."

"What does that have to do with you?"

"Never mind. It's too complicated." She shook her head. "But who called me? How did he know to impersonate you?"

"That's easy. My byline goes on all the stories I've written about you. Obviously we know each other."

"But how did he know about the stallion? And something else has been really bugging me. He could never have gotten close enough to Arrow to get a rope on him. I can't figure it out."

Joel took her hand. "I think he knows a lot about you and about animals. The guy is really dangerous. You can't mess around in this. Let the police find him."

"The local police aren't even looking. I guess since I wasn't killed, they aren't too interested. My dad, his Indian tracker friend, and the sheriff from Sedona are the only ones searching right now . . . and Wally."

Her mother brought them some lemonade. "Would you like to stay for lunch, Joel?"

"No thanks, Mrs. Shepherd. I'm on my way to cover an incident in Mesa. Robbery. I just wanted to check on Meadow after you told me about her abduction." He gulped down the drink and stood. "Take care of yourself and don't go off alone anymore."

Mom sighed. "Same thing I've been telling her for years."

"I had a really good reason . . . ."

Meadow walked Joel to his car, then went to check on Foxfire. Her mare had eaten all her hay and was alert. She swung her head around and flicked her ears forward at the sound of riders coming in.

"Did you find any clues?" Meadow rushed to Shadow's side.

"A couple of interesting things came up." Her father's jaw was tight.

"I found something, Meadow!" Wally triumphantly pulled out a small dart-like object and handed it to her.

She turned it over. "Looks like a syringe."

Sheriff Dave nodded. "They're used for sedating animals. Shot out of an air rifle."

"That's how he captured the stallion!"

"Yes, he must have two guns. It was a regular rifle he used on Foxy." Dave dismounted and tied his horse to the rail. "That's not all we found, though."

Wally broke in. "We found the skeleton, Meadow! It was in the mine."

"If we can link the killing to your captor, he'll be put away for years," Dad said.

Dave started toward the house. "I need to phone the police, so they can collect the remains and photograph the area."

Meadow approached Nueme. "Did the tracks tell you anything?"

"The man has a distinctive gait. One stride a little shorter than the other."

"He did have a funny walk. Are you talking about a real limp?"

Nueme rubbed his chin. "Not necessarily. It may not be very noticeable unless you're looking for it."

"After his leg was crushed, he probably *does* limp."

Her father turned from loosening Shadow's girth. "I don't know, Meadow. We checked the rockslide where he was. No sign of blood or a struggle to get loose. It's hard to figure. Are you sure he was pinned?"

She nodded. "Positive. He was trying to get free when we galloped away. I didn't hang around."

"I'm glad you didn't." Her father put his arm around her and they walked to the house.

The next day, Linda called, inviting Meadow to come and stay. At first, Mom was reluctant to let her go.

"Please, Mom, I'm so bored here. You won't let me ride and I haven't seen Linda in ages. A change of scene would do me a world of good."

Her mother smiled. "I guess you're right. But Kelsey and Foxy stay here. I want you to rest, not gallivant around playing with animals."

Meadow huffed. "Okay. Foxy deserves a break after being shot, and Kelsey can keep her company."

The Bowmans pool was pure bliss and Meadow made good use of the diving board and slide before swimming a few laps. She swam across, did a flip turn at the edge and started the back stroke.

Linda, sunning herself on the deck, called to her. "Hey, you're supposed to be resting. I promised your mom."

Meadow floated to the side, climbed out, and grabbed a towel. "It feels good to get some exercise. Mom made me lay around for two whole days."

"You can't blame her. It was pretty traumatic being tied up in a mine overnight. Parents tend to worry about things like that."

"Being active helps me think. I have to figure out who the hooded man is. Someone that knows me, understands animals, and can appear suddenly."

Little lines puckered Linda's forehead. "A magician."

"Yeah. And he seemed familiar, like I know him. Something about the way he walks. A slightly weird gait. Nueme noticed it in the tracks he found."

"Let's not worry about it right now. Dinner is about ready and we need to get dressed." Linda led the way into the house.

They sat in the dining room and were served several courses by the new cook, Celeste, a youngish woman with dark, curly hair. To top off the meal, she brought in chocolate mousse in parfait dishes and ceremoniously set them on the table. "Will there be anything else, *mademoiselle*?"

"No, that'll be fine. Have fun tomorrow."

"Yes, *mademoiselle*. I will see my intended. He looks a little, shall we say . . . different, but very dashing." She put on a sly smile. "We meet in a secret place."

Celeste left the room and Linda leaned in, saying in a hushed voice, "She's a gourmet French chef, according to my mother. But the food is too rich for my taste. I prefer Lupe's cooking at the ranch."

"Me too. Celeste put sauce on everything."

After the meal, Meadow sat across from Linda in the den, catching up on all the news. Linda's parents were out of town on business—Bill in Mexico and Mary at her New York City gallery. Brett wouldn't be back from military school for another three weeks. Meadow refrained from asking about the divine Tiffany. She didn't want to know.

Linda shifted in her seat. "Some things you said earlier about your captor have been troubling me. He walks funny, understands animals, and appears suddenly. Plus he wore all black with a hood. I just realized who it might be."

Meadow came to attention. "Who?"

"First, I want to show you a photograph." Linda rose and began rifling through her father's heavy walnut desk. She located a large manila envelope. "Here it is." She pulled out a picture, and handed it to Meadow.

She looked at it and gasped. "It's him! The same clothes, boots and everything." The image was of a man, dressed in a hooded black costume, standing next to a fierce-looking tiger on a pedestal. "Who is he?"

"He called himself 'The Amazing Ninja' back then, when he performed in a circus. Gave up the act when he was mauled by a tiger and lost his lower leg. He became the caretaker of Fort Apache. My dad got this photo from the former owner when he bought the place. I had forgotten all about it until you started describing the man who captured you."

Meadow stared at her with a thumping heart. "It's creepy Clay."

"He did magic tricks and trained animals. It explains the strange comings and goings and his ability to sedate the stallion."

"But how did he get out from under the rockslide . . . oh, you said the tiger mauled him, I bet he has a fake leg." Goosebumps appeared on Meadow's arms. "I have to call my dad right now. Clay was at the Fort when I left."

"Use the phone in here."

Meadow dialed the number waited. Wally's voice came on. "Hi, Meadow. Your folks went out. Your mom left food on the stove for me."

"Wally, this is really important. When they come home, tell them I need to talk to them about Clay."

"Clay? He's right here, Meadow. Do you want to talk to him?"

"No! Don't say anything to him. And lock the door when he leaves. As soon as my parents get home, have them call me. Understand?"

"Sure, Meadow. I'll have your parents call right away. And I'll lock the door when he leaves."

Meadow frowned as she hung up. "Clay probably heard every word. He was standing right there."

Linda grabbed the phone. "I'm calling the police." She spoke for a couple of minutes, then slammed the receiver down. "Your dad's right. This police department is worthless. They said to bring the picture in tomorrow and they'll investigate. I wish Dave were here, but he's on his way back to Sedona."

The wait was agonizing. The Bowmans huge house suddenly seemed to close in on Meadow as she paced and fretted waiting for her parents to call. Linda suggested a game of cards, and it helped pass the time but wasn't easy to stay focused. It was close to eleven when the phone finally rang, making them both jump.

"Dad, it's Clay! Linda has a photo of him in the same clothes!"

"Calm down, Meadow. I'll go talk to him right now. I'll let you know what I find out."

"Please be careful. He's a killer!"

"Don't worry. Nueme's here, and I'm taking my revolver."

It wasn't long before her father called back. The tension in his voice came across loud and clear. "He's gone. The call to Wally must have tipped him off." He paused. "Nueme and I are going after him. He locked Kelsey in the tack room . . . and took Foxy."

Chapter 32

Waiting

Meadow collapsed into Bill Bowman's chair, dropping her head onto the desk. Linda came up from behind and squeezed her shoulders. "Don't worry, sweetie. They'll find Foxy. Your dad and Nueme are a formidable team."

"What if he hurts her? What if he ambushes Daddy? He's a killer." Meadow raised up a tear-stained face and stared at her friend. "I've got to do something. It's me he wants."

"That's exactly why your father told you to stay here, where it's safe."

"I'm not good at just waiting."

"I know, but that's what the killer wants—you to go look for Foxy. What was it that he said? He wants to question you about something?"

Meadow nodded. "He never said what it was about. I don't know anything."

"Think—something only you know . . ."

A dark curtain dropped down. The events of the past few days overwhelmed her and she couldn't control the shaking and sobbing. "I don't know, I don't know."

Linda hugged her close. "Shhh. It's okay, don't think about it right now. I'm going to make you some warm milk with honey. Then you're going to bed. A good night's sleep is what you need."

After drinking the milk, Linda tucked her in, then tiptoed out of the bedroom. Meadow did feel calmer, and a dreamless unconsciousness claimed her.

In the middle of the night, her eyes flew open to pitch blackness. The amulet was warm against her chest. What woke her? She listened, and heard a faint scratching against the side of the house. What was that? It happened again. She let out her breath. It was just the wind blowing a branch. She was as jumpy as a new foal.

Oh well, can't sleep now. She turned on a lamp, and started thumbing through a Western Horseman magazine left on the nightstand. Suddenly, her breath caught and the magazine slipped through her fingers. Of course, that hooded monster, Clay, was in cahoots with Wendell! They were after the Indian Medicine Chest. It all made sense now. She was the only one, besides Colt, who knew where the treasure was hidden.

She got up and went to the window. The eastern sky showed faint signs of light across the desert landscape, outlining a huge saguaro nearby. Good, it was almost daylight. Her parents would be up, and she could call home.

After pulling on cut-offs and a tee shirt, Meadow found her way to the den and dialed the fort. Her mother answered. "Nothing yet, honey. They lost the trail last night, and just left again. I reported Foxy's theft to the police. They're sending someone out today."

"I'll come home and talk to them."

"No, honey, your father wants you to stay put for the time being. When Linda takes the picture in, you can make a statement. Try not to worry, I'll call the second they find her."

Meadow set the phone down, stalking around the room for a few minutes. Geez, this was horrible—the eternal waiting. With nothing else to do, she went to the kitchen. It gleamed with every conceivable appliance known to man. Celeste was off today, so no coffee brewing. She looked around for the coffeepot, Linda might want some. Anyway, it smelled great even though to her it tasted nasty. Behind a little sliding door she found the plug-in kind. At home, her mother still used an old-fashioned percolator. She found a can of Folgers, then read the instructions on the coffeemaker. By the time Linda wandered in, she proudly poured her a cup of the fresh brew.

"Thanks, you're a doll. I need this." Linda drizzled in some cream and sipped. "Umm. Even better than Celeste makes."

Meadow offered a wan smile. "I needed something to do." She tapped her fingers on the counter, then blurted out, "I figured out why Clay wants to question me. It's about the Indian Medicine Chest."

"What? No one knows where it is."

"I do." She purposely left Colt out of it. She didn't want *him* in trouble. It was bad enough to have kept the secret from everyone.

Linda's eyes widened. "When did you find it? Why didn't you tell anyone?"

Meadow squirmed and looked down.

"Oh, never mind about all that. The important thing is, how did Clay find out about it?" Linda asked.

"Wendell must have recruited him. Last summer he had a whole gang of thieves, remember? He likes to direct things, not actually do the bad stuff. I'm sure he's behind it all. I've been getting weird phone calls for months, and Joel said the police traced him to Phoenix."

"Oh, sweetie, why didn't you tell anyone?"

"At first, I thought it was just a prankster. And then, after Lisa died, I didn't want to worry my parents. I think her death is related to everything else."

"And without parental restrictions, you thought you could track down whoever it was."

"Something like that."

"It's time to tell everyone in order to catch the killer. This morning we'll take that photo of Clay to the police. But first, I'm going to call Dave and fill him in. If Wendell is involved, he should be here to help. He's been working on the artifact case since the beginning."

The police were very polite to Linda and even asked Meadow pertinent questions. They examined the photograph, the burns on her wrists and made copious notes. A couple of officers were dispatched to Fort Apache to follow up. It was about time the police took them seriously.

It was noon by the time they finished, and Linda treated for lunch at a swank restaurant. Meadow didn't have much appetite, but the food was wonderful when she tasted a few bites. To make Linda happy, she ate more than she wanted.

Linda watched the waiter clear their plates away and prepared to leave. "Listen, I have class this afternoon, but will be home by five. Even though Celeste has the day off, our stableman, Sam, will be there. So you won't be alone."

"Quit worrying about me. I'll be fine. With swimming and all the books you have there's plenty to keep me busy. Or maybe I'll take a nap after this huge meal."

Linda laughed. "That'll be the day, you taking a nap."

After her friend dropped her off and left for college, Meadow dove into the pool. She swam a few laps, then dressed and wandered out to the stable to say hello to Sam. Her chest tightened when she saw the horses poking their heads over the stall doors. Where was Foxfire?

She was petting Brett's horse, Calypso, when Sam found her.

His weathered face broke into a smile. "Hello, Missy. I haven't seen much of you, lately. I'll saddle up one of these broncs if you want to ride."

Meadow swallowed. "I wish I could, Sam. I'd go right out and look for Foxy."

He patted her shoulder. "I'm sorry, miss. What kind of a dirty rascal steals someone's horse?"

"He's more than a rascal—he's a full blown assassin." Meadow clenched both fists. "I won't rest till I find him if he hurts Foxy." Then her voice caught. "He already killed Lisa."

Meadow turned and stumbled toward the house, before she totally broke down in front of Sam. It was too painful around the horses, a sharp reminder of her missing mare. She wandered through the house, and as usual, was drawn to the well-stocked library. She picked up a book, but after a little while put it back down. Too hard to concentrate.

Back in the den, she stared at the phone for a minute, steeling herself against bugging her mother again. The Arizona Republic lay on the desk, and she opened it to the crossword puzzle. When a half-hearted attempt at a solution resulted in a host of blank boxes mocking her, she threw the paper down and started pacing. It took ten minutes to get all the way through the house. There were clocks in many of the rooms, but none of them seemed to make the time pass more quickly. Finally, she avoided looking at them altogether. She was taking one more lap through the house, when the grandfather clock in the living room chimed five times and simultaneously the phone rang. She raced to get it.

It was Linda. "I'm sorry, Sweetie, I'll be a little late. Fender bender on Scottsdale Road and I have to wait for the cops to get here."

"Are you okay?"

"Yeah, nothing serious. A weird coincidence, though—it was Celeste who rear-ended me. She said she was distracted by something or other. Anyway, I shouldn't be more than an hour or so. Any news?"

"Not really. Mom called to say I had to stay here at least another night."

"Stay as long as you like, you're good company. I'll bring home take-out for dinner and we'll make a party of it. See you soon. Oh, tell Sam to stay late tonight, until I get home."

"Okay, 'bye." She hung up and headed for the stable. Sam was probably feeding by now. She walked toward the barn, then stopped at the entrance and stuck her head in. Where was he? "Sam? Are you in here?"

A whinny broke the silence and she saw a familiar chestnut head with a perfect star, looking over a stall door. She ran forward, blinded by sudden tears. "Foxy!"

Just as she got to Foxfire, a steel grip reached out, and iron fingers closed around her throat. Pale, dead eyes bored into hers. "You're lucky, kid. Instead of a last meal, you get a last ride."

Chapter 33

Ride of No Return

Meadow jounced along, Foxfire keeping pace with the mammoth mule's long-striding trot. Her hands were tied in front, probably so she wouldn't fall off. It was hard enough to balance at this gait as it was. At first, she rode frozen in fear, her heart thudding. Gradually, the terror abated and anger took over. She glared at his back. He wouldn't get away with this without a fight.

Her mind worked feverishly to come up with an escape plan. She thought about sliding off, but the brute had a death grip on Foxfire's reins and there was no way she would let him steal her mare a second time. Besides, he would catch her quickly enough and kill her on the spot. Maybe there would be a chance to flee when they got to wherever the heck they were going. She could tell they were heading east from the slant of the setting sun, but didn't recognize the desert they were passing through.

Clay sat deep in the saddle and ramrod straight, never looking left or right, totally focused on his evil intent. He never uttered a word. From behind, his left leg stuck out at an odd angle in the stirrup. His artificial foot. It was a wonder he could ride so well.

After trotting for hours in twilight and then darkness, the light began to change. Ahead of them a full moon swelled up over the horizon, illuminating the stark landscape. The pale light made the saguaros cast long shadows like an army of green giants marching into battle. How long had they been traveling? Someone must be looking for them by now.

They came up over a rise, and far down the other side, a faint light flickered. It took at least another half hour to reach what turned out to be a camp with a fire ring in the center. Clay's old army jeep was parked nearby. Flames licked the charred mesquite, emitting a familiar odor like when her father started up the barbeque. A sob caught in Meadow's throat as she thought about her family and how worried they must be. It seemed she was always a source of worry lately.

Clay reined the big mule to a halt next to the campfire, and a young woman emerged out of a tent. "Douse the fire," he growled at her, dismounting.

"Of course, *mi amour*. I wanted to make sure you could find your way. You should appreciate my thoughtfulness. After the police detained me, I had to drive like a crazy woman to beat you out here."

He turned slowly to face her. His voice, low and measured, was chilly as a mountain spring. "You *are* a crazy woman. Quit yappin' and do like I told ya."

Celeste narrowed her eyes and took her time, swinging shapely hips over to the jeep. She retrieved a canvas water bag off the front, then trickled the contents onto the fire, making it hiss and steam.

Meadow gritted her teeth. So that's why Linda had been delayed. Celeste purposely ran into her car. It had all been part of the plan to make sure she would be alone at the Bowman estate. Almost alone. She hoped Sam hadn't been injured.

Clay watched Celeste's rebellious display for a moment, then turned his attention to Meadow. He wrenched her off Foxfire, allowing her to fall into a heap on the hard earth. Pain shot through her side as she landed like a sack of oats. Foxfire snorted and bared her teeth, snapping at Clay viciously. He rammed his elbow into the mare's jaw and jerked at the reins, jamming her bit down. Blood oozed from Foxfire's mouth, as he continued yanking, forcing her to back away from him.

"Stop, you're hurting her!" Meadow's cry went unheeded as the monster kept up the torment on her horse. Clenching her jaw against the pain, she managed to get to her feet. Without thinking she ran at Clay and kicked as hard as she could at his prosthesis, hoping to loosen it and tip him over. It made a dull metallic sound, but had little other affect. He brushed her aside as he might a bothersome insect and she stumbled to the ground.

Celeste rushed over and untied the restraints on her hands. Meadow rubbed circulation back and glanced up to see Clay grab a rope from the jeep. He looped it around Foxfire's neck, then around one back hoof, tying the ends together so her foot was held up off the ground. He yanked on the rope, while Foxfire struggled against the restraint, her eyes wild. She lost her balance, fell heavily and was unable to rise.

Meadow, peering through tears, attempted to go help her mare, but Clay pushed her back down. Celeste approached and gave him an accusing look. "I thought you were just going to ask the girl a few questions. Why abuse her horse?"

"Stay out of this if you know what's good for you. Come to think of it, you've pretty much outlived your usefulness."

For the first time, a hint of fear played across Celeste's face. "What do you mean? You said you loved me. That we were going to run away together. Why else would I double-cross my employer and help you bring this girl out here?" She went to him, wrapping him in her arms. "We love each other, remember, *mi amour*? Remember all the sweet nights together? Making plans?"

Clay stood like a statue, never altering his chiseled look. Celeste stepped back and scanned his face, and her expression changed as the truth dawned on her. She began beating on his chest, screaming in French.

Meadow took the opportunity to creep away on all fours, heading toward Foxfire. With a sudden shove, Clay sent Celeste reeling into the fire pit. She flung out her arms to break the fall, then screamed in agony as her hands came down on the still-burning coals.

Clay ignored his girlfriend and caught up with Meadow, hauling her back. Hot tears coursed down her cheeks. "What do you want? Please untie Foxfire. I'll tell you anything, just let her go."

"Tell me where the Indian Medicine chest is hidden, and I'll untie your horse. Otherwise, I'll cut her up in little pieces, and feed her to the buzzards." He whipped a wicked blade from the sheath at his waist and held it in front of her eyes.

Meadow tried to buy time. "How do you know about the chest?"

Behind him, Celeste had clawed her way out of the pit and snuck away into the tent. In a moment she was back out and running toward Clay, brandishing a shovel. She made the mistake of cursing as she ran, and he turned to fend her off. He dropped the dagger, ripped the spade from her hands, and used it to whack her across the side of her head. The woman's eyes rolled back and she sank into the dirt at his feet, still as a corpse.

Meadow scrambled to pick up the knife and sprinted toward Foxfire. The monster was right behind, and grabbed a handful of her hair, snapping her neck back. He pinned the offending arm behind, and the blade fell with a small thump. She kicked out, helpless to do more. He laughed in a sick sort of way. "Do you really think you can get away from me?" He abruptly quit laughing and got close to her face, so close she could smell his foul breath. "Now tell me where it is."

She gulped and blurted out, "First untie Foxy."

"You agree to cooperate and I'll untie her. Or else you'll watch her die a slow, painful death. Which will it be?"

"Untie her and I'll tell you everything. Promise you won't hurt her and I promise I won't run."

His cold, colorless eyes appraised her for a moment, then he nodded and let her arm go. She stood by as he loosened the rope and Foxfire regained her feet, gingerly placing her rope-burned hoof on the ground. He tied her to the jeep, then faced Meadow. "Talk."

There was no choice. She clenched her jaw, then said, "It's in the secret room at the cliff dwelling."

"Does Wendell know where that is?"

"Yes." So Wendell *was* behind this whole thing.

Clay again stared his deadly stare, then turned from her, apparently satisfied she was telling the truth. He re-sheathed the knife and retrieved the shovel, placing it in her hands. "Over there." He indicated a spot a little ways from the campsite. "You get to dig your own grave, just like in the movies."

The air whooshed out of Meadows's lungs and sweat beaded on her brow. "But I told you what you wanted to know!"

"Don't worry, it'll be quick, just like your girlfriend, Lisa. Be glad I'm not going to torture you. Believe me, I'm an expert at that."

"You cut her girth?"

"Who else?"

Meadow kept talking, trying to delay the inevitable. "I knew it! Everything that's been happening is connected. Did you make those weird phone calls?"

Now that the evil monster had his information, he became almost chatty. "No, that would be Wendell. He's a scary guy. A master at coming up with complicated strategies. He told me all about the original plan to steal the artifacts. You were the only fly in the ointment. Now he wants you eliminated."

The pit of her stomach was sour and her legs threatened to buckle. Need to be strong, need to keep him talking. She forged on. "What about the skeleton? Is that the remains of your partner, George Edwards?"

"You know, kid, Wendell's right. You're too smart for your own good. Stop here. Dig."

The desert floor was packed tight, but Meadow obediently shoved in the spade. After she dug a little deeper, it started loosening up. She waited until she had a full shovel, then turned, flinging it at the monster's face. But he was too quick and dodged the load. He slapped her hard, the impact knocking her to her knees, the sting radiating throughout her body.

"That should knock some of the fight out. Now get up. Keep digging."

Blisters formed and her shoulders ached from the repetitive motion, but every time she slowed, Clay administered another mind-numbing slap. The hole was nearly a foot deep, when he finally stopped her.

"We're out of time, kid. That's deep enough. The coyotes will dig you up anyway."

With the extreme fatigue, her muscles ceased to scream and her brain became quiet, accepting of her fate. She prayed it *would* be quick, like he said. He gripped the nape of her neck with one hand and removed the dagger from his waist, raising it to her jugular.

She looked into his dead, colorless eyes without fear, as when a deer is in the clutches of a mountain lion, knowing that a struggle is useless.

Chapter 34

The Hunt

The evening light was waning by the time Shep clomped into the house with Nueme and Sheriff Dave trailing behind. They followed their noses to the kitchen where Rose was taking a roast out of the oven. Her welcoming smile faded when saw their faces.

"No luck finding Foxy, I guess?" she asked, more statement than question.

"Not a trace. That scumbag covered his tracks well." Shep pulled out a chair and sat heavily. "Glad Meadow's not here. Have you heard from her?"

"It's been a couple of hours, which is strange, since she'd been calling constantly."

"Linda's probably keeping her occupied. Dinner almost ready? We haven't had a bite since breakfast."

"Just need to put the biscuits in. You fellas wash up and we can start on the salad." Rose got out the olive oil to mix up the dressing.

There were hardly even any scraps left for Kelsey after Shep and the other hungry men finished dinner.

"Thanks, Rose. That really hit the spot." Nueme pushed back from the table.

Shep turned to Dave. "Any other ideas? We covered the mine area thoroughly today."

"I've already put out an APB. The force is on the alert for a horse trailer or truck. He won't be able to get her across the state line."

Rose jumped up to grab the phone when it rang. "It's most likely Meadow," she said over her shoulder. As she listened, her face paled. "Shep, it's Linda. You'd better hear this."

He took the receiver. "Hello, Linda. What's up?"

"Meadow's missing." Linda's voice was strained, scared.

Shep clenched his fist around the phone. "What happened?"

"My car was rear-ended, so I was late getting home and couldn't find Meadow. I went to the barn and our stableman, Sam, was bound and gagged in a stall."

"Did Sam see who it was?"

"I'm afraid not, he was hit from behind and knocked out. But they left on horseback."

Oh my god. The nightmare begins. "I'll be right over."

"I'll call the police."

Shep slammed down the phone and turned to the other men. "Meadow's been kidnapped from the Bowman place. They left on horseback. Linda's going to report it, but it'll be faster to hunt for them ourselves. I don't trust that dimwitted police department to get their act together. Nueme, load the horses; Dave, you can follow us in your Land Rover."

"I'll come along," Rose said.

"No, you'd better wait. There might be a ransom call."

Her lip trembled. "Oh . . . right." She grabbed his arm. "At least take Kelsey. She'll find Meadow."

"Good idea." He opened the gun locker, loaded his Winchester, and strode out of the house. Kelsey eagerly joined him and Nueme in the cab.

Shep gunned the engine, and Gertie lurched forward, as though surprised to be have such rough treatment. He drove at a reckless speed, heedless of the honks and dirty looks from the few other motorists they passed.

No police cars were around when they reached the Bowmans. Sam met them at the barn and watched the horses being unloaded. The stableman held an icepack to his head. "I'm sure sorry Mr. Shepherd, the bugger clocked me before I knew anyone was here."

Shep tightened his cinch and grunted, "Not your fault, Sam."

Linda rushed out of the house. "I just got off of the line with the police. They said for you to wait for them."

"I'm going to find my girl." Shep stepped into the stirrup. "Let's ride, boys."

Shep sank into the saddle and rode Shadow like he was pursued by a demon. Or, he thought grimly, to put it more accurately, pursuing a demon. Aided by Dave's high-powered flashlight, they were able to make good time following the hoof prints.

Before long, though, they were forced to slow down. The terrain became increasingly rocky which didn't offer much in the way of tracks.

Shep reined in and whistled for Kelsey. "Find Meadow, find Foxy." She raced to the front and sniffed around briefly before leading the way at a trot. Thank the lord Rose had made them bring Meadow's dog.

It was agonizing every time Kelsey lost the scent and had to circle back. Shep grated under the slower pace, swearing under his breath. What would that maniac do to his daughter? It had been hours since her abduction. God, he prayed they would be in time.

Nueme and Dave rode up abreast of him, offering silent support. They were the best companions he could wish for in a crisis.

The time passed, on and on they rode, farther and farther into the desolate desert. Anger, mixed with dread at what they might find, burrowed deep in Shep's being. It was so much like searching for Meadow last summer, it was uncanny. That turned out all right. But this time she was with Clay, a real sicko. The tension made his back ache as if he'd been breaking rocks in the hot sun.

Where the hell had that brute taken her?

Kelsey suddenly growled and gave a low woof as they topped a rise. Dave shone his light ahead, then quickly shut it off. "Hold up," he said. "It's a camp. If it's the kidnapper, we need to approach cautiously."

Shep breathed deeply, his hands itching to circle the killer's neck and squeeze the life out of him. He didn't know if he could restrain himself.

Chapter 35

The Warrior Prince

Meadow's stomach churned from Clay's fetid breath as he held her tightly. She closed her eyes, waiting for the dagger to pierce her vein. He seemed to enjoy dragging it out.

That's strange, the amulet began to warm against her chest. Peace floated over her, and she could see the Medicine Woman, Meda, hold out her hand.

Had he sliced her jugular? Was her life blood ebbing away?

An unearthly sound, like a war cry shattered the night, and her eyes flew wide.

As if in slow motion, an Indian warrior was bearing down on them astride a dark horse. Was it her last wish come true, a vision of Colt?

No, it *was* Colt, riding Smoke. His arm held aloft with a lance decorated with black-tipped white feathers. Smoke skidded to a halt in a swirl of dust and Colt threw the spear into the ground, where it stuck within inches of Clay. It quivered for a moment, glowing eerily in the moonlight.

Colt had the appearance of an other-worldly god, beautiful and invincible.

"Let her go." His voice was soft, but the impact strong. Clay sucked in his breath and his hands dropped to his side. His eyes unblinking, as if mesmerized, the killer stood as though rooted to the spot.

Her savior vaulted from Smoke's back and cradled Meadow to his chest. She inhaled his earthy forest scent and felt his immense strength.

The feeling was so heavenly, she wondered if she *had* died, and this was the afterlife. Things like this just didn't happen in the real world. The illusion was disrupted when Colt drew back from her and became practical.

"We have to tie him up. Your father, Nueme and the sheriff are not far behind me. Is there a rope here?"

Meadow, unable to find her voice, nodded toward the jeep. Colt pulled his lance out of the ground and marched Clay in front of him. Still lying near the fire, Celeste groaned and moved. The sound brought Meadow back to total focus, and she ran to her side.

"Celeste, are you okay?" The woman moaned and her lids fluttered, but she didn't wake up.

Colt, finished with gagging and hog-tying Clay, came over and kneeled next to them. He lifted Celeste's eyelids and rubbed her hands. No response. "She must have a concussion. When the others get here, someone can drive her to the emergency room." He turned to Meadow. "Along with you."

"But I'm all right, now that you're here."

He smiled and gently took both hands, turning them over. Angry blisters swelled on her palms, some already burst and oozing. "And not just your hands, you should see your face. It looks like you've been in a train wreck. You need medical attention. No arguments."

Meadow nodded meekly. "Anything you say, Kemo Sabe." Colt burst out laughing, and she frowned. "What's so funny?"

"Please don't quote the Lone Ranger, or his sidekick, Tonto. In my language, *Kemo Sabe* means 'soggy shrub'. Of course, *Tonto* means 'stupid', so you have to consider the source, I guess."

Her eyes widened and then she giggled along with him. It felt good to laugh after so much suffering. She laughed and then suddenly she was crying, great gulping sobs. Colt silently enfolded her in his arms, sensing her need for release.

She finally pulled back, wiping at her tears. "I'm sorry. I'm not usually so emotional."

"Don't be sorry. You've been through more than many people could endure."

In the aftermath of her breakdown, she began shivering.

Colt stood. "The night is cool. I'll replenish the fire. It'll be a beacon for your father." He brought her a blanket from the tent, then began gathering wood.

Meadow hugged the cover around her and watched Colt work. His movements were lithe, effortless, and like a creature of the forest, untamed and wild. Before long, the flames danced and swayed through the mesquite. The warm, hypnotic effect soon had her eyes growing heavy. She must have nodded off, because the next thing she knew, Foxfire nickered.

Horses were approaching.

Chapter 36

The Wrath of Shep

Shep touched Dave's arm. "The campfire is blazing. No kidnapper would advertise their whereabouts." A spark of hope lit in his gut. "Maybe someone found and helped Meadow."

"Who? We haven't run across another soul in this wasteland of cactus spines and rock," Dave said.

Nueme smiled. "Maybe the gods were looking out for her."

Shep quickly surveyed the campsite as they neared. Thank the Lord. Meadow rose stiffly from in front of the fire. She seemed to be all right, wrapped in a blanket. Clay was hogtied near his jeep and a woman lay unconscious opposite the campfire. Where was the Good Samaritan?

He leaped off of Shadow, tossing the reins to Nueme. "Meadow, are you okay, sweetheart?"

She nodded while he hugged her to his chest. Into her hair, he said, "What happened here? Who helped you?"

Meadow pulled back from him with a dreamy expression. "It was Colt. He's right here." She gazed around, then seemed puzzled. "Or he was a minute ago. Didn't you see him?" The firelight played across her features.

What the hell? Shep cupped her chin to get a better look at her face. Long rows of angry, swollen welts crisscrossed from her scalp down to her neck, like meat pounded with a tenderizing mallet. He drew in a harsh breath. The spectacle of such cruel treatment ignited the firestorm of rage that had been smoldering just below the surface. Aside from the obvious, what else did that brute do to his little girl? He gently released his hold on her, then stomped to where Sheriff Dave was bent over Clay trying to get answers. "Untie him."

Sheriff Dave looked up with a question in his eyes. "What for? Might as well take him in like this. It's a darn good job. A wild bronc couldn't escape."

Shep's voice was dark and deliberate. "Untie him. Now. And get him to his feet."

Dave did as he was told and in short order, Clay stood before Shep, colorless and unrepentant. At the sight of Shep's clenched fists, he said, "I have no quarrel with you. You've got your kid back, what else do you want?"

"You dirty bastard!" Like a mad bull, Shep bellowed his fury, and at the same time, his right hook shot out, connecting with the man's nose. Blood sprayed out in a crazy pattern over his shirt as Clay's head snapped back and he stumbled to the ground. Shep saw only red as he dove onto the fallen man, and began systematically beating him, a blow for each one he had inflicted on Meadow. Clay squirmed and tried to fight back, but all that did was fuel the fire of Shep's unrelenting anger. Sweat trickled into his eyes, but Shep had no intention of stopping until he felt restraining hands on his arms.

"Easy, Shep. I know you want to kill 'im. So do I, but let's leave him to the authorities and the Great Spirit to deal with." Nueme's words, spoken softly, began to calm the torrent of blows.

Shep took a great swig of air and his vision cleared enough to see Nueme's wisdom. Except in time of war or in self-defense, a person had no right to take another's life. He slowly regained his feet and turned his back on the child beater. He heard the click of handcuffs and Dave maneuvering his prisoner into the back of the jeep. Shep walked over to a wide-eyed Meadow.

"Wow, Daddy."

"Sorry you had to see that, sweetheart." He took her hand. "Now what was this you were saying about Colt?"

"He saved me. Said he saw you coming to get me."

Shep exchanged a glance with Nueme. "We didn't see anyone on the way. But someone tied up that scumbag."

Meadow faced Nueme. "You didn't see him? How did he know you were coming?"

Nueme wore his usual inscrutable expression as he gazed off into the darkness. "He saw us, but we couldn't see him. That's the way it is sometimes."

Meadow grabbed Nueme's arm, her stance rigid, intense. "When you see Colt, tell him our secret is no longer safe. He'll know what to do. Please, Nueme, it's really important."

"Yes, when I see him."

Shep frowned and looked from his friend to his daughter, and saw her shoulders relax, as if a burden had just been lifted. What the hell was that all about? He decided not to question it. Time enough later. Right now there were more pressing issues.

He strode over to where Foxfire was tied and ran his hands down her legs. "Some rope burn, but she looks fit enough to travel." He nodded toward the woman, still lying in the same position. "I'll drive Meadow and this woman to the emergency room and then Dave can escort the lunatic to jail. Nueme will bring all the horses back."

The woman moaned when Shep lifted her into backseat of the vehicle, propping her to one side. Dave climbed in between her and Clay, and put his arm around the injured woman to support her during the bumpy ride across the desert. Meadow sat in the front, close to Shep, her head resting on his arm, with Kelsey half on her lap.

The only sounds on their journey back were engine rattles, the swishing of tires against sand and the occasional whistling *hoo hoo hoo* of a pygmy cactus owl.

Chapter 37

Foiled Again

Wendell marched behind the burly guard, his elevator shoes clacking on the polished concrete floor of the county jail. He knew he looked the part in a pin-striped suit topped off with a fedora pulled low. Black-rimmed glasses framed his face, giving him a bookish appearance. The guard swung open a heavy metal door and gave a curt nod to indicate it was okay for Wendell to enter the room.

Seated on a wooden chair, Clay bent over a table, head in hands. His bristly hair reminded Wendell of a white clothes brush. The door clanged shut, and the albino flinched, lifting his chin. His colorless eyes stood out starkly from the purple bruising underneath them, and his nose appeared flattened, covered by a large bandage.

Wendell raised his brows. "What happened to you? Don't tell me you tangled with Shep?"

A flicker of interest flitted across the stony countenance, and Clay peered at him. "Wendell? Good disguise." Then the pale, dead eyes glittered. "Yeah, it was that son of bitch. If I ever get out of here, I'll gladly kill him *and* his precious kid for you."

Wendell chuckled without mirth. "Don't say I didn't warn you."

"What story did you give the officer to let you in here?"

"Said I was a defense attorney and needed to question you to see if I wanted to take the case. I tested this disguise out on Lucy when she went to the grocery store. Approached her to ask where the mustard was located. She didn't have a clue it was me in these shoes, plus the toupee and mustache. Even got a little flirty, dumb broad. I figured these cops are every bit as stupid as

Lucy, and I was right. Just gave them a fake card and they led me right to you."

"Why are you here? Afraid I'll implicate you in this fiasco?"

"Actually, I'm not worried about that. You're not the type to squeal. Besides, I have the goods on you and there's no evidence against me. You did all the dirty work." He narrowed his eyes and growled, "But you didn't finish the job."

Clay's face twitched. "I remember."

"What happened? The plan was working perfectly." Wendell paced the small enclosure, which wasn't easy in two inch heels. The action didn't help his temper. "How could you screw it up? We had her, all you had to do is get the information and squash her like a cockroach!" He closed his eyes, inhaled, and consciously lowered his voice. "Did you at least find out where the chest is?"

"I think so."

"You *think* so?" Wendell massaged his temples. "You *think* so! Either she told your or not, you imbecile!"

Clay clenched his fist and stood, still towering over Wendell in spite of the high-rise shoes. "Why should I tell you? What good will that do me? I'll be stuck in prison for years if they convict me of kidnapping."

Wendell stepped back. "Calm down. I'm working on that. You may have to spend a few weeks in the hoosegow, but if you don't make trouble, I'll get you out. Then you can complete the job as ordered. At least tell me what happened. Next time, the plan has gotta be foolproof."

"You probably won't believe me. I hardly believe it myself." Clay shook his head, rubbing a hand over the white bristles. "After the kid talked, I playcd games with her for a while—not *real* torture—just for my own amusement. She's a tough little broad."

"Yeah, yeah, get on with it."

"I had her at knifepoint, just about to slice her open . . ." He paused, staring into space.

Wendell huffed impatiently. "Well?"

Clay's eyes went weird, even weirder than normal, trancelike. "I don't really know what happened. Suddenly, there was a bright light . . . well, not exactly a light, but kind of an aura. About the same time an Indian spear stuck in the ground next to me, then something or someone landed smack on me, knocking me senseless. Next thing I knew, I was gagged and trussed up like a turkey." He faced Wendell. "How do *you* explain that?"

"Are you crazy? I knew you were a little demented, but I didn't think you were completely nuts! You got tied up and don't know how it happened?"

The label of crazy didn't seem to faze Clay, and he shrugged. "Later, Shep, his Indian buddy, and the sheriff showed up. That's all I know. Take it or leave it." He sank back down on the chair, returning his head to his hands.

The walls seemed to close in on Wendell, one concrete block at a time, and he pulled at his necktie. What was it about that Meadow? Somehow, when she was in his grasp, she always managed to slip away. A chill started at the top of his head and ran the length of his body and he shuddered. Then he slitted his eyes and clenched his jaw. Snap out of it. She's just a bratty kid that's unusually lucky. But her luck was about to run out.

He clomped to the door and rang the buzzer for the guard, already plotting. This time the scheme would be so clever, she'd never wiggle out of it.

Even if he never obtained the Indian treasure, revenge *would* be his.

Chapter 38

The Prodigal Returns

Meadow jolted awake, confused. Where was she? People scurrying around in white coats. Slowly, her brain cleared. Oh, yeah, the hospital.

"Better take care of this woman." Her father nodded toward the still unconscious Celeste.

The orderlies whisked Celeste away on a gurney. Another crew came for Meadow and placed her in a little room with all sorts of beeping, flashing machines.

She longed to just go home to her own cozy bed, but after the examination, the doctor insisted Meadow spend the night. She wanted to put up a fuss but one look at Dad warned against it. Besides, exhaustion had taken all the fight out.

A nurse led her to a shower room, placing an open-backed gown, and a little kit containing a toothbrush and comb on a plastic chair. "Here you go, honey. Take as long as you want. It will relax you."

The nurse was right. Her aching muscles appreciated the long, hot shower, and her eyelids began to droop as she toweled off. She forced herself to brush her teeth, even though it hurt to move her mouth. As she picked up the comb, Meadow made the mistake of glancing into the mirror. She cringed at the image reflected there. A grotesque, distorted face with red, swollen cheeks and bloodshot eyes stared back at her. No wonder the doctor wanted to watch her overnight. She looked like something out of a Frankenstein movie.

Several times during the night, she was awakened by unfamiliar noises and nurses bustling around. How could anyone rest and get well with all that going on?

Fortunately, the doctor released her the next day, giving strict instructions to her parents about enforced rest for a few days. Meadow was relieved she didn't have to go to school with her hideous, bruised face. The confirmation of Clay's abuse was preserved forever, though. The police photographer shot multiple views of the bruises after the detective took her statement.

A week later, Meadow yawned and stretched like a contented cat. She was getting positively lazy. She lay there, basking in the stream of sunshine bursting through her window. Her mouth broke into a grin. Soon they'd be heading for Brighten. Beautiful, wonderful Brighten. How she had missed it—especially lately. And, best of all, Mike was coming home today. There was a definite hole in their family with him gone. She couldn't wait to compare notes about his time in jail and her nightmare. He was the only one she *could* talk to about it. The rest of the family was still too freaked out and she had no close friends, now that Lisa was gone.

A cloud dimmed her sunny outlook as she thought back to recent events. *Wendell.* She crinkled her forehead, clenching her fists. He was behind everything and still on the loose. She wished there was more proof against him, but the attorney told her Clay hadn't implicated him. And without Clay talking, there wasn't enough evidence to arrest Wendell. The sneaky toad. Once more he escaped without a scratch. At least that slime ball, Clay, would be put away for years. Her testimony, along with Celeste's, made sure of that. And the medicine chest was safe, even if Clay *had* told Wendell where it was. She knew Colt would take care of it.

Her mind flashed to the terrible ordeal, thinking of what would have happened if Colt hadn't arrived at exactly the right moment. Her body would be strewn about the desert, coyote bait by now. Where had Colt disappeared to so suddenly? She squirmed in bed. Why did he always vanish before she could introduce him to anyone?

The door popped open and her mother came in. "Rise and shine, Sleeping Beauty. We have to be on our way to pick up Mike. Then we're going to the Bowmans for brunch. I'm not sure what that is, but Mary Bowman insists it's the latest thing."

Meadow screwed up her face. "I'm sure it is if Mrs. Bowman came up with it. Do we *have* to go? It would be nice to have Mike all to ourselves for a while."

Mom sat on the bed. "I know, but there'll be plenty of time later. Mary planned this as a welcome home party for Mike. I would have said no if she'd asked me first. We'll just have to make the best of it. After all, we owe them so much."

"Can I at least wear jeans?"

"Suit yourself, but Mary said there was some kind of surprise." Her mother wore a sundress with a light sweater over it.

"Shoot. I guess I have to find something decent to wear," she muttered as her mother left. Meadow rummaged around in her closet and found the red dress with large buttons at the shoulders. She hadn't worn it since the Scott incident in front of her classmates. "This is perfect. No one at the Bowmans will unbutton me."

Her mother smiled when Meadow appeared, ready to go. "You look lovely, honey. Most of the bruises have already faded.

"The two prettiest gals in the county, I'll wager." Her father offered them both an arm and escorted them to the Ranch Wagon. Monty was waiting, already behind the steering wheel. Wally, beaming like the sunshine, occupied the back seat. Her parents slid in next to Monty, and she climbed in beside Wally. "Oh, boy, Mike is coming home!" he said.

They arrived at the bus station early, and Meadow sat fidgeting on a bench beside her mother while her father paced around, peering down the road. Monty slouched against a nearby wall, feigning indifference. Wally bounced around asking, "Will he get here pretty quick?" As though one of them had the magic answer that would make it happen sooner.

Everyone stood and gathered when a speck on the highway grew larger and finally materialized into a long Greyhound bus. It rolled to a stop in front of them, the brakes whooshing out air, and the door folded open. Several nondescript passengers alit and wandered away, some being greeted by family or friends.

Meadow swallowed, staring at the doorway. Where was he? Did he miss the bus? Did they change their minds about letting him out?

At last, one more figure shuffled down the steps, carrying a duffle. Head down, wearing a gray shirt with a thin black tie and gray pants, he didn't look anything like the brother she loved so well. But it was.

Mom surged forward and clasped him to her, tears streaming down her face. Dad, Monty, and Wally surrounded them like a protective barrier from the outside world. Mike raised moist eyes. With the back of his hand he wiped at the wetness.

Meadow felt as if she didn't know this person, a shadow of the old Mike. *What have they done to my brother?* She sniffled, and they all turned toward her.

With a touch of his old bravado, Mike said, "What's the matter, Med? I'm out now. They wanted to keep me, but the warden was so sick of me telling them how to run things, they finally stuck me on a bus and here I am. Almost good as new." He raised his arms and pivoted for all to get a good look.

In spite of herself, Meadow laughed. "You know, Cynthia wanted to come along to meet you, but I said no way."

Monty snorted, and her father said, "As if we'd let that little hussy ride with us."

Then they were all laughing and talking at once. During a pause her mother said, "We're going to the Bowmans for a little get-together. They all want to see you." She wore a worried pucker, searching for Mike's reaction.

"They want to see a real jailbird up close, I guess. At least I look the part." He tugged at the ugly tie.

Her mother smiled and pulled out a western shirt and jeans from her bag. "I brought you these to wear. You can change in the men's room."

"Oh great. I get to take off my clothes in the men's room of a bus station." Mike rolled his eyes in mock dismay, but obediently started for the restroom, with Wally trailing like an adoring puppy.

Mary Bowman had decorated the patio of their Scottsdale estate with balloons and streamers, even hanging a large sign that read "Welcome home, Mike!"

Thankfully, only family was invited, with the exception of Sheriff Dave and Nueme. They were like family anyhow. Everyone gathered around Mike giving him hugs and backslaps. Linda led him to a table laden with sausages, salads and all sorts of sweet rolls, and something called 'quiche.' Mike spooned out a huge plateful and ate like he been starving for three months.

Meadow took the opportunity to corner Nueme. "Did you give Colt my message?"

Nueme smiled. "Colt always does what is needed."

Her breath came out in relief. "Thanks, Nueme. Have you seen the stallion up north? He must have taken the herd back to Brighten by now."

`"Haven't seen him, but that doesn't mean he isn't there."

Mike finished eating and made his way to Meadow. Nueme excused himself to join the group of adults sitting near the pool. Meadow linked her arm with Mike's and maneuvered him to one side. "Are you okay? Really okay?"

"I am, now that I'm back home. But it was hard, and I met some sad characters that didn't have great parents like we do. Made me appreciate them."

"Was it pretty rough, though? I bet some of the other kids were really mean."

He shrugged. "Yeah, some of them had been in street gangs. Had to fight the hoods a couple of times. No big deal. They left me alone after that." He squeezed her arm. "But what about you? Monty said Clay kidnapped and tortured you. I knew there was something fishy about him. What a weirdo. I would've loved to see Dad punch him out. I would've helped."

Meadow averted her eyes. She had longed for a confidant, but now it wasn't so easy. "It's kinda hard to talk about. I get it all muddled up in my brain. It almost feels like a bad dream instead of reality . . . I dunno, maybe it'll sort itself out in time. One thing for sure—I'll be glad to get back to Brighten for the summer."

"Me too. But it'll be strange without Monty there."

"I know. When he told us he was going with Mr. Sims as assistant trainer for the summer in Prescott, you could have heard a feather drop. It's not very far from Sedona, though. We can go to the horse races over there and see him. It'll be fun."

Their conversation was cut short by the drone of an airplane circling at low altitude, just above the Bowmans' place. Bill rushed out and began waving his arms to a newly cut-in landing strip, just behind the arena.

Linda hurried over to Meadow and Mike, her face flushed. "This is the surprise! Brett's home!"

Then Meadow saw another banner had been hung while she and Mike were deep in conversation. It read, "Welcome home, Brett!"

She was suddenly glad she wore her red dress.

Chapter 39

The Cave Revisited

Meadow's heart thumped as Brett made a pass over the landing field, dramatically waving the wings of the airplane.

"What a showoff!" Mike said, laughing.

They watched the plane circle back around, then touch down smoothly. It rumbled to a stop while the propeller sputtered and slowed. Brett swung open the door and stepped out looking like a World War II flying ace. He wore a black bomber jacket and a military style cap tipped cockily to one side. Just like a movie star, Meadow thought, a little thrill shooting through her.

Bill Bowman hurried toward Brett and clapped him on the shoulder. "How does she fly, son?"

"Great, Dad! Thanks for the present. I know you said I'd get a surprise when I got my wings, but never dreamed it would be a De Havilland Beaver."

"I had an ulterior motive. This plane can be put down in remote areas. Like the ranch at Brighten. When I have a business appointment in Scottsdale, you can fly me down. It'll be a real time saver."

Mary Bowman came forward with a pinched look. "Just so you know, Brett, I was against the idea. I think you're too young to be flying such a thing."

"Don't worry, Mother. I got professional flight training at Eaton. Remember, it was *your* idea to send me away to military school."

Meadow suppressed a smile at the exchange, and Brett winked at her over his mother's head. Brett noticed Mike standing to one side. "Hey, Mike! Good to see you. C'mon, you wanna take a little spin?"

"Heck, yeah!" Mike practically trampled everyone to get over to the plane.

"Monty, you wanna come?" Brett asked. "Wally?"

"Sure!" They said in unison.

Meadow watched with a sinking feeling as the four guys clambered in and slipped on their headphones. Crap, a boys-only club.

Dad came and draped his arm around her.

After the takeoff, everyone filed back onto the patio and the party continued. Meadow plopped down at the edge of the pool, kicked off her sandals and dangled her feet in the water. Mary Bowman's new maid served Mimosas to the adults in fancy stemmed glasses.

Mom eyed the girl, then turned to Mrs. Bowman. "How's Celeste doing?"

"She's slowly recovering from her concussion. She'll be fit to testify by the time the trial rolls around."

Dave shook his head. "It's hard to believe she got taken in so thoroughly by that slimy Clay."

"Women do all sorts of foolish things for love." Dad's face was grim. "Look at how many of them write to convicts in prison and fall in love with them."

Mom got a pucker between her brows. "But it's an open and shut case, right, Bill?"

"My attorney assures me Clay will get thirty years, minimum."

Meadow kicked her feet violently in the water. "I hope they throw the book at him and he never gets out!"

Linda smiled at her. "Amen."

"Dave, is there any new evidence to implicate Wendell?" Nueme raised the question Meadow had been wondering, but was afraid to hear the answer.

"Not yet, but I won't give up."

Linda put her hand on Dave's arm. "Are you going to tell them the news, or should I?"

Mrs. Bowman turned a sickly shade of green, and Linda laughed. "Don't worry, Mother. It's not *that* kind of announcement. Tell them, Dave."

Dave stood and cleared his throat, waiting for all eyes to be on him before he began. "As you know, Sheriff Lodge is retiring, so in the interest of keeping the peace, and not to mention law and order in the great state of Arizona, I've decided to run for Yavapai County Sheriff." He grinned as he sat down. "Please excuse the formal speech, but I need to practice in front of audiences."

Everyone laughed and clapped, except for Mrs. Bowman. She still looked a little put out.

Bill Bowman shook his hand. "You've got my vote. I'm sure you'll do a great job, in the tradition of Sheriff Lodge." He turned to Dad. "I know you've been transporting horses from Fort Apache to Brighten for the summer. How's it coming along?"

"Just fine. We'll be ready to open on time next weekend."

Meadow couldn't help but breathe a happy sigh at the very thought of Brighten. Just one more week of school, then freedom for three whole months! Fort Apache had been closed since the middle of May, when the weather turned hot. It was a nice break to have a couple of weeks off. She wouldn't have to work so much at the stable this summer, either. They had a new hand to help out, one of Dad's old ranching buddies.

Everyone searched the sky when the drone of an airplane broke in on the peaceful scene by the pool. Her father said, "Ahh, nothing like the sound of a radial engine."

Meadow raised one eyebrow. How did he know about airplane engines? Geez, parents were so weird sometimes. But at least he was acting more normal lately.

The plane rolled to a stop and the boys-only club alit, one by one. She ignored Brett when he came over to the pool and sat beside her. He tilted toward her and whispered, "You look awfully cute in that dress, but it's not appropriate for flying."

She whipped her head around. "I can change. I have jeans and boots stashed here from when I stayed with Linda."

Brett laughed at her enthusiasm. "Okay, I'll be waiting."

In the bedroom, Meadow yanked off her dress, pulled on jeans and hopped through the house with one boot on, trying to pull on the other. This would be her first time in an airplane and her heart raced.

Brett was standing by the wing and handed her into the right seat. Meadow looked to the rear seats. "Who else is coming?"

"No one. It's just us. I was saving the best till last."

Meadow swallowed and Brett helped her adjust the headset. She held her breath and gripped the seat during taxi and takeoff, then relaxed as they gained altitude. Pretty soon, she could see the craggy rocks and treacherous cliffs of the Superstition Mountains not far below. She loved the delightful sensation of soaring through the clouds, light as air. Wonderful, but not quite as perfect as flying on Arrow, the Sky Horse.

Then Brett made a turn and flew due north. It didn't take long for them to see the red rocks of Sedona. Meadow's breath quickened. "Are we going to the ranch?"

Brett smiled at her. "Even better. I'm taking you to the cliff dwelling. We'll land on the high mesa above it and hike down. That's the real reason I wanted you to change clothes."

Meadow laughed. "I wondered about that. I never heard of a dress code for a private plane."

"Ha, you always see right through me."

"I wish."

Meadow held on, tense as a bedspring, while the Beaver descended, then bounced and thumped to a halt on the uneven ground of the mesa top. Brett helped her out of the plane and they began the hike to the entrance of the cave.

As she climbed the stone steps and entered the dwelling, Meadow was overcome by the feeling that she was home at last. The amulet warmed her chest as she ran her hand along the walls and traced over the petroglyphs. She inhaled deeply; the faintly aromatic odor of herbs still permeated the place, even though the furnishings were gone.

Brett broke the spell. "It's still pretty cool, even without all the artifacts."

Meadow touched his arm. "C'mon, Brett. I don't think you've ever seen the Medicine Woman's secret room." She led the way down the steps, past the underground lake and through the maze of tunnels. The hidden door moved against their weight and opened a slit. Meadow squeezed through and stopped, sucking in her breath. Just as when she had first seen the chamber, a shaft of light illuminated the wall painting of Arrow.

Brett pressed in behind her. "Wow, that's beautiful. It reminds me of . . ."

"Of Diablo." She finished his thought.

"Yeah, I guess it does, in a strange sorta way."

Meadow scanned the rest of the room, then sighed in relief. Colt had taken the Medicine Chest to a new hiding place. It was safe.

They made their way back to the main room and sat next to each other, looking out at the red cliffs. It was awe-inspiring and serene at the same time. Arrow was out there somewhere with his herd. She wished she could see him, just to know he was all right.

After a little while, Brett turned to her, touching her face. "I heard about what happened. I'm sorry you had to go through that. It must have been terrible."

Her gaze dropped to the rock floor. "Yes."

Brett lifted her chin, mesmerizing her with his slate-blue eyes. "You're the bravest girl I've ever known. I have something for you." He pulled off his class ring, and taking her hand, put it on her finger. "I'd like you to wear it."

Meadow had dreamed of this happening, but now that it had, she was frozen at the controls. She blurted out the first thing that came to mind. "What about Tiffany?"

He frowned. "What about her? You're worth ten of her. She can't even ride a horse, for cripes sake. Just tell me if you don't want to wear my ring."

She smiled, reaching for his hand. "Of course I do." She wiggled it on her finger, then put it in her pocket. "It's too big, but I can wrap yarn around it to make it fit. Like all the girls are doing."

Brett leaned in and Meadow felt his lips on hers. At last, a proper kiss. It was heavenly. She began to melt into his arms, but just at that moment, Meadow heard a loud shrieking whoop. She cranked her head back and stared down into the canyon.

"What are you doing?" Brett's voice had an edge.

"Did you hear that?"

"Are you crazy? Hear what?"

"It sounded like an Indian war cry."

"I didn't hear anything."

"Look, there . . . Do you see him? It's Colt galloping Smoke down the canyon!"

"Colt? That's impossible. You're hallucinating."

"Don't you see him? He's plain as day."

"I don't see anything and you ruined a perfect moment."

Meadow grabbed his hand. "C'mon Brett, maybe we can get to the opening before he does!" She started for the steps, pulling him along behind her.

They were both panting by the time they reached the top of the ladder and gained solid ground. She searched the surrounding area. "Darn! We must have just missed him."

"You're looney. He was never here. It's not possible. Go ahead and look if you want to. I'm going back to the plane." Scowling, Brett turned on his heel and headed up the trail.

Meadow sighed as he rounded a corner. Shoot, he'd never forgive her. She was just about to follow Brett when the amulet warmed and a low whicker stopped her cold. Out from behind a boulder pranced Arrow, magnificent as always. He tossed his head and a cascade of silver mane floated around his arched neck.

The stallion stood as she threw her arms around him and buried her face in his neck. "I've missed you so much." She stroked him, dreamily. "After next week, I'll see you all the time."

It wasn't long before Arrow gently butted his head against her, then whirled and vanished into the brush.

Meadow gazed after him with a lingering smile. With the whole summer ahead, the possibilities were endless. She and Colt would ride the range together, and he'd tell her all his secrets; Wendell would be tracked down and put in jail where he belonged, and she'd get her father to acknowledge their Indian heritage.

And maybe she could even patch things up with Brett.

THE LEGACY BOOK THREE

Back at Brighten, Meadow renews her quest to uncover her father's secret. She is tested to the limit as she bravely forges ahead, outwitting criminals who will stop at nothing to gain the treasure. Will she be able to protect Arrow?

The stunning revelations will forever change her life and the lives of those she holds dear.

About the Author

Melody Huttinger grew up with horses as her best friends. She learned to train them, tutored by her father, who rescued many so-called untrainable and neglected animals. Her family owned and operated various riding stables throughout the years, providing inspiration for Arrow, the Sky Horse series. Many of the characters in the story are drawn from the colorful collection of characters she met as a young dude wrangler.

From her family home in Northern Arizona, Melody has carried on the tradition of re-training Thoroughbreds off the track and has owned and trained various other breeds, including Arabians, Quarter Horses and wild Mustangs.

As a child, Melody read every horse story available, but times became disappointed in the lack of knowledge that many of the authors displayed. She set out to write her own story depicting horses in a more realistic light.

Arrow the Sky Horse series, although partly fantasy, is based on her own experiences growing up with a family in the horse business. She hopes all readers, young and old, will be entertained and enjoy the stories about the animals so close to her heart.

Acknowledgements

A big thank you to my Dad, Mom and brothers who provided a colorful background and memorable characters for these novels.

Thank you to all my good friends, too numerous to mention by name, for all your encouragement and moral support in writing the Arrow series. Especially helpful is my writing critique group for providing great feedback.

I would like to acknowledge my husband Jay for his patience and understanding in this process, not to mention his invaluable help in editing the final draft.

Thanks to you all!

Made in the USA
Columbia, SC
09 June 2021